The Poisoned Passover

Susan Van Dusen

Aakenbaaken & Kent

Aakenbaaken & Kent

Poisoned Passover

ISBN: 978-1-958022-03-0

DEDICATION

To George, Danny and David, who have supported me in the writing of this book.

A tisket, a taskit
Chopped liver in your basket
I added poison just for you
Though you never asked it

Chapter One

"So, would you kill him or not?" Julia asked, taking a sip of Dr. Brown's Root Beer.

"It's hard to say," her best friend from childhood, Shayna Grossman, responded thoughtfully, popping a pitted black olive into her scarlet lipsticked mouth.

The women were sitting at a tiny table for two at Sophie's kosher delicatessen in Crestfall, Illinois, just south of Kankakee, where Julia Donnelly lived with her husband Harold, the mayor, and their two sons, Jordan and Sammy. Sophie's was the place for the real old-time Jewish food grandparents used to love; where a pickle was packed full of vinegar. None of that pale green cucumber pretending to be a truly brined dill.

"Remember," Julia repeated, leaning forward, "this man is beating up an unarmed slave. It's not a fair fight. There's no one else around. Would you kill the bully?" She was interested in her friend's reaction to murder, whether in some situations it's acceptable in a civilized society.

"I don't even like to kill spiders let alone another person. You tell me, Julia." Shayna pressed her friend's buttons the way she always did, forcing Julia to think more deeply than she had intended. "What would it take for you to kill someone?"

Shayna picked up her onion roll, ready to be adorned with all the accoutrements of a pastrami sandwich. The two women were sitting in the *fleishidik* (meat section) of the deli which had separate entrances, separate kitchens, separate cookware and dishware from the *milchedik* (the dairy side)

It was actually two different side-by-side delis owned by Sophie. Jews who kept kosher did not mix milk products and meat products.

"That's not the point, Shayna. We're talking about the Passover story here."

"I know," Shayna said stubbornly, her brown eyes piercing Julia's. "But what would it take for you to kill someone? Could you really do it?"

"Okay." Julia was up for the discussion. She pointed her pickle spear at Shayna. "If someone tried to harm me or my family, I'd murder him or her right on the spot."

Shayna put down her onion roll and folded her arms across her massive chest. Julia assumed she was imagining someone getting the drop on her husband Sol. The man was short and thick through the chest, but strong as a bull. "I guess I could, too," Shayna said, "if it came to someone holding a knife to Sol's throat. I'd definitely do something about it if I could."

"Now we've got a baseline," Julia was getting excited. "We both agree to kill someone who's threatening our loved ones. But did Moses know this slave who was getting beaten?"

"No."

"So why would he kill for him?"

"Because the man was an innocent victim?" Shayna's voice went up about an octave as she answered querulously. Usually she was more assertive.

"Because he felt a kinship with the person being beaten," Julia said, slathering yellow mustard on her rye bread. "The victim was a Jew, and though Moses had been brought up as an Egyptian, he knew in his heart that he was Jewish." Julia raised her mustard-splattered knife for emphasis. "Plus," she reminded Shayna how Rabbi Fine, their Torah study teacher, had set up the story: "If Moses doesn't kill the guy, there's no reason for him to anger Pharaoh, and if Pharaoh isn't angry at Moses there's no reason for him to flee, and if he doesn't flee, he never talks to the burning bush and—

"I know, I know," Shayna interrupted. "Sometimes, I almost regret ever bringing you into the Torah group." She laughed.

Julia could never say no to Shayna. She was very persuasive. For a four-foot-nine *zaftig* woman with thick ebony black hair, she could make a Navy SEAL squirm. Julia had once joined a gym because Shayna wanted an exercise partner. They had shared a trainer, which meant that each got half a workout. That suited Julia fine. She was breathing hard simply contemplating lifting a five-pound weight. Then, they did Korean Yoga together. Julia thought the trainers were perverse, having them lie on the floor while the instructors pressed and probed their stomachs. Shayna left their sessions energized. Julia felt violated, wondering if she should notify Police Chief Scarpelli about the practice. He looked into it, he told her, but came up with nothing except a relaxing massage.

Several months ago, Shayna decided Julia's spirit was drooping around the edges and needed something to give it some zest. She dragged her to a Torah study meeting composed of an eclectic group of religious women taught by an Orthodox rabbi. Since Julia considered herself at the lowest rung on the "Jewishness ladder," she figured it couldn't hurt. It was slow going at first, but after returning a few more times, her once dormant brain started to awaken. The rabbi's words stimulated Julia to question things she had not thought about in years. She felt freer, happier. Now she was trying to bring more Jewish tradition

2

into her own home with varying degrees of success.

Torah group became a place to expand her mind, where Julia could ask any question and find some kind of an answer or a new avenue of thought. For the first time, she no longer felt a stranger to Judaism. Also, she felt a stirring, a tiny stripling of an idea that there was more to life than sweeping the kitchen floor, washing clothes and schlepping sons from one sports activity to another. Hope had entered her vocabulary.

Julia responded to Shayna's dry comment ruing the day she ever introduced her to the Torah group.

"I'm even more surprised than you that I like the group," Julia said. "It's different from being the Mayor's wife or the mother of Jordan and Sammy. It's mine. Not that my life is empty, as the wife of the mayor of Crestfall, with all the rubber chicken dinners Harold and I attend, and being an active member of two PTA's. Finally this is something that I can call my own. And I won't apologize for enjoying the Torah sessions. At least I get to think independently and express my own ideas, hopefully without political retribution."

Julia rose to go to the silverware dispensers to pick up more napkins and heard an argument coming from the kitchen area. *Hmmm*, she thought, *that's not typical*. She'd never heard cross words between store employees, certainly not here in such a family kind of place like Sophie's. *I wonder what's going on?* she thought. Curiosity had always been her curse. A part of her always wanted to know the what and why of things. Suddenly there was a big crash, as if a slew of pots and pans were being thrown on the floor.

She craned her neck toward the sound of discord then caught herself. It's not your problem, Julia, she told herself. Let it go.

Returning to the table Julia observed her friend preparing a sandwich.

"Shayna, what in heaven's name are you doing?"

"What are you talking about?" Shayna sounded a bit defensive. "This is merely ketchup, an actual vegetable in the parlance of our erstwhile president Ronald Reagan." She bristled. Shayna was very serious about her food.

"That's not just ketchup, Shayna," Julia said patiently. "It's a crime against mankind." She stared at her best friend who was wearing what could only be called a bright yellow moo-moo tastefully decorated with large green hearts, which covered her Rubenesque figure from neck to ankle.

"Never in my life have I seen anyone put ketchup on a pastrami sandwich. It's almost worse than putting ketchup on a hotdog. And I think that's an imprisonable offense in Chicago."

3

"Hah," Shayna responded triumphantly, placing first a piece of red onion, then a juicy tomato slice atop her mountain of meat. When her concoction was finally constructed, she pointed a finger at Julia. "Here's where the pot is calling the kettle black." Her long black curls bobbed up and down with conviction.

"And what's that supposed to mean?" Julia asked, acknowledging to herself that perhaps she could also lose a pound or three, though she had only gone up one dress size in the past ten years. A straight twelve for her wasn't so shabby, she thought.

"Just look at your own delicacy." Shayna pointed to Julia's towering salami on rye. It had to be three inches thick. "Tell me that's a healthy meal."

Julia admitted salami on rye was not on the skinny girl's diet. Processed meat, however, when piled up slice upon slice, felt like dental ambrosia as one's teeth traveled through it. Her father liked hard salami, and sometimes he preferred it soft, so the family always had at least two long salamis hanging by string from nails on the kitchen wall. Whenever he walked by, he'd take a bite out of whichever one hit the spot for the day.

"It's not a healthy meal," Julia admitted, "but we don't usually do this."

"I agree," Shayna said righteously. "Besides, *Pesach* is just three days away, and we won't be able to eat foods made with *chametz* for eight days."

"That's right," Julia said. "When are you and Sol leaving for Passover this year?"

"We're flying down to Miami tomorrow." She licked a glob of ketchup from her finger. "The kids are going to meet us there. The hotel serves a *Pesachdik* dinner, so I won't have to do any of the crazy cooking or cleaning this year. Even so, I did have a professional cleaning crew come to my house and scrub it from attic to basement. And," – she looked angelic – "I got rid of all the crispy, crunchy crackers and other things not permitted at *Pesach,* just in case Sol and I want to return before the holiday is over. The kids think I'm crazy"

Shayna's children were already in their twenties. Harold and Julia had married later than Shayna and Sol. After years of failng to conceive, the Donnellys had adopted their two sons. Jordan was fifteen, going on thirty, and Sammy was a solid ten.

"What's on your agenda this year?" Shayna asked.

"Devorah just invited us to her house for a *seder*," Julia said.

Devorah was a member of their Torah group. She had been studying Torah for several years and could even read much of it in Hebrew. Julia was happy that she wouldn't be facing her family's obvious ennui with Passover

4

customs.

Harold, who converted to Judaism from being a Catholic, had never thrown himself into Jewish tradition. He accepted Judaism on a purely pragmatic level. The boys had followed in his unenthusiastic footsteps. This upset Julia. She wanted the whole family to enthusiastically share their religion, at least to the degree to which they observed it. Since her own sister lived in Nebraska, she usually had a simple little Passover in their home, and counted it as a success if they could get through the *seder* without the boys flicking wine drops at each other during the ten plagues, or excessive burping as they drank cups of grape juice and Mogen David wine.

Lately Julia was beginning to realize that it was unfair of her to expect Harold to excitedly participate in something that was very strange for him. He had been brought up as a Catholic. He had never experienced the satisfaction of a well-done Passover *Seder* or the joy of a Purim party. How could she hope that he would accept something that was so foreign to him? Still, she wished that he could push himself to support her efforts in that direction.

"You better be prepared," Shayna warned her.

"Prepared for what?" Julia asked.

"Devorah and her husband have a very traditional *seder*," Shayna explained. "First, you eat the whole meal on the floor, lying on big pillows."

"What?"

"Yeah. The *Hagaddah* says that since we aren't slaves anymore, we get to recline like the higher ups in those days, and they used to lie on pillows."

"Do we at least use utensils?"

Suddenly the normal white noise of people responding to their order numbers being called was shattered by harsh words. Sophie, the owner of the deli, was giving out customer samples from a platter when an angry twenty-something man burst from the kitchen and stomped up to her. His scowling mouth was surrounded by a dark five o'clock shadow on a swarthy face, and he was clutching a knife, the kind that cuts fat off of brisket and corned beef. It's funny what you notice when you're paralyzed in fear.

"You're going to be very, very sorry," he threatened, jabbing the knife at her face. "I've always worked hard for you." Then he threw the knife on the floor, turned, and marched out of the deli.

There was a flurry of action. Some customers in line to buy food, frightened by the scene, scurried out. Others gathered around Sophie like jackals trying to find out what had just happened. A third category stayed at their little tables, refusing to be parted from the meals they had just purchased.

"Sophie," Shayna pushed herself into the ghoulish group surrounding the deli owner, and relieved her of the platter. "Come here. Sit by us."

A fireplug of a woman who must have been in her late sixties trudged toward them. She wore a thin hairnet over a tightly pulled back black bun. Shayna dragged over a chair.

"Sit," she commanded Sophie, running off to the coffee machine, bringing back a steaming cup to the table. Julia had never seen her friend move so quickly.

Sophie was breathing hard. She was trying not to cry. "Sophie, meet Julia, the wife of Mayor Harold Donnelly. Julia, Sophie, owner of this wonderful deli."

"Now," she continued, "what was that all about? Should we call the police?"

"Oy," Sophie sighed, one fist pushing away a tear. "That was nothing. I mean it was something, but I can't do nothing about it. Carlos, he's one of my best meat counter men. You tell him you want one eighth pound lean corned beef, that's exactly what you'll get. No more, no less. But since the fire, I can't hire back all of my old workers. I can't afford him now. Maybe in a few months when the rest of my customers come back, but not now. He got a little angry with me," she sighed.

Fire? Now Julia remembered. About two months ago there was an article in the newspaper about a fire at Sophie's Deli. She had to shut down and redo the basement where they prepared the corned beef.

"Did they ever find out what caused it?" Shayna asked.

"My son, Milton, thinks it probably was an electrical fire caused by old wiring," Sophie said. "But the fire chief believes it was arson. He found something, a quickener or —"

"You mean an accelerant?" That was the extent of Julia's fire-starting knowledge.

"Yeah," she answered. "But we got no idea who could have done it."

"Well," Shayna puffed out her ample chest, "my friend Julia is quite good at solving crimes. Just a few months ago she found a very valuable piece of jewelry that had been taken from me, and then she solved a big mystery about a stolen heirloom with our Torah leader Rabbi Fine."

"Shayna," Julia cautioned. Their eyes met. Shayna shut her mouth.

"I don't know," Sophie murmured. "There is so much happening at one time. It's getting to be too much for me to take."

"What's going on?" Shayna leaned forward and took Sophie's hand.

6

"First, the fire. Insurance says they're not going to pay me nothing until we find out how it started. Can you believe it? They think I did it for the money. And my son, he's *hocking me a chinek* to give him the store. He wants to turn it into a billiard parlor. Imagine that. A place where grown men hit little balls with wooden sticks! 'Ma,' he says to me, 'Crestfall doesn't have any place for young people to go and have fun, play pool, have a few drinks.' He even wants a little area for children so when their parents are making balls fall into holes, the kids can watch cartoons." Sophie raised her hands in frustration, then settled them on her ample thighs. "What am I supposed to do for the rest of my life? That boy! When God gave out brains, Milton was sleeping." Sophie's tone hardened. She leaned forward as if to tell a secret. "I didn't survive the war to retire. I know people who retire. Three weeks later, they have nothing to do, they die. No thank you very much. I'm not giving Milton nothing. He can't even hold one job for more than a month."

"I'm sorry to hear that," Julia said, preparing herself to learn all about this poor woman's life in the next ten minutes. Being the mayor's wife was akin to being the wife of a minister or rabbi. People tended to spill out their problems with nothing more than a "Hi, how are you?"

"Then," Sophie continued, "there's this Lester Pintner. Have you ever heard of him?"

"The name's familiar," Julia said.

"He's some hotsy-totsy land developer person. He buys low and sells high. He wants me to sell this store so he can build up the block and make it nice for rich people. Some of my neighbors already sold to him."

"What have you told him?" Shayna asked.

"I told him I don't want no chocolates that he sends, no flowers, or his fake worries about my health." Sophie sniffed. "I'm as strong as a horse." She hit her chest with her fist. "I keep saying I don't want to sell, but he won't stop bothering me. He even offered to put my deli in his brand-new building. You think this old place will fit into a skyscraper?"

She motioned the women to come close to her. "He's the kind of man," she lowered her voice, "who wants you to pay him for blowing his nose. I knew vermin like him from Russia." Her lips puckered with distaste. "I'll tell you what I told the fire chief," she whispered. "Pintner has a man, a mean looking so-and-so who works for him. This no-neck *shmendrick* walks around the block and scares people."

"How does he scare them?" Julia asked. She hated to think this was happening right now in Crestfall. She made a mental note to talk to Harold about it.

"He does things, maybe little things at first. Rosenblatt, the shoe repair man next door, he says that this guy comes into his store and tries to make trouble. Once he spit on the floor. Rosenblatt told him to get out. The man laughed and told Rosenblatt he better look behind his back from then on. Rosenblatt called the police, but they told him they have to catch the guy doing something wrong. So Rosenblatt tells me, if I find him beaten up or dead, I should tell the police that no-neck did it."

"I'm so sorry that you have to be going through all of this," Julia said. She wished there was something to do, perhaps talk to the fire chief. But, it appeared he already had made up his mind.

Sophie patted Julia's hand. "Dolly, I've been through worse. Life is hard," she said, "then it gets worse." She laughed bitterly. "I better get back to work. But first, I want to show you something."

Sophie motioned to various corners of the store. "I put in some spy cameras," she whispered. "Some in the back and some in the front on the *milchedik* and *fleischidik* sides. Now, if someone tries some hanky-panky, I'm gonna see who's doing what."

"Have you told anyone else?" Julia asked.

"No." She pretended to lock her mouth with a key. "It's our secret. If something happens to me, you'll know. No one else."

Julia was astonished that Sophie would pick her and Shayna to share her secret, but Shayna had been going to Sophie's for years, and Sophie knew that Harold Donnelly was the mayor of Crestfall, which made his wife trustworthy by association.

Sophie picked up her tray. "Here," she plopped two little sample containers on their table. "I'm giving out tastes of my chopped liver. I'm trying to drum up more business because of the fire, you know? Each day I give out a different sample from each side of the store. One day it's a knish. The next day a bagel. It's beginning to work. Mrs. Teplitz, she comes in for a box of Tam Tam matzah crackers. I suggest the chopped liver would be tasty to put on it. She buys a pound." Sophie's smile was like a beam of sunshine.

A sigh escaped from her chest. "I'm even thinking of taking out some advertisements. A few months before the fire, this greenhorn, Nathan Nachel, comes to me and says, 'Sophie, I want to buy your deli.' I say back to him, 'That's nice, but I don't want to sell'. He says, 'If you don't sell to me, I'm going to open up my own deli a few miles away.' I say, 'It's a free country, mister. You want to open a store, be my guest. I haven't worked here forty years for nothing.' So, he opens his store. Bam! I have a fire and have to close for two months. Now he's got a lot of my customers, and some of them like his fancy-shmancy place with shiny new counters and tables. They don't want my old pickle barrels and Formica tables no more." Her face seemed to dissolve into itself.

"Don't you worry," Shayna patted Sophie's shoulder. "We'll keep coming here, and I'll make sure my Torah group shops here, too," she said.

"Thank you, sweetheart," Sophie said, holding back her tears. "Well," she sighed and slowly got up, "the show must go on." She shuffled off to another table.

Shayna and Julia wrapped up the remainder of their lunch (Sophie was known for her large portions; they always saved half of the sandwich for lunch the next day), put on their coats and bussed their own table. Julia popped her sample of chopped liver into the sandwich bag as they walked out to the parking lot.

"Wow," Shayna said. "That was something. You sure you wouldn't like to look around and find out who started her fire?"

Julia counted to ten before responding to her friend. She said, "Shayna, arson is a real crime. Serious. You have to know lots of scientific things; use special equipment; send things out to be tested. How could you even think I could find out who started Sophie's fire? And," she was getting hotter under the collar, "who gave you the right to almost offer my services to Sophie? I don't know anything about solving crimes except what I learn from TV."

"You could have fooled me," Shayna shot back. "You found my missing stickpin. From nothing you found it, no clues, no bread crumbs, just the 'little grey cells' in your head, as Hercule Poirot likes to say."

That was true. A few months ago Shayna called Julia crying. Shayna never cried. Shayna made other people cry.

"What's the problem?" Julia asked, thinking something had happened to her husband or one of the kids.

"It's my stickpin," she sobbed.

"Your sticky what?" It was difficult to understand what her friend was saying.

"My stickpin that Sol gave me as an engagement present. It's gone."

"Shayna, slow down. First of all, what is a stickpin?"

"You don't know what a stickpin is?" She hiccupped.

"No. Never heard of it; never had one."

"It's a piece of jewelry, well known in the east."

"The East like in China?"

"No," she said frostily, "like in Brooklyn Heights."

"Okay. So?"

"So, when Sol and I were engaged, I told him I didn't need an engagement ring like everyone else. I said that the most important thing to express our love would be a wedding ring."

"Very romantic," Julia offered.

"But Sol wanted to do something for our engagement, so he bought me a beautiful diamond stickpin; a decorative pin with a half-carat diamond surrounded by rubies. You wear it on the lapel of a suit jacket or on a blouse collar. Now I've lost it, and it's close to our anniversary, and I always wear it on our anniversary. What am I going to do?"

"Have you looked everywhere you went when you wore it the last time?"

"You sound just like my mother, of blessed memory. Of course I did."

"Have you looked on the lapel of every jacket, blouse and sweater in your house?" Julia asked.

"Actually," Shayna sniffed, "I have."

"You've looked through all your pockets, your purses, under all the beds, and on the car floor?"

"Ditto," she started crying again.

"Let's just think this through," Julia suggested.

Shayna kept her stickpin in her jewelry box, which sat on her dresser.

"Could someone have come into your house and taken it?" Julia asked.

"Who would do such a thing?"

"Who's been at your house since you last wore it?"

"Julia, it's been at least a month since I wore it."

"Has anyone come to visit?"

Shayna's eyebrows knit together when she thought deeply. "Faigie came with two of her girls. My niece Rochelle had some dolls and books that her kids outgrew. She asked me to give them to Faigie."

Faigie was an ultra-Orthodox member of their Torah group. She had enough children for her own baseball team from the ages of one year through eight.

"Aha. Now we've got something," Julia crowed.

"I doubt that Faigie would take my stickpin," Shayna said icily.

"I know, but she had children with her. Never put it past a child to do something unexpected. How old were the kids she brought?"

10

"I think she brought two girls, one maybe five, the other one four. They played dolls together, dressing them up, then putting them in their pajamas and singing them lullabies. They were precious. They made me want to call my kids and tell them to hurry up and marry and have grandchildren for me!"

Julia got up from her kitchen table and wiped down the counters while holding the phone to her ear. "Did they roam around the house at all?"

She could picture Shayna shrugging over the phone. "I'm sure they did at one time or another. Faigie and I were talking. She says she's decided to stop having children, no matter what her husband says."

Julia suggested they pay Faigie and her daughters a visit. "You talk to Faigie, and I'll talk to the girls," Julia said.

A brisk late March wind blew the two friends to Faigie's home that afternoon. As Shayna and Faigie had some tea and coffee cake amongst the babies either crawling or running around the small living room, Julia asked the two girls to take her on a tour of their bedroom. It was a small room painted in light aqua with two sets of bunkbeds that Faigie's daughters shared. Were it not for the toys, one might think it was some sorority dormitory. Play things were placed not so neatly in bins according to subject. Games were in one bin, dolls in another, dress-up clothes in yet another, and a large bin for art projects with construction paper and colored markers.

"Do you have any dolls?" Julia asked. "I have boys and I never get to play with dolls."

"Yes," Sarah answered. She was about five, fair skinned, with brown curly hair. At times, she still sucked her thumb.

She and her sister Esther, a smaller identical version of Sarah, brought out two dolls that they had received from Shayna's niece.

"These are beautiful," I said. "They're in their pajamas. Could we dress them up?"

"Yeth," Esther said. She had a delicious lisp that Julia hoped for her sake would disappear as she grew older.

Esther put a red-and-white gingham doll dress on her doll. Sarah was trying to tug a worn blue denim dress over her doll, but was having difficulties.

"Can I help you?" Julia gently took the doll and the dress and saw the problem. There was a long pin stuck in the dress that kept Sarah from pulling it on her doll.

She removed the pin and put the dress on the doll. Sarah was pleased. Julia examined the pin in her hand. It was a diamond surrounded by rubies. Shayna's stick pin.

11

"Hey, Sarah," Julia was the epitome of calm, "where did you find this?"

"At Shayna's," she said with the pure naïveté of a child. "It was in a big box on her dresser. We thought it would look pretty on the doll dresses we got from her."

"Did you ask permission?" Julia asked softly.

Sarah and Esther looked at each other, guileless. "No. We thought she was giving us things. Did we do something wrong?"

They both looked ready to cry.

"No. Just a problem in communication," Julia said. "Let's go in and show Mommy and Shayna our dolls."

Needless to say, Shayna was thrilled to get her pin back, a mortified Faigie taught her girls never to take anything without first asking, and the minor mystery was solved. Julia thought that Shayna made it seem much bigger than it was. "It was more like a serendipitous confluence of events," Julia noted airily.

"Oh, we are sounding so grand and righteous with our terms, aren't we? Did you or did you not locate a missing item?"

"You know I did." Julia responded.

Shayna knew how to press her buttons.

"And didn't you and the Rabbi solve the mystery of who stole Malka's ancient heirloom, and the whole ugly story behind it? If that's not all absolute fact I'll eat my purse. And it's real leather!"

Julia gave her friend an impatient *tsk*. "All I'm asking is that you don't go around telling people about it. And don't offer my services without my permission. Remember, I'm the Mayor's wife. I don't need any stories about my super sleuthing powers flying around town."

"Alright, already," Shayna conceded. "I stand corrected. I won't talk about my best friend's ability to solve mysteries anymore, but I must tell you it was all very impressive."

She pursed her lips and nodded her head.

The women reached Shayna's car first. It was obvious that she still had something on her mind, like a dog who refused to give up a bone. They stood face to face like sumo wrestlers assaying each other's strength.

"Julia Donnelly," Shayna added with great intensity, "there is something special about you. I can't say what it is, but you see things other people don't notice. I see a new ice cream parlor opening up; you see more sales tax accruing to the city. That's why you were such a great reporter in the old days. And I think you could use your "uber-logic" to find out about who set Sophie's fire."

Before Julia could jump in with a response, Shayna went on. "Can you believe everything that's happening to Sophie? It seems like a dark cloud is rolling over her head."

"It does seem like a coincidence having Nate's Nosh opening, and suddenly Sophie has a fire." Julia agreed.

"And don't forget all the other stuff she mentioned, the so-and-so who wants to buy her building, and that mean man, and her good-for-nothing son," she added knowingly, "and then that meat cutter. Do you think he'll follow through on his threat to her?"

Julia was frustrated. "Shayna, how should I know? I can't solve all the mysteries of the world. I've got my own *tsuris* to take care of. You know. You used to have kids in your house. They need food, water, and sun to grow, and my kids require a lot of attention."

"By the way, has Jordan taken the car lately?" Shayna was trying to shake her cavernous purse to locate her keys.

"No," Julia crossed her fingers. Jordan, her fifteen-year-old son had decided to take her car for a ride recently without permission. "He seems to be on the straight and narrow since we addressed his last felonious fling."

"Good." Shayna found her key. "So, officially we have finished discussing Sophie and Jordan's troubled lives. Now for a new subject."

Shayna opened her sandwich bag and brought out her container of chopped liver, opened it, and dipped in a finger. "Umm, delicious," she *kvelled*. "Take a taste." She offered some to Julia. "Don't blame the liver for your bad mood."

Julia took a half-hearted dip, tasted, and then her eyes lit up.

"Is this the best chopped liver you've ever had?" Shayna proclaimed.

"Absolutely." Julia restrained herself from reaching into her purse and eating her entire sample right on the spot.

"So," Shayna asked, nonchalantly, "what are you bringing to Devorah's Passover *seder*?"

"I don't know," Julia said. "We don't keep kosher, so I can't cook anything myself."

Her friend dramatically pointed her keys at the little white container in her hand as if she were a model hawking her wares in a television commercial. "Why not chopped liver as an appetizer with matzoh crackers?" she gushed.

"What a great idea. This is as good as it gets," she laughed.

"Chopped liver it is."

"Sophie's is the best," Shayna smiled like the Mona Lisa. "It's got a sliver of sweetness that makes it taste more like pâté. I could eat a pound of it slathered over a nice *parve challah*, but that would be rather piggish of me," she giggled, opening her car door and stuffing herself in.

Mother hen to the last, Shayna waited until Julia was in her car and belted in before she zoomed out of the parking lot.

Oh my, Julia thought. An hour with Shayna was as exhausting as two hours of hard labor, though she loved her friend to death. She knew her so well. It might seem silly, but Julia had felt alive while working through the process of finding Shayna's stick pin. Since then, the ennui of housework, homework and chauffeuring was weighing down her self-worth again.

Then she interrupted her dark thoughts and remembered what Shayna had once told her to do when she was depressed, "Don't think about your boring life, because problems are sure to come along that you didn't expect. Remember, that nice girl on Saturday Night Live who played Roseanne Rosannadanna once said, 'It's always something'."

Shayna was right.

It was close to two p.m. when Julia got home. She parked her van in the driveway and took a deep breath. It was the end of March. The air was still nippy, but it was clear spring was coming. Tiny green tips from hostas plants peeked up from her so-called garden. She was the mistress of perennials, plants strong enough to live through weeds and her waning enthusiasm as the growing season progressed. Julia loved flowers. She just didn't appreciate planting and pruning.

Her head was spinning with the idea of Passover, the Exodus of the Jews from Egypt. This wasn't just a fairy tale, though Harold and the boys didn't take it literally. A friend from Israel had told her that Israeli students were taught the Bible as history. And Rabbi Fine had reminded the group that Egypt was not only a geographic location, it was also a state of mind. In the last class he had said, "Going out of Egypt refers to each individual's personal departure from everything that interferes with the full expression of his or her potential spiritual state."

She remembered him explaining that *Mitzrayim*, the Hebrew word for Egypt, was related to the word *maitzorim*, boundaries or limitations. Through Torah and *mitzvot* (commandments and good deeds), a Jew can go beyond the limits of his or her physical existence and become more closely connected to *HaShem,* another name for God.

Heady thoughts on a sunny March day, Julia thought, light heartedly. The Torah, like a tree, was quietly growing its roots within her. And that made Julia very happy. Since quitting a writing career after adopting the boys, Julia was feeling as though she was losing her edge. Being a member of the Torah group had turned on a switch, making her think about existential questions such as, "What are we supposed to do with our lives?" And lately she had been adding a few traditional trappings to her own home. Careful was the word, since Harold didn't like change. Very slowly, she was pushing toward being kosher without anyone at home really noticing. Meals were becoming all meat, or all dairy. In Judaism, the two aren't mixed. She was putting pots and pans for meat dishes in a different cabinet from the dairy pots and pans. As long as Harold didn't cook or clean up the kitchen, and she couldn't see that situation occurring any time soon, her little experiment was safe.

Julia entered the front door and noticed Sammy's shoes on the rug. Did school let out early, she wondered?

"Sammy," she yelled, "I'm home."

15

"So am I," he yelled from his room.

Rather than continue shouting, Julia decided to go upstairs. Sammy, her dear ten-year-old was lying on his unmade bed reading a Batman comic book.

"Hi, there," she said. "How come you're home early?"

"Didn't want to stay at school anymore."

Say what? That one came out of left field. Sammy was the quiet one. Jordan, the oldest, was the one who gave the Donnellys gray hair. He was always into something. A few months ago, he "borrowed" Julia's car to pick up a friend of his. No license. No permission. A long grounding and some sessions with a shrink to discuss why he felt the need to act out so much, and he seemed to have calmed down a bit. Even he was surprised by his *chutzpah*.

On the other hand, Julia always worried that Sammy, the obedient, eager to please son, would someday erupt. And maybe, she thought, it's his turn now.

"What exactly do you mean you didn't want to stay at school any longer?"

"I couldn't take being there anymore, so when the bell rang to go to the next class, I walked home."

Interesting. "Didn't anyone see you?"

"I guess not."

"Didn't anyone try to stop you?"

"Maybe." He continued staring at his comic book, though he had probably read the same page once or twice during their chat.

"Maybe?" She asked, her eyebrows almost touching in disbelief.

"Well, a hall guard asked where I was going, and I sorta said I was going to meet my mother outside."

"And?"

"And, she's in my grade, so she said, 'Okay,' and I walked out."

Julia sat down on Sammy's bed. His skin and bones body was taut. This was a very worried boy, but he wouldn't put down that comic book; it appeared to be glued to his hands, and he wouldn't look at her.

"Kiddo," she said, choosing her soft, nurturing voice, "tell me what happened. I promise I won't get angry. I just want to understand what's going on." This was her sensitive child, the one who had great empathy for others, the one who held his own troubles deep inside.

Julia went through the mantra of terrible things that could traumatize a child into doing something unacceptable to adults.

"Is someone bullying you?"

Silence.

"Did you forget to turn in your homework?"

Nothing.

"Are you having trouble with a teacher?"

Zilch.

Suddenly, there it was, the quiver. The sign that was ready to open up and say something spine-tingling. He turned his head toward his mother.

"I've decided I'm not going to school anymore."

Julia stammered. "But why? I mean there's a law, Sammy. All kids have to go to school."

"Not me," he said. "Not anymore."

He put down the comic book, turned onto his side, and curled up in a fetal position. No coaxing on Julia's part could move him to talk further. She called Harold. His cell phone was off, as usual, so she left a message. She also called his office, but his secretary had no idea where he was. Harold had a love/hate relationship with his phone. He had begrudgingly agreed to have a cell phone, but kept it off at all times. At certain points of the day he deigned to check his messages.

"What if there's a real emergency?" Julia once asked.

"My office always knows where I am," he replied.

Not. As. In. Today. Why, she asked herself, *am I always the one left holding the bag, or in this case, Sammy? What am I supposed to do? Harold's incommunicado.*

Unbidden, a dark thought crept into her head. *Why,* she wondered, *does he never answer his phone?* Like the archetypical, dueling spirits, one on each side of her brain, the angelic one said, '*I haven't the faintest.*' That however was a lie. The truth simply hurt too much.

'*The 'ruler of Crestfall' doesn't want to get into a family fracas,*' sneered the devil. '*Sometimes home is harder to figure out than a budget for 30,000 people. You don't really need Harold. What would your next step be if he wasn't in the picture?*'

"I'd call the school," Julia responded.

'*There you go.*' The devil disappeared in a puff of smoke.

'*You know what to do, as usual,*' his voice echoed from above.

Julia called the school, told them that Sammy was at home, and decided to calm down.

She chose to do what Shayna had told her a long time ago. '*If you've done everything you can, chill.*'

Julia sat by the kitchen table and picked up her notes on Passover. The Torah meeting was that night. It was only Wednesday, but the holiday began on

17

Friday, and Thursday night, people would be too busy cooking and still cleaning. Perhaps she could immerse herself in the Passover story to soothe her troubled soul.

One of the points Rabbi Fine had made about Passover the previous week was that each person is obligated to see himself, or herself, as if he had personally gone out of Egypt. "This is the birth of the first Jewish generation," he explained. "During this time, we bring a sense of renewal as our houses are transformed from top to bottom and declared *Pesachdik* (kosher for *Pesach*)."

In other words, this was a time for an extreme version of spring cleaning. "No simple vacuuming and dusting here," he stressed. "It is a search and destroy mission against *chametz*. All leavened products, anything with yeast in it, must go." Actually that meant all wheat, barley, oats, spelt or rye, anything that became wet for more than eighteen minutes, would begin the leavening process.

In order to be absolutely certain that no *chametz* was left, many people turned out the pockets of every piece of clothing in the house. They sent their clothes to be cleaned. Others removed everything from all cabinets and closets and cleaned them out. Refrigerators, freezers, and ovens had to be cleaned. Afterwards their shelves would be covered with tin foil to assure Passover pots and pans would be pure. Special covers were placed over stove burners. Separate sets of dishes, silverware, pots, and pans were used during Passover.

Julia had known about these things in theory, but was taken aback when she learned at the last meeting what the women in the Torah group were doing.

Malka, a large outspoken woman with teased black hair went on about removing every single bread product from her pantry.

"I put it all in bags and take them to the Rabbi," she said. "I pay him for the privilege of holding my *chametz*."

"He wouldn't be able to own your *chametz*," Devorah noted. "He'd probably sell it to a non-Jew until the holiday is over."

Chaya, Malka's diminutive sister, had a different interpretation of holiday preparations. "I take everything that's objectionable, put it in my spare room, and tape it off. Otherwise, with two young kids and a job, it's too much work."

Bubbe, their grandmother, added, "My favorite part is looking through the pockets of every jacket, skirt or pants to make sure there's no *chametz*. Last year," the eighty-plus year-old bragged, "I found ten dollars in change at Malka's house."

"When all the cleaning is done," Rabbi Fine told them, "we must work

18

still harder to eliminate *chametz. Bedika chametz* is the formal search for *chametz* on the night before *Pesach.*"

Julia decided to do that with Sammy. He owed her for the predicament they were in now, so he would just have to take part in this "new" home tradition the next night.

The kitchen door squeaked open. Someone's got to oil it this millennium, Julia thought. Harold was home. He entered with that "Boy do I have a lot of work to do tonight" look on his face. He stopped at the kitchen table, took one look at Julia and said, "What's wrong?"

"How could anything be wrong," she said icily, "except that you were too busy to pick up the phone when I called to tell you that your son has decided he's not going to go back to school again. Ever."

"Wait, you're angry with me and I didn't do anything?" He sounded exactly like their older son, Jordan, gearing up to offer a barrel-full of excuses.

"Do you understand how upsetting it is that if an emergency happens I have no way of contacting you?"

"Was this an emergency?" Harold's eyes opened wide behind his thick tortoise-shelled glasses. "Is Jordan Okay?"

"It's not Jordan this time. It's Sammy, and the term emergency has many shadings," she said ominously. "Sammy just walked out of school today. And informed me that he would never return."

Julia lifted her hands then let them fall back onto the kitchen table.

"Well, he's simply got to go back," Harold said. "It's the law."

"You go and talk to him about it," she suggested, returning to her Torah group notes, not fooling Harold one bit. Words swam before her face without meaning. She wanted him to deal with a serious kid issue for once. Julia was tired of being the bad guy with the boys all the time.

Harold climbed the stairs with a heavy tread. Each step sounded like a sigh. When he was in Sammy's room, Julia tiptoed up and listened outside the door.

"Sport, Mom tells me you won't go back to school."

"Yeah," Sammy mumbled.

"Why?"

"Don't want to talk about it," Sammy said.

"Look, every problem has a solution. Sometimes not everyone is happy about the whole solution; that's when you know it's probably fair."

"Dad, I can't stand being there. Okay? Are you satisfied?"

"No, Sport, I'm not. Tell me what the problem is and I'll leave you alone for now."

"The kids are so dumb. The teacher has to repeat everything to them over and over, and they never even listen to her."

"Well, that's just the way school is taught with a group of students, Sammy. You're already in the top class. I'd think that your classmates would be more interested."

"They're not, Dad. They talk all through the lessons and the teachers don't do anything. One teacher, Mrs. Schmidt, even takes out the newspaper and reads it when the kids get too obnoxious. I can't stand it."

Julia imagined Harold pushing his glasses up on his nose. He always did that when he was nervous. "There's got to be something we can do about this, Sport. Mom and I will talk to the principal and see what's going on."

Sammy's voice suddenly became very strong, strident, angry. "No, you can't," he yelled. "You'll just make it worse for me. You want to know what's really wrong, Dad? It's you. You're the problem."

Silence for a second. Harold was taken aback. Sammy began to cry miserably, then a shuffling of feet as he ran into his closet and closed the door. Harold tried to calm Sammy for a few more minutes before he came out into the hall.

"This could be serious," he said as they walked downstairs together. "What do you think?" he asked.

"What do I think?" Julia echoed, facing her husband on the bottom step. "I think we need to talk to his school counselor."

"I agree. We'll have to find out exactly what Sammy meant when he said I'm the reason he doesn't want to go to school anymore," Harold continued, his brow furrowed. "Do you want to call now?" he asked.

"Not particularly. Why don't you?"

He raked his slender fingers over the top of his thinning hair.

"You're really better at this than I am," he conceded.

Julia sighed. He was right. She called and made an appointment with the counselor for the next day. Sammy would be there for the appointment, too.

Chapter Three: Torah Night

Sammy's decision to quit school lay heavily on Julia's chest as if she had eaten an entire New York cheesecake. It hurt, particularly since her sons were adopted. She always related their problems to the fact that she and Harold weren't the boys' birth parents.

That was especially true for Sammy, her youngest and most vulnerable. When he was a little boy, Julia had lain in bed with him at night, telling stories in the dark. He was always the knight who would use his brains to solve challenges rather than use brute strength as his brother would. That was the main difference between the boys. Jordan was the lion whose muscular roar would frighten the evil dragon.

Sammy was the thoughtful one who would work out life's puzzles. He would find the princess and whisk her away while the dragon was asleep from eating a magical potion Sammy had invented.

That's why Julia was worried. Sammy had always talked to her. He hadn't gotten to the age when parents are the enemy. Recently, though, now that she thought about it, he had become more remote.

We aren't telling stories like we used to, she realized. He preferred to read alone for his before bed routine. It killed her to know that he had been suffering and she hadn't a clue.

Julia felt like a stale washrag. She had little motivation to go to Torah group that night. Harold stayed home. "Go to your Torah thing," he urged. "Maybe it'll take your mind off of Sammy."

As if that was possible, Julia thought. She might still harbor resentful feelings that she had given up a career to bring up the children, but Julia really wouldn't change a thing. These boys were her life, and she would do anything she could for them. Sammy made that point painfully clear one night during one of their bedtime talks. They were lying together on her bed and he asked how far she would go to save him if he were in terrible trouble. She told him about the woman who lifted a car off of her son to save him from being crushed.

"I'd do the same for you in a second," Julia told him.

"Mom," he protested, "you can't even open a can without Dad's help."

"But if you were in the can, I could," she had replied. He seemed satisfied with that.

Harold was worried, too. He kept poking his glasses up on his nose. Both parents were nervous about their school appointment. They didn't know what to expect. That particularly bothered Harold. He liked to be prepared, know what the different possibilities were when facing an issue. That's one thing Julia loved about him. He was a rock, dependable, unflappable. With their experience talking to school administrators about Jordan in the past, Julia always had the feeling that they were being pushed into decisions. She didn't want that to happen to Sammy. In his situation, as far as she could tell, he hadn't done anything wrong. Julia wanted to make sure his case would be treated with respect and patience.

That evening before the meeting, Julia drove to Shayna's house early to help her set up the dishes and have a quick chat about Sammy. She always had the same feeling driving up to her friend's home. As houses in the Torah group went, hers was medium, a red brick with a triangle-shaped front. For some reason it always reminded Julia of a gingerbread house with white painted shutters on each window and a white storm door with scallops around the top pane.

Inside, Shayna had white walls and light wood floors. She added color with things she and Sol had brought back from their many trips abroad. They had removed the wall between their dining room and kitchen, and had added on to the house to create a large, completely open great room.

Ringing the bell was unnecessary. On Torah group nights, everyone left their doors open.

"Hello, my adopted sister," Shayna said, entering the room like a model showing off a new outfit. Upon seeing Julia, she stopped.

"What's wrong," she bent her head to one side and stared, then enveloped Julia in a huge maternal hug.

"I'm sorry." Julia said. "I didn't know it was so obvious."

Julia did tend to wear her heart on her sleeve. Living with a very logical, tacit man stimulated her at times to over emotionalize, just to get a rise out of her husband.

"We've had a shock with Sammy and my mind isn't all here," she said.

"Tell me." Shayna was able to do the impossible, give her complete attention to a needy friend while she brought carafes of coffee, tea, and a pitcher of iced water to the table. As she bustled around, making the final touches to her dining area, Julia confided what had happened earlier.

"It's not bullying?" She asked.

"No." Julia said.

"Not because he can't understand what's going on in class?"

"No. He's a smart boy."

"He mentioned it was Harold's fault?"

"Yes," Julia said, awaiting her thoughts.

"You've got a problem on your hands."

"Tell me."

"I just did," Shayna responded, folding her arms across her chest. "It's got something to do with Harold. Harold is not a grocer or a shoemaker. He is the mayor of Crestfall. What's so important about being mayor? I'll ask you another question: Why do children of pastors and rabbis and policemen frequently have problems?"

Julia was finally getting her drift. Of course, children of pastors and rabbis and policemen were always held to a higher standard. Maybe Sammy felt pressure because Harold was the mayor. On the other hand, some of them act out just to make sure other kids see them as normal.

"You may be right," Julia offered. "I never thought of it in that way."

"If it's because of that, you're going to be the proud owner of yet another psychologist bill for a while," Shayna said ruefully. "Poor Sammy."

Julia purposely tried to compartmentalize Sammy into another part of her mind like men are able to do. She focused on Shayna's teak Danish dining room table with a colorful red runner going down the middle. It was stacked with paper dishes, plastic utensils, fruit and candy. No *chametz* here, and no early Passover goodies, either. She had read somewhere that you weren't supposed to eat food made for Passover before the holiday. At times her mind was so over-ridden with religious restrictions that the actual beauty of Judaism was lost.

"So," Shayna was dressed in a bright pink and red tunic over black tights, "what did you think about Sophie today?"

"Sophie?" Julia had almost forgotten. Was that only this afternoon? It felt like a week.

"Sophie has big problems. She needs help to solve them, maybe like hiring a detective or someone professional." Julia raised her voice and enunciated carefully, "Someone who knows how to investigate arsons."

Shayna gave her a meaningful look. Julia knew that look. Julia also knew she was going to tell Shayna to mind her own business Then the screen door squeaked open as Torah group members began to show up.

Lilah came in wearing a tight black skirt that reached above her knees with black and white striped tights and a tight green sweater with sleeves pulled up to her elbows. The women hugged. This group was very big on hugging.

"Anything new?" Julia asked.

Lilah offered a faint smile. She and her husband had been trying to have a child for three years. "Same old, same old."

Faigie was right behind her. She was still mourning the loss of her unborn infant a few months ago and the deeds of Mel, her errant husband, but slowly, she was showing signs of life again. The mother of eight had decided to lose weight and take some time out for herself. In the last three months, she had lost close to twenty pounds. Now she was wearing a peach colored tam on her head instead of a *sheitl,* a wig, which is worn by some very observant Jewish women.

"Oh," she stepped away from Lilah and took Julia into her arms. "Esther and Sarah have been asking to see you. They want to play dolls again. Maybe you and your family could join us for dinner one night. That's if you can take the tumult of all the children," she laughed.

"Let's make a plan for after Passover," Julia said, hoping that Harold and the boys would come with her. That would make about fifteen around a very noisy table. Still, many Orthodox Jews lived by the *mitzvah* to be fruitful and multiply. In fact, Shayna had told her you get extra points for doing it over *Shabbat.*

As the women hovered between the kitchen area and the great room, trying to help Shayna, Devorah came in. One of those women who doesn't have a clue as to how beautiful she is, her face was almost hidden behind big black framed glasses. Long, dishwater blonde hair was simply held in place by a barrette on each side. As usual, Devorah was wearing a long plain grey skirt with a white blouse covered by a grey cardigan sweater.

She immediately ran to hug Julia, whispering, "I can't wait until the *seder.* David has all kinds of plans up his sleeve for the boys."

Julia was excited, relieved that the weight of having a perfect *seder* wouldn't be on her shoulders this year. In truth, preparing for a seder, even if one isn't extremely religious, is like preparing for a war. There are so many hoops to jump through, a special *seder* plate with symbols explaining the story of the Jews' escape and exile from Egypt; the several boxes of matzoh one must use instead of bread; the dishes one cooks that aren't usual the rest of the year. And that's nothing compared to the preparations around the house that the more observant Jews do.

Last, but certainly not least, were the three musketeers, Malka, Chava, and Bubbe, two sisters and their grandmother. As usual, they were bursting with loud conversation.

"I'm telling you the man is so dumb, he couldn't put a tail on a cat," Bubbe groused.

"Bubbe, enough," Malka shushed her while hanging their coats in the closet.

"Don't you shush me, you shusher. I used to powder your bare *tuchus* when you were a baby. Have some respect."

Suddenly, the older woman was all smiles. "Julia, my *shaina maidel*, how are you," she bolted across the room and took Julia's face into her hands. "Look at this face. Did I ever tell you girls what a wonderful person our Julia is?"

"A thousand times," Chava smiled. "Hello, everyone. Are we late?"

She looked around. The rabbi wasn't here yet, as usual. This was the Torah group that Shayna had cajoled Julia into. At first it was a group of strangers, women who believed deeply in Torah and followed its 613 commandments along with additional laws handed down through the ages. Julia felt like a stranger in a strange land. But, little by little, she was coming to see some of the reasoning behind the Orthodox view of Judaism. Not everything she gleaned from the Torah was acceptable to her personally, but it was fascinating to learn it.

One of the reasons for Julia's recent appreciation of Judaism was because of Rabbi Fine. He had been assigned to teach Torah by the *Kollel*, a group of very Orthodox men who sent rabbis around to educate generally Orthodox women about Jewish concepts. Rabbi Fine was a delightful, energetic soul, accepting each woman at her own level, sharing his thoughts about Jewish laws and lore, then letting them jump in with questions and comments.

"Since Rabbi Fine is late," Shayna yelled over their voices.

"As usual" Bubbe added.

"Why don't you all sit down and talk amongst yourselves. That way I can finish bringing things in without falling over you," Shayna was joking but serious at the same time. She liked to put out her dishes by her own high standards.

The women all settled in at the dining room table, shelling pistachio nuts and dishing gossip.

"Just so you know, that man puts his thumb on the scales," Bubbe was continuing her rant.

"You can't say that, Bubbe," Chava countered patiently. "It's *lashon harah*. Gossip. And we're not supposed to do that."

"I know what I know," Bubbe threw back.

"How do you know he cheats?" Malka asked. Today she was wearing a light mango and puce horizontal striped tunic with black tights. Her outfit almost outshone Shayna's. Malka was the older of the two sisters. She was a big woman with a big voice and thick frequently teased black hair.

"From all the years we've been going to Sophie's, I know what a pound of lox looks like, and I know how it feels," Bubbe insisted, a white-haired tiny imp of a woman in her eighties. "This *gonif,* Nate, he puts more paper under the lox when he weighs it on the scale. How do I know he doesn't tape three quarters under it? Then, when I get home with the lox, there's only one piece of paper, and the lox feels too light." She sniffed with distaste.

"So why don't you go back to Sophie's?" Shayna asked as she placed a bowl of herring in sour cream, onions and chopped apple on the table.

"We should," Chavah said. "It's just that when Sophie's place was closed after the fire, we switched to Nate's Nosh. I forgot Sophie's opened again."

Chava, the second sister, was smaller and more demure than Malka.

"Yeah, you and lots of others," Shayna noted. "Julia and I were in there earlier today, and she's hurting. She needs her loyal customers back."

"We'll switch back to her after the holiday." Malka spooned a generous portion of herring onto her plate. "Besides, I've heard that Nate cuts corners. I'm not so sure that everything in his deli has a *hechsher.*" Julia had learned that a *hechsher* was a sign on a product, a "K" or some other mark, proclaiming that it was kosher.

"No!" Faigie's eyes opened wide. "But we've been buying our deli meat there since Sophie's fire. Have we been eating *traif?*" She looked close to tears.

"Just wait a minute," Devorah jumped in. "Before we accuse Nate of doing anything wrong, we should check it out. We can ask the Rabbi for help. He can go and see where the meat's coming from. If Nate wants to quash a rumor, that's the way to do it."

"Did you hear about the bomb scare in Parkerton?" Lilah asked, changing the subject.

"A bomb scare?" Malka's booming voice silenced the group. "When did that happen?"

Lilah, shy about having the floor, lowered her voice to a whisper. "Parkton officials didn't want anyone to know, but my brother-in-law was at the police station, checking out their boiler. Our company is competing for their heating business. He heard the policemen talking about someone calling in a bomb threat. It was for a vacant building in the factory district, and they had to send in bomb sniffing dogs and men wearing those thick suits searching for bombs."

26

"Did they find anything?" Chava asked.

"They found a note. My brother-in-law told us it said, 'Jews aren't welcome here'."

A collective gasp from the group.

"And no one told the public about this?" Malka was furious.

Lilah shrugged. "They didn't find any bomb, and they don't know if this is a real threat or not. Why start a panic?"

"Why start a panic?" Bubbe was beside herself, almost jumping up from her chair. "Because if we ignore it, they will come again. They always come again," she almost yelled.

"Bubbe, it was a scare, not anything real," Chava soothed.

"That's what they said in the Old Country. 'It's nothing serious. Don't worry.' And look at what happened?"

Malka tish-toshed the rumors. "When something serious happens, I can assure you we'll know," she pronounced.

"Will you tell us if anything like that happens in Crestfall?" Devorah looked at Julia.

It's always like that. When someone wants to know what's going up at a building site, when someone has a bone to pick with the city, or when someone wants a traffic ticket fixed, they always turn to the mayor's wife. Julia couldn't do anything for them, though not for their lack of trying. 'She's the wife of the mayor,' they would say to themselves. 'Of course, she must have some clout.' What they didn't know was that this particular mayor wouldn't even fix a ticket for his lovely wife. "I'll do what I can," she replied. "I promise."

The door opened, Rabbi Fine came in at a fast clip. He looked like a running wrinkle factory with his white shirt almost completely hanging out in the front, his black jacket partly off, his arms overflowing with papers sticking out at all angles. He was rotund without being fat, had a short, wispy auburn beard with *peyis*, very long sideburns that he wore behind his ears, and a *yarmulke*, a small, round, suede skull cap which he usually wore under a black fedora. He always dressed in a black suit with a white shirt, and a tie that frequently exhibited whatever he had eaten for lunch. This evening, he had forgone the tie.

"*Sleecha, sleecha*, pardon me, ladies. Something came up at the last minute."

"Rabbi," Malka at least waited until Rabbi Fine took his seat, "we have a question about Nate's Nosh. There's a rumor going around that Nate doesn't always use kosher deli meat. Is there any way to find out if that's true?"

She didn't mention that she was the one stoking the rumors.

"Well," Rabbi Fine scratched his ear, "I suppose I could go talk to him or to the *mashgiach*, the rabbi who watches his kitchen. He's got to attest that everything at the store is kosher."

"And, by the way," Malka continued, spearing a plump slice of melon that matched her tunic, "I heard about a Passover mix that lets you make pancakes without flour. Is there anything wrong with that?"

"I just found another mix that lets you make donuts on Passover. It doesn't use any yeast," Faigie piped up. "Is that okay?"

Julia was stunned. Every day of the year, these women observed the tenets of Jewish law. They kept kosher homes, fasted on fast days; some went to the ritual baths to purify themselves each month, and yet, take away their donuts or their favorite grain cereals for a week during Passover, and they went bonkers.

Rabbi Fine pulled on his short beard. "If the ingredients are okay for *Pesach*, then the answer is yes. But," he raised his finger to the air and began talking in his sing song voice, "there are some who feel that even if the ingredients are acceptable, it is the intent that should be honored."

"What do you mean?" Lilah asked.

"I mean, if the Torah says you shouldn't have things that can be leavened, why make up something that generally has those grains? Why not just stick with the program?"

Yes, Julia said to herself, that's exactly what I thought. Why have pretend pancakes when real pancakes are banned? It made no sense.

They began the Passover lesson. When just about ten minutes remained, Rabbi Fine said, "Please close your books. I want to talk about something *Pesachdig* that relates to us as individuals."

They all sat quietly.

"I'm going to ask you a presumptive question." He looked at each of them before going further. "There is no right or wrong. And after I ask this question, we'll take some quiet time to think about it before talking again."

Julia's interest was piqued. Usually the class was more informal about their conversations.

"Okay," he said. "Here it is. Imagine you are in Midian as Moses was. Consider that you have just walked up to a burning bush in which the bush really isn't being consumed, and that through this fire, God has told you to go to Egypt, tell Pharaoh to let the Jews go, and then to lead them into the desert. What would you do? How would you feel?"

28

Silence. No one wanted to go first.

Malka was the first to speak. "I'd go home and pack." The rest of the women tittered.

Shayna said, "If I'm looking at this bush inside of a fire, but the bush isn't burning up, I'd probably accept that it's a message from God, and I'd have to do what He said."

"Maybe it isn't God," Faigie ventured. "Maybe it's something evil. I don't think I'd do what it said." Her recent experience with a philandering, abusive husband had made her a less trusting soul.

Julia jumped in. "I think I'd do what Moses did. I'd say that I wasn't the right person for the job, that I didn't have the experience to walk up to the leader of the Egyptians and tell him to let my people go."

"And yet," Rabbi Fine said, fixing his eyes on her, "God chose you. He knew that even though you didn't have the best resume for the job, there was something inside of you that made you the best choice."

The intensity of the rabbi's stare got to Julia. She cleared her throat and broke eye contact. Was it merely an active imagination, or was this question really directed at her?

Devorah entered the fray. She leaned in toward the table, "Moses refused God's request for seven days."

"That's correct," Rabbi Fine agreed. "Moses brought up three reasons why he was not the right person to send." He held up one finger. "He insisted that he was a bad speaker. You remember the story about him when he was a baby?"

"Oh, yes," Faigie interrupted. "Pharaoh's court set a test for baby Moses by putting two plates before him. The belief was that his future could be told by which he reached for first. One plate contained precious jewels; the other red hot coals. The baby reached for a coal and touched it to his tongue. For the rest of his life, his speech was affected." She fell back in her chair. It was rare for her to speak out at Torah.

"That's right," the Rabbi agreed. "And God's response was that his brother Aaron could speak for him."

"Moses also said no one would believe him," Bubbe added. "I wouldn't. This man, a total stranger walks up to me and says, 'get your stuff together, God told me Pharaoh's going to let us go.' Foolishness, I would think."

"And," Chava added, "he didn't want to step on his brother Aaron's toes. Aaron was already a leader among the Jews in Egypt."

"Yet God persisted," Rabbi Fine said. "Why?"

Julia thought to herself, *if I were Moses, the constant requests from God would have caused a lot of self- examination. He might ask himself what was it that God saw that convinced Him Moses was the right person for the task?*

Julia began thinking about herself, and the fact that sometimes she had to be dragged into situations that ultimately were right for her. Like Shayna's pushing her into this Torah group, for example. Why had the rabbi brought up this particular point?

Afterwards, while helping Shayna clear the table, the two women continued discussing the Passover story in preparation for the *seder* on Friday night. The rabbi had reminded them of the tradition of the feather, the candle, and the wooden spoon. One should go around the house with a lit candle to find crumbs, sweep them up with the feather into the wooden spoon, and burn them outside the night before Passover. Julia still felt she might be able convince Sammy to do that if she told him he might find something like an action figure at the end. Bribery aside, it would at least introduce him to something interesting about their religion.

Blast it, she thought, why am I the only person in the house who cares about being Jewish? Of course, it was so easy to blame it all on Harold. He did Judaism like a zombie, no affect, no outward signs of enjoyment. The boys took it all in. What could I do to change it, she pondered? Obviously her perky, positive attitude was a turn-off to the kids. If only she could put Judaism on an X-Box game, her problems would be solved.

As Julia drove back home that night, she wondered why Rabbi Fine told that story about Moses? It seemed as though he had been specifically looking at her. Did he want her to do something? If so, what? Shayna would probably say, 'I'll bet he wants you to do your thing.' My thing? Julia swerved to avoid hitting a car that had jumped the stop light to her side. What's my thing?

'Your thing,' she could imagine Shayna saying, 'Yeah, your thing…solving a mystery.'

'I may criticize, nudge, give kudos, yell, maybe, but I never lie to you,' she could imagine her friend saying in a very serious voice.

Solving a mystery, Julia thought. She had really perked up when she had worked out who had taken the missing stickpin from Shayna's house. Although it was little more than armchair logic, and she had, indeed, been lucky, it was an exciting experience. And that's not even considering the unbelievable work she and Rabbi Fine had done in finding Malka's *yad*, a jewel encrusted rod adorned by a hand with a pointing finger to help people read Torah. That case required real hunting down and eliminating suspects. Julia figured she should put up a sign saying, Julia Donnelly, finder of lost things. She'd have to further research the Jewish writings on lost and found objects.

Julia had been so involved with thinking, the car had practically driven itself home. She parked in the driveway while pondering if there was any basis to accept Shayna's musings. Then she walked inside to a manic scene.

Sammy was in the living room crying, yelling at Harold who was standing over him. Jordan was sitting in a chair as though watching a play, occasionally laughing, sometimes shouting out encouragement to his brother. Jordan was almost always the one being yelled at. Julia could see he was enjoying being on the other side of the fence for once.

"I'm not going to school tomorrow, and you can't make me."

"I told you, Mom and I will be there with you to see what we can do about your—"

Harold, red-faced, was trying to find the right word that wouldn't offend Sammy, "your problem."

"I don't have a shitty problem," Sammy shouted. "You're the problem," he sobbed. "The whole world's the problem."

He'd never said a swear word in their presence before. As parents, Julia and Harold weren't stupid. He probably knew more swear words than they did, but he'd never crossed the line to curse in front of mom and dad.

What in heaven's name was going on here, Julia wondered, standing in the living room doorway. As she had many times, she tried to rush in and make it all better, but Sammy would have none of it. He pushed her away. It was the first time her baby didn't want his mother. Julia wanted to cry, but being a parent sometimes means you have to tamp down your own feelings. She remembered Sammy as a dear, little infant so many years ago, cuddling his head in the crook of her neck. What had happened to make him act this way? As soon as they handled this outburst, Julia was going to lock the bedroom door and cry her eyes out.

"Look," she said, "we can agree to disagree here." Julia turned to Harold. He looked like he wanted to punch a wall, and Sammy was a puddle of angry tears.

"He won't listen to any reason," Harold was breathing heavily. The only time he got emotional was when they were smack in the middle of a Jordan escapade. Never with Sammy.

"Sammy," Julia interjected before anything violent occurred, "you will go to school tomorrow. We'll meet with the counselor, but I promise you, we'll all come home after the meeting. We have to decide what to do with you, then we'll put that plan in action next week. You will not be staying in school," She enunciated quite clearly. "Do you understand?"

He nodded, looking miserable. Julia could usually appeal to his reasonable side, but in this case, he was stonewalling them. Suddenly he ran up the stairs and slammed the door to his room.

"Harold," she folded her arms across her chest, "this subject is closed for the evening. A new bottle of merlot is calling our name from the basement fridge. Why don't you open it? We can both use a glass or two. And as for you, Jordan—

"What? What did I do? I'm going to school. I haven't done anything wrong," he stammered.

Knowing Jordan, Julia was pretty sure he had done something and was terrified that she had found out about it.

"Why don't you be a good big brother and try to calm Sammy down? We don't know exactly what set him off, but if one of us is hurting, it affects the whole family." That was a concept that Rabbi Fine had taught the Torah group. It certainly applied to this situation.

Jordan looked at his mother with surprise. She was treating him like an adult. This was at a higher level of needing his help than carrying groceries into the house or mowing the lawn.

"Okay, Mom," he said, and went upstairs to Sammy's room. The door closed. It was a rare occasion that the two boys were on the same page.

"Why are you looking at me like I did something wrong?" Harold asked. "You're always complaining that you have to be the bad guy and I get off scot free. Well, this time I took charge because you weren't here, for a change. So what's your beef now?"

"Nothing," Julia said, walking down to the basement refrigerator for that bottle of wine. She never, ever, drank alcoholic beverages beyond religious holidays and family functions. This hullabaloo had made her too tired to think of anything except having a glass of merlot, taking a hot bath and getting a good night's sleep. Tomorrow's meeting was going to be brutal, but Friday night they'd be going to Devorah's for Passover. At least that was something to look forward to.

It was like one of those football games where they say one team won ugly.

Sammy refused to get dressed. For a skinny kid, he sure had a lot of fight in him.

Harold announced that they would take him to school in his pajamas. That didn't faze Sammy.

He refused to leave his room. Since Harold weighed about 165 pounds to Sammy's 60, he was able to carry the struggling child down the stairs. The screaming was blood curdling. In between the kicking and hitting, Julia idly wondered what the neighbors might think. Then, she had a bright idea. If Sammy was so hysterical about going to school, why not bring the school to him?

She told Harold to halt and let the prisoner go. Sammy made a beeline for his bedroom and, no surprise, slammed the door. Luckily there was no lock on it. Julia called the school counselor and she agreed to come to them. Then, proud of her coolness under fire, she took a breath.

Mrs. Finiken arrived twenty minutes later. Sammy wouldn't come downstairs, so Mrs. Finiken went into his room alone, came out some ten minutes later and sat in Harold's favorite living room chair. She didn't look like Julia's old teachers who used to wear about three different dresses a year, one black, one navy blue, and another deep purple. She most likely was five years out of college, an attractive woman if you like perky cheerleaders, and seemed very understanding.

"He won't tell me what the deeper problem is," she explained, "but apparently, he thinks he's wasting time in class because the teacher repeats things over and over again when he gets it the first time. He says he wants to smash his head on his desk in desperation."

"So, that's public school," Harold said. "You've got to make sure every child understands the concepts being taught."

But Sammy is in all of our accelerated classes. He's at the top of what we offer," Mrs. Finiken shrugged her shoulders. "I brought his records with me." She opened a manila file. "Though he tests high, these results may not even show the extent of his capabilities."

"So you're saying that maybe he's too bright for your school?" Julia was sitting on the sofa quietly wringing her hands.

"I'm not saying that at this point," Mrs. Finiken said. "But it bears more study.

"If Sammy's right, then sitting in a class where he knows the answers before the teacher asks the question is like torture to him. As to the other, deeper problem he mentioned," she looked at Harold, "I think you might consider taking him to a psychologist. You've got a very unhappy child up there."

"I seem to remember that it's the school's responsibility to educate each child based upon that student's need," Harold was pacing around the room. "Even if he's in all accelerated classes, the school still has the duty to give our son enrichment materials, or even additional curricula to meet his needs."

"We'll cross that bridge when we get there," Mrs. Finiken remarked. "Right now we have to discover what his problems are."

"Well," Julia asked, "what are we supposed to do now? He should be going to school."

Mrs. Finiken smiled. "We do have a tutoring service. We could send teachers here to teach him two or three times a week for each subject. That way he won't fall behind. In the meantime, we can retest him. If the results show that he is above what our school offers, I can give you a list of private academies to look into."

She closed her file and rose from the chair. "I'll come back on Monday to test him, and I will begin sending tutors on Tuesday. Let's see how that works." Mrs. Finiken put her hand on Julia's shoulder. "It will be alright. If you were to see some of the cases that come through my office, you'd realize that Sammy's suggests a very positive outcome. Just be patient."

After she left, Julia dropped back onto the flowered camel-back sofa. Harold had reclaimed his chair. His brow was furrowed.

"How do you think it went?" he asked.

"I can't think of anything more to do than to call the same shrink Jordan sees. We ought to get a family rate," Julia sighed.

"Do you think the kid's some kind of genius?"

"I don't know," Julia responded. "I wish we knew something about his birth parents." Sammy had been left in front of a Planned Parenthood office door with no information. They had no idea what health problems to look out for, no clue as to what illnesses were in his family tree, or his parents' IQs. Still, when Julia saw him just five days old, she knew that he was meant to be their son.

Harold looked at his watch. "I've got a meeting in twenty minutes. Is it okay to go?"

"Sure," Julia dragged herself off of the couch. She was used to playing back-up. "I'll go and explain what's going to happen. You do what you have to do."

Satisfied that he was free to go, Harold picked up his briefcase and made a run for the back door. Julia went upstairs, knocked on Sammy's door and went in.

"Here's what we're gonna do," She put fake cheer in her voice and explained the testing, tutoring and shrink ideas.

"And I won't have to go to school again?"

"Well, maybe not that school, depending on your test scores. If your brain's too big for public school, we'll find another place that will challenge you rather than bore you to death. I'm so sorry," she said. "We had no idea that school was so horrible for you."

Sammy's face crumpled. "I'm different from the other kids. They always act so silly, and I just want to learn stuff."

"But why did you say that Dad's the problem."

He looked at me. "I'll talk to the shrink about that, Mom." Even though the issues remained, Sammy seemed lighter, as though a huge weight had been lifted from his shoulders.

"Alrighty, then." Julia rubbed her hands together. "Well, tomorrow is Passover, Kiddo, and since you're home you're not going to be a slouch. First you're going to get dressed, eat a good breakfast, none of that sugary cereal for you today. We're going to buy a special kit with a feather, a wooden spoon and a candle. It's for some Torah group stuff. Then you, Jordan, and I are going to do it in the house tonight unless Dad's home, then we'll all do it together." He rolled his eyes. "After we get the kit, we'll swing by Sophie's deli and buy a delicious lunch to eat at home. And tomorrow night," she said, feeling her enthusiasm rise, "we'll all go to my friend Devorah's house for a real old time *seder*. And no long face, okay?"

"Okay, Mom." He allowed a ghost of a smile to reach his lips. Julia opened her arms and held Sammy tightly as he fell into her embrace.

They arrived at Sophie's at lunchtime, never a good idea if you're in a hurry.

"Here." Julia took a number and gave it to Sammy. "You order the sandwiches. Get me a salami on rye with regular mustard and a dill pickle. Take it from those barrels over there. You can get whatever you want."

Happy to have his own responsibility, Sammy waited in the human sea of impatient people trying to make their final purchases before *Pesach*. Julia went over to the freezer section to choose a half pound of chopped liver for herself, and a pound container for Devorah. There weren't going to be too many people at her *seder*, so a pound was more than enough. Other than Julia, the Donnelly family wouldn't touch the stuff, so that half pound was more than enough for her at home. A man blocked Julia's way to the freezer. He was dressed oddly. Though it wasn't cold out, he wore a hat low on his face and a heavy coat that hid his body. He looked like a street person. She wondered why he was hanging around this part of the freezer section, since chopped liver was pricey. Finally he finished whatever he was doing and hurried out of the store. When Julia thought about him later, she couldn't recall him actually taking any liver out.

Sammy's number was called. Lunch and liver were paid for, the errands were over, and mother and son drove home. They sat at the kitchen table eating their sandwiches on the wrapped paper from the store so they wouldn't have to wash dishes.

"Boy, you sure picked the perfect pickle," Julia announced with juice dripping down her chin.

"The regular pickles we buy in the jars are kind of tasteless," Sammy said, proud that his choice had pleased her.

"Yup," she responded. "The old dills like this have a sharpness to their taste as they go down your gullet. But it takes a long time to get this taste. Today's delis don't want to wait so long for their pickles."

"Were all the delis and grocery stores like Sophie's back in the olden days when you were a kid?" he asked. "I've seen some old-time pictures with guys wearing big mustaches that remind me of her place."

The fact that her son thought that she might have been around in the 1920s was somewhat distressing, but at least this was a real discussion about something more substantial than which super hero was the strongest of them all. Julia suddenly realized it was rare for her to spend time with just one son. Usually the Donnellys went to events as a family; rarely having enough alone time with each son. She would offer Sammy and Jordan snacks when they returned from school; she'd ask each how their day had been, often receiving a grunt, or a 'fine.' Then Jordan would go off to his room to play computer games and Sammy might get a head start on homework. Apart from finding out where they were going when they tried to leave the house, there was little depth to their daily communication. That's got to change, she decided.

After a cheese lasagna dinner, Julia informed Jordan and Sammy that they would be participating in the "*bedikat chametz.*"

"That's Jewishy stuff," Jordan balked. "You know I'm not into that."

"Mom, do I have to?" Sammy whined.

She gave each of them the omnipotent stare every mother has that wordlessly expresses further remarks will be to no avail. The deed will be done. Thus says THE MOTHER.

The trick is to use the look so rarely that the boys wouldn't question it any further.

As a result, Sammy, Jordan, and Julia stalked the house for errant breadcrumbs. She had left trails of crumbs around the house while the boys were in their rooms after dinner. Jordan held the candle while Sammy used a feather to scoop up the crumbs into a wooden spoon. They went along with it for Julia's sake, then were completely surprised at the end of the sortie when the breadcrumbs led Sammy to the newest action figure for his collection and Jordan to a crisp ten dollar bill.

"Hey, cool, Mom. Count me in any time." Jordan neatly placed the bill in his wallet.

"That wasn't so bad," Sammy admitted. "Can we do it again next year?"

"Sure." Julia's heart almost burst. This year an action figure, a ten dollar bill. Next year a more in depth discussion of why we do this. Sometimes progress is slow, but the journey is worth it.

"But there's more," she announced. Both boys stood still as statues as they waited to hear what other fiendish activity their mother had planned for them.

"Tomorrow morning, before you leave for school," she said, "we'll burn the crumbs, the feather, the wooden spoon and the bag. I'll recite a prayer and we're done."

Usually a statement that required more effort from the boys would have resulted in slumped shoulders and peeved looks on their faces. This time, Jordan yelled, "I get to do the fire."

Sammy piped up, "I decide where we're making the fire, and I get to throw in the feather and the wooden spoon."

Amazingly, there was peace. 'S*halom bayit*,' they call it in the Torah group. At the same time, a quote jumped into Julia's head that a journey begins with a first step.

Sammy went upstairs to play with his new figure, a monstrosity, in Julia's opinion. It looked like a green samurai warrior with several arms, each of which held a different weapon. And even though Julia was full from dinner, she snuck to the refrigerator and took a couple of generous tablespoons full of Sophie's chopped liver. Ambrosia. Shayna was right. It was a perfect appetizer for the *seder*.

"Welcome to the Kasbah." Devorah laughed as the Donnelly family entered her large living/dining room. The floor was awash in huge woven Kilim pillows in Turkish and Afghani red and brown designs alongside bedroom pillows in colorful cases. They were propped against the chairs and sofa. Julia could almost imagine they were in some nomadic tent in the desert except for the surrounding walls of books and art.

"I'm just very happy you could come." Devorah hugged Julia so hard, she almost squashed the chopped liver container between them. "This is such a treat. David loves leading a *seder* with children," she whispered in Julia's ear. "Our family lives on the east coast, so we only see the nieces and nephews on bar and bat mitzvah celebrations or the occasional visit."

Sammy awkwardly presented her with a bouquet purchased earlier in the day.

Devorah accepted it with a small bow. "Thank you, kind sir. Chivalry is not dead."

Sammy blushed.

Julia left Harold and the boys under David's ministrations while she and Devorah dodged pillows and made their way to the kitchen.

"Julia, this is my Aunt Rose and her friend Tzippi, whom I consider an aunt, too."

"Pleased to meet you," Rose piped. She was a tiny, elfin woman with a helmet of white hair tinted blue. She was currently placing carrot slices on top of pieces of home-made *gefilte fish.*

"And I'm Tzippi," a lively bird-like presence added. At eighty-plus years old, her orangey-red hair was arranged in tight curls showing her scalp. "Rose and I have been neighbors for what?"

"Thirty years," Rose answered, "give or take a decade."

"You know, we made the *gefilte fish* by ourselves," Tzippi piped in.

"Right," Rose agreed. "No fish balls in a jar for us. Only fresh."

"Oh, what's that?" Tzippi pointed to the white container Devorah carried. "Chopped liver."

"From where?" Rose asked.

"Sophie's," Julia responded.

The two women shared a knowing look and smiled at an inside joke.

"The best," Tzippi *kvelled.* "We've been buying from her for years."

"So sorry about the fire," Rose added. "She's such a wonderful cook."

Tzippi reached for the carton. "May I?" she asked, taking off the top and sticking in a tablespoon.

"Yum," she crooned, putting her hand on her chest. "Do you have any Tam Tam crackers?"

Julia had brought a box of the Passover Tam Tams in her tote bag.

Rose dipped in a cracker to take a taste. "Sophie must have added an additional ingredient this year," she noted. "It's a little different, but still delicious."

When Tzippi went for a third taste, Rose slapped her hand in a good-natured way.

"Don't eat it all, Tzippi. Leave some for the others."

The others meant Devorah and David. Julia's family wouldn't think of eating chopped liver, vegetarian or otherwise, and she had already been sated on the liver she'd bought earlier.

Rose removed the liver from the carton and put it onto a small platter. She quickly shaped it into a dome with a spoon, then surrounded it with matzoh crackers.

"There," she looked at her work critically. "Now it's ready to be served."

"Not so fast, Auntie," Devorah said. Methodically she studded the liver with pitted black olives. "Now it's ready to go to the guys."

Tzippi nodded in Rose's direction. "That one rushes so much, she'll probably be early to her own funeral," she joked.

"Stop it," Rose snapped. She spit three times and knocked on the wooden table. "It's bad luck to mention such things."

"Let's see," Devorah murmured to herself, "what's left to be done?"

It was then Julia noticed the earthy aromas of the brisket coming from a covered platter, fragrant apricot, sweet potato and prune *tzimmes*, a dish that cooked forever and just got better with time (another dish Julia's family would skip, even though she loved it). Bright green asparagus was covered by freshly squeezed lemon and pepper. Julia sensed the redolence of sweet and savory matzoh and farfel kugels. Eying the other covered dishes was like an exciting game of 'what's under the foil?' She was reminded of her grandmother's kitchen when she was a child, a comfortable steaming jumble of moist plump raisins, fresh cherry and pear compotes and flourless chocolate cakes topped with raspberries. This meal promised to be a gustatory delight, if nothing else.

"If the *seder* plate's ready, so are we," Rose looked for the dish with indentations for Passover's ceremonial ingredients.

Devorah discovered it behind the *gefilte fish* sitting on the stove. "Okay," she said, "*karpas, beitza, maror, charoset…*"

"You know what it all means?" Rose asked kindly. She was treating Julia like a non-Jew, which wasn't far from the truth.

"I know what to put on the plate when I have a *haggadah* in my hand, Julia said. "I just don't remember what they signify. I do know that *maror*, the bitter herbs, reminds us of the bitterness of slavery."

"Good, dear," Tzippi said. She had just returned from the living room and was finishing another Tam Tam cracker with chopped liver.

"Tzippi, stop already. You won't have an appetite for dinner if you keep hitting the liver. Devorah will be so disappointed all her cooking will be wasted on you."

Devorah hid a smile as she placed the *zroah* on the plate. "This," she explained, "is the shank bone representing the special lamb that was brought to the Temple in Jerusalem on Passover as an offering to *HaShem*. It also reminds us that *HaShem* 'passed over' our ancestors' houses in Egypt awaiting the plague of the death of the first born."

"The boiled egg, the *beitza*, round and smooth, symbolizes new life that comes with the season of spring," Tzippi added.

Charoset, Julia already knew, was a delightfully sweet mixture of apples, honey, wine, cinnamon and walnuts which represent the mortar for the bricks our ancestors used building pyramids for the Egyptians. That's the one seder dish that everyone in her house loved. She had to chop copious amounts of apples the night before their *seder* so the boys could eat the tasty dish as a snack the next few days.

"And *karpas* is parsley, a sign of spring, which we dip into salt water to remind us of the tears and sweat of our ancestors when they toiled as slaves," Rose noted somberly.

"Though I frequently use lettuce," Tzippi said.

"But parsley is more accepted." Rose put in her two cents.

"I disagree," Tzippi sniped.

"Those two have been bickering like that since I was old enough to understand," Devorah whispered. "They married two brothers, who, unfortunately died years ago. Such a loss." She sighed, then called out to David, "Pour the wine, Honey, everything's set. And don't forget Elijah's cup."

Elijah was a prophet said to travel to every *seder* in the world, a heavy duty job. Each table had a cup of wine for him, and many children watched that cup all evening to see if the spirit had taken a sip before going on to the next home. A *bubbemeisah*, an old wives' tale, swore that if a child fell asleep at the

Passover table, Elijah might take him away. The children never knew where, and no one ever fell asleep to anyone's knowledge.

Julia walked into the dining room. The men were standing in a corner, talking in low tones. She sidled closer.

"Devorah told me about the bomb scare in Parkerton," David said.

Harold looked uncomfortable.

"Has anything happened in Crestfall?"

"Not yet," Harold replied, "but so far three surrounding towns have received some kind of threat. No real bombs were found, but one fake bomb was located at a park. People were told there was a gas leak and left quickly. Police found the bomb at the bottom of a slide. Imagine if it had been real, and a kid had slid into it?"

Harold put his hand over his mouth and shook his head. "Why isn't anyone saying something about this?" David asked.

"Because what these people want is recognition, scare power. This could be the work of a couple of teenagers for all we know. Should we set all of our communities on edge because of some stupid kids?" Harold put his hand on David's arm. "Rest assured, we haven't had anything happen here, yet, and if it's serious enough, we'll tell the public. For now, we wait. Each town has a task force that's doing nothing but searching for who's doing this."

"But," David murmured, "if we say nothing, they may continue their scare tactics, raising the level each time they're ignored."

"Right now, this is what the mayors have agreed to do. Tomorrow is another day. I don't like to keep the public ignorant on this, either."

Devorah came in, her face red from being in a hot kitchen. "*Seder* time," she called.

They all arranged themselves on the pillows. Sammy and Jordan reveled in the fact that the *seder* service would be on the floor, their favorite place as they generally lounged in front of the television set in the Donnelly family room. Even the aunts looked comfortable in their elastic-waist pants. The *seder* plate was placed in front of David.

"So, Davidleh, let's get going," Tzippi said. "We don't need a three hour performance. I've only got so long to live!"

Julia's eyebrows must have risen past her hairline. "Don't worry, Aunt Tzippi, I've timed it at two hours and fifty-five minutes," David responded with a straight face.

Sammy, Jordan, and Harold looked stricken. Devorah nudged Julia's foot and whispered, "Don't worry. They do the same thing every year. They like to

46

scare our guests."

They ran through the beginning blessings of the *haggadah,* the book that explains how to conduct a *seder.* Harold and Jordan's faces were blank. Julia assumed that Harold had zoned out to consider some budget matter and Jordan was thinking about girls in bikinis or whatever. Only Sammy seemed to be listening carefully.

At last they came to the story itself, the tale that is told in every Jewish household in the world on Passover; how God took the Jewish people out of Egypt, removed them from slavery, and brought them to the Promised Land. David eventually came to the Hebrew words that were etched in Julia's mind, "*Avadeem hayeenoo l'faroh b'mitzrayim.* We were slaves of Pharaoh in the land of Egypt, but the Lord our God brought us out of there with a strong hand and an out- stretched arm."

David glanced at Sammy. "What?" he asked. Sammy hesitated.

"It's okay," David said. "Kids are supposed to ask questions tonight of all nights."

"It's just that," he hesitated, "do you really believe all of this stuff happened? I mean, the ten plagues, the clouds of fire, the parting of the Sea of Reeds? And the story of the Jews walking through the desert for forty years? How come so long? How could they eat? How could they drink?" Sammy appeared to be embarrassed that he had said so much to a room full of adults.

"You know, you're not the only one to doubt. I did once, too, a long time ago. But," David went on, " in Israel this is taught as actual history."

"Can they prove any of it?"

"Yes," David responded with certainty. "Of course, there are many theories of where these things happened, but I prefer the one I am going to tell you now."

Julia could tell by the look on Harold's face that he had just decided he was in the presence of a religious kook, but for her sake, was going to hold his tongue. In fact, earlier that day, as Harold was putting on his pants in their bedroom, he had calmly announced, 'You're going to owe me big for this one.'

"I beg to differ," Julia said, buttoning her blouse. "I seem to recall going with you to at least a hundred rubber chicken dinners and smiling vapidly at rooms full of literal strangers just to help you out with your career."

"But this isn't as important as a career," he said. "It's just for one of your 'Torah friends.'" Special emphasis on Torah friends, as if they were freaks.

"They're just as important to me as your constituents are to you," Julia retorted. Was that true, she asked herself? Was she giving the Torah group that much weight? Did it really mean so much? She didn't know at that moment.

They finished dressing in silence. Julia's mind clicked back to David, as he had continued talking.

"Let's take some of your questions." He stretched out his long legs. "You asked how they could eat and drink during their trek in the desert. The Torah mentions times in which the Jewish people demanded that Moses find water for them. Well, I've got two for you, and you won't believe where they are. First is a place called Marah, which means bitter. Three days after crossing the Sea of Reeds, the Jewish people were wandering in the desert, parched. Finally they came upon water, but when they drank, it was bitter to the taste. What good is bitter water?"

"Not much," Jordan said.

"It might make you sick," Sammy added, scratching his head.

"Right. So, Moses cried out to *HaShem* for help, and *HaShem* basically pointed out a tree to Moses, and told him to throw it into the water. Suddenly," David said in hushed tones, "the water tasted as sweet as honey, and all the people drank."

"How do you know that's true?" Sammy demanded. "Because it's a lake bed of clay, no sand. Water coming up through clay is alkaline, bitter."

"What's alkaline?" Jordan asked.

Julia was amazed he was following this.

Harold broke in. "It's a salt mixture that has a bitter taste. It dissolves easily in water and is present in some soils of very dry regions."

"How did you know that?" She was awed by her husband's knowledge of the arcane.

"Comes from sharing info with other mayors. Some people have clay wells out west; their water is bitter. The cities have to pipe in better water which raises taxes."

Sammy directed another question to David. "You said there's another story?"

"Yes," David continued. He crossed his legs camp style. Sammy did the same. "The Torah notes that on the way to Mt. Sinai, Moses and his people camped by Elim, a place with seventy palm trees and twelve springs of water. Today it's called Al Bad, and it's about half way from the coast of the Sea of Reeds and Mt. Sinai. They're both in Saudi Arabia." he paused. "Now, today it may not have twelve actual springs, but the palm trees are still there. It does exist. It is a geographical fact." David noted. "You can check it out."

"How can these places be in Saudi Arabia and not Israel?" Sammy wanted to know.

48

"I'll tell you in a minute. But first, you asked about food. The Torah tells us that God provided manna every day early in the morning. Each family would gather just enough for its household. I've researched this, and there are several different scientific explanations of what manna was and still is. Some scientists say that the manna actually was similar to mushrooms, which we know are breeding grounds for insects that decompose quickly. The fungi produce molecules that resemble human neurochemicals, and appear as small fibers that look like hoarfrost."

"Shrooms," Jordan had awakened from his stupor. "Cool."

"Another type is turkey oak manna formed by aphids, and appears in a white form. Still, a third kind is made of the crystallized "honeydew" of certain scale insects. In the desert, this sweet tasting crust dries quickly in the desert sun, and must be collected before sunrise each day."

"David," Devorah interrupted, "enough about plant lice before dinner."

"Okay. We'll change direction. You've heard of Mount Sinai where the Hebrews received the Ten Commandments? That's no fantasy. It's still there. Some scholars believe it's located in Saudi Arabia and they call it Jabal al Lawz. If you look at a map, you'll see Marah, Elim and Mt. Sinai in the proper order. All I'm suggesting, Sammy, is to keep an open mind. There are other professionals who have different interpretations of where these places are located. The most important thing, though, is that they believe these sites exist.

"And," David said, "as for your question of why they had to wander in the desert for forty years, consider this. What were the Jews when they left Egypt?"

"Slaves." Julia's eldest son was still with them. He was into aliens who make humans slaves in his video games.

"Do you think slaves would immediately understand the concept of being free after four hundred years of servitude?"

"Maybe not," Sammy said.

"They were used to bowing down to Egyptian idols, living like Egyptians. They had to learn what it was to be their own people. In fact, many of the original slaves died during the trip. Those who remained accepted Jewish beliefs and the Jewish way of life. The forty years of wandering prepared them to be Jews." David paused. "Does that answer some of your questions, Sammy?"

"Yeah," he replied, sounding more relaxed than he'd been in the last two days. David was like a magic elixir for him.

After finishing the first part of the *haggadah*, it was time to eat. All of the women got up to bring in dinner. The food was delicious. For some reason, even though Julia cooked some of the very same dishes at home, her sons seemed to enjoy Devorah's food more than hers. She felt a prick of jealousy at the back of her neck On the other hand, she was more than pleased that her sons seemed to be enjoying themselves. Just before the boys were going to search for the *afikoman*, all hell broke loose.

Suddenly Aunt Tzippi gave Harold a glassy stare and whispered in a trembling voice, "Edward, you've come back. You've been gone so long."

Rose quickly put a hand on her shoulder. "Tzippi, Edward's been gone for ten years. He died, dear."

"No," Tzippi pointed a shaking finger at Harold. "Thass him," her words were slurring.

Julia watched as her glassy eyes began rolling up in their sockets. "Breathe..." she gasped before passing out.

David jumped up. "I'm calling 911," he shouted. "Devorah, keep her breathing. Do CPR, anything," he ordered urgently.

In less than five minutes EMTs arrived and took Aunt Tzippi out on a stretcher. Devorah and Rose drove off to the hospital. David urged the Donnellys to go home.

"I'm not leaving all this food to spoil," Julia told him. "We'll wrap everything in tinfoil and put it in the refrigerator. You go to the hospital with your family."

He quickly showed them how to lock the front door, then ran out of the condo. Julia, Harold, and the kids brought their plates to the kitchen and worked in tandem to clean up. They'd never done anything like that as a family before. The boys were in shock. Harold and Julia were, too. Tzippi had seemed to be such a lively person. What had happened to her?

When all the dishes were in the dishwasher, even though it was *Shabbat* and the first night of Passover, a time Orthodox Jews would refrain from using electronics, Julia turned it on. She didn't want Devorah to return to a house with dirty dishes. They locked the door, went home, and broke out the ice cream. Tzippi had gotten ill just before dessert. Some people can't eat when they're upset. At the Donnelly house, unhappiness meant a refrigerator raid on the most unhealthy junk food around, like ice cream.

"Sammy," Julia commented, as they ate butter pecan ice cream, "those were really good questions."

"Yeah." His mouth was full of his favorite flavor. "David is kind of cool. You know, he talks to kids like we're equals or something. I wouldn't mind going over there again."

"It wasn't totally boring, like our *seders*," Jordan added.

50

"What made it so different?" Julia wanted to know.

"Like he believed that Passover is more than a story. In Sunday school, it's like everything is a fairy tale," Sammy said, "but to David, it's real life history."

Surprise. All Julia had to do was get a degree in Judaic studies, relate it to her children, and maybe then they wouldn't throw bits of mitzvah at each other during their *seders*.

On the other hand, Julia was proud of how the boys had acted during the *seder* and the frightening scene with Tzippi. After the family polished off a quart of ice cream, Julia reminded herself to call Devorah on Sunday when Shabbat would be over and prayed that Tzippi was well on the road to recovery.

Just before going to bed, Sammy asked Julia to come into his room.

"Mom," he asked in a voice that took her back to his early years, "what do you think's going to happen to Tzippi? Is she going to live?"

Julia sat on his bed and took his hand.

"Honey," she said, "I don't know. I hope she's okay. The doctors will do everything they can for her."

"Is there anything we can do to help her?"

"Pray," Julia said. "Not something you may have learned as a kid in Sunday School, but real thoughts from your heart."

"How do you know that God will hear me?"

"How could God not?" she said, thinking hard about saying the right thing. This was one of those moments a parent does not want to screw up.

"God hears all," Julia fervently hoped her statement was true. "That doesn't mean your prayers will work out the way you want, but I doubt that He'll ignore words from a pure soul like yours."

She kissed her son on the forehead.

"Mom," he said.

"What, sweetheart?"

"I love you."

And that is all a mother can ever ask for.

Devorah called from the hospital on Saturday night, just after the first three stars appeared in the sky. That's when Julia knew that the Shabbat restrictions were over.

"Julia, you won't believe it. Tzippi almost died Friday night."

"Almost died? What happened? One minute she was fine. The next, she was hallucinating."

"The doctors don't know yet," Devorah said. "They ended up pumping her stomach, giving her charcoal. They're going to analyze her stomach contents to see what might have caused it. Julia," her voice broke, "I can't believe that anything I cooked could have made this happen. I mean, we all ate the same thing."

"You can't blame yourself, Devorah. We don't know if something reacted to some medication she was taking. Is she okay now? Can she have visitors?"

"They're going to keep her here for a few more days. She's so dehydrated from everything they did last night. Aunt Rose is a basket case. They're like sisters." Devorah began to cry into the phone. "I don't know what I'd do if anything happened to her. My mother died when I was only sixteen. Rose and Tzippi have both been like mothers to me all these years."

"Look," Julia said. "She made it this far. Give her time to heal. The doctors will work out what happened. Go home. Rest. She's probably sleeping it off anyway. I'll try to visit tomorrow when she's stronger. And don't worry. We put everything away Friday night. Probably in all the wrong places, but at least you won't come home to a messy kitchen."

"Bless you," Devorah laughed. "I'm sure everything will be all right. I'm just so confused. David and I are fine. Was anyone sick at your house last night?"

"No."

"*Baruch Hashem.* Thank God. Well, I'll go now. Thanks for listening."

"Call me if you need anything."

"Thank you, Julia. You're a good friend."

As soon as she hung up the phone, Shayna called from Florida.

"Your line was busy forever," she whined. "Who were you talking to for so long?"

"Devorah." Julia explained what had happened on Friday night."

"Whoo boy," she exclaimed. "Something strange is going on, maybe a coincidence, maybe not. You won't believe what I'm calling about. You know a lot of our acquaintances come to this Florida hotel for Passover. They really do a great job; a wonderful rabbi, fantastic food, you can't imagine. And the desserts are to die for," she gushed.

"And so?" Julia wanted to pick up the pace. Shayna wouldn't call to just *kvell* over the matzah ball soup.

"So, this evening, two people I know got calls from Crestfall. Members of two families have ended up in the hospital gravely ill from some kind of food poisoning. I was calling to see if you're okay."

"We're all fine, thank God."

Shayna was right. Could it be a coincidence that so many people would end up with severe stomach problems on the same night? There had to be some connection.

"Do the doctors know what the cause is?" Julia asked. "No," Shayna yelled. She always yelled over the telephone like the fact that she was all the way in Florida meant her voice wouldn't carry over the phone lines. "It's a mystery," she said, with a meaningful pause.

"What's going on in your little head?" Julia wondered out loud.

"I just thought…you know."

"You know what?" Julia countered.

"You might do a little snooping when you visit Devorah's Aunt Tzippi. See what's going on."

"For heaven's sake, Shayna, I have no business sneaking around the hospital looking for I don't know what. Let's wait till the doctors find out if the cases have anything in common. Then we'll know what's happening." Julia let out a long, exasperated sigh.

"Okay," Shayna warned, "but watch out. Something *meshuge* is going on up there. I'll call you tomorrow and let you know if I find out more."

Something crazy was going on but, Julia convinced herself, it had nothing to do with her.

Hospitals always got to Julia; the astringent smell of alcohol, the memory of painful allergy shots, the sickly sweet suckers the doctors used to give her when she didn't cry after a visit. Still, it was important to go to the hospital to see Tzippi. Devorah had informed her Aunt Tzippi was alert, worrying about who would water her plants. As Julia walked down the hallway, following the receptionist's directions, she saw a familiar face. Rabbi Fine. He was walking toward her at a fast clip, looking worried and more distracted than usual.

"Ah, Julia," he said, as though raised from deep thought. "Just the person I wanted to see."

"Me? Did I do something wrong?"

She was always apologizing for the silliest things. Even when she slammed a door by accident, she would unconsciously say, 'Excuse me.'

"No. Of course not. I'm sorry. My mind's full of other things. Who are you here to visit?"

"Devorah's Aunt Tzippi. During the *seder* Friday night she became very ill and we had to call 911."

"Another one," he murmured.

"Another one what?" Julia asked, a feeling of distress growing in her chest.

"Julia," he hesitated, then decided to say what he wanted to say, "I've just visited two members of one family. One of their Friday night *seder* guests died yesterday. But that's not the end of it." His face was ashen. "We have an informal rabbi's hotline between the synagogues in Crestfall and the surrounding towns. This morning I found out there are four more victims from two other *seders*; all with similar symptoms; all had their stomachs pumped. By my count, including Devorah's aunt, that's eight people, and so far three have passed away."

"Oh no." Julia's hands automatically went to her face. She was horrified.

Rabbi Fine looked haggard. "I don't believe in coincidences. Do you?"

Julia had a sick feeling. She knew what he was going to say and tried to head him off before he made the request. She turned toward him with her palms held up in submission.

"Rabbi, what could we possibly do?"

"That's the ticket." Suddenly he was glowing with enthusiasm. He raised a fist in a sign of victory. "What can we do to solve this enigma? I knew you would understand, Julia. We have a case."

"Wait, Rabbi." Hands in submission danced a quick ballet, rapidly turning into her hands held out, as though warding off something bad. Rabbi Fine had turned her meaning completely around. What could we possibly do, he asked? Julia countered, "We can give this to people better acquainted in the ways of death and dying." This was definitely a matter for the police was what she meant, not that she and the Rabbi should jump into an investigation. Julia was feeling like a cornered cat. She could just imagine Harold's response if she went home and announced she was going to work on a "case" in solving life and death! At least locating Shayna's stick pin hadn't used up too much of her time, and locating Malka's *yad* wasn't too terribly dangerous except for one black eye and some sore muscles.

They were passing the women's wing. Rabbi Fine led Julia to a chair in the maternity ward. Julia had never felt comfortable in maternity wards. They brought back the memories of her inability to become pregnant, to fulfill what she believed was the inherent gift of being a woman. She was equally uncomfortable now, knowing the rabbi was going to convince her to do something she knew would get her into a lot of trouble.

"Look," he said, leaning forward in a nearby chair. The entire room was filled with soft pastel colors and whimsical photos of little animals posing in human clothes. It felt like a bizarre zoo. "What if some terror group is targeting Jews by poisoning them? The question is how could they get so many people to eat the same thing? Most of the meal is cooked by the different hostesses and their guests. Some people do fish or chicken. Not everyone has brisket. And most people make their own matzah kugel. Some use apples and raisins. Some use potato. No. It has to be something that people usually buy in a store. But," he pondered, "there are so many stores. How could anyone know where everyone is shopping?"

He was unconsciously *davening*, moving his body rhythmically back and forth the way the religious say their prayers. As he stroked his short beard, Julia was reminded of a lesson in which he had described the way he taught Torah as a loose definition of "*pilpul*." *Pilpul*, she remembered him saying in his sing-song voice, is a method of analyzing the similarities or contradictions between different *Talmudic* texts when studying a particular principle. "If you look at this text's explanation of a point, then it follows that X will be true. But," he went on, "if you look at a different text's explanation of the same issue, then Y will be true."

He was mumbling to himself. "Maybe it's one store? That's right. It must be one store." He slapped his knee. The rabbi had answered his own question. He turned to Julia. "All we have to do is find which store everyone shopped at, narrow down the food choices, and if what I posit is true, we'll have at least found what made people sick. But," he continued *davening* again, "what if someone purposely poisoned the food, like the Tylenol killer?" He stared at Julia as though he was seeing her for the first time.

"Do you remember the Tylenol killer?" He asked. "Someone poisoned Tylenol capsules and people died. They never found out who did it."

"Rabbi, listen to me," Julia interrupted, "This is for the police to solve."

"The police won't know this is a serial crime unless we tell them. Otherwise, they'll think that eight people got food poisoning. Nothing more. It's a big night for eating out."

He looked at her expectantly.

"Well," Julia was reluctant to say it, "I could call the police chief. I know him through Harold, and we could tell him what we think."

"Excellent." She thought Rabbi Fine was going to give her a big hug, he was so pleased. Of course, observant Jewish men cannot embrace any woman other than their wives and children. They can't even shake hands with a female.

"Make an appointment for today or tomorrow, any time, and we'll tell him our suspicions," he said.

"Then what?" Julia asked.

"Then we'll see what we will see." He jumped up, and as he was rushing away, called out, "Tell Devorah I'll visit her aunt tomorrow."

"Will do." Visions of getting involved in another "case" danced through Julia's head.

Was she looking forward to another hunt, horrified at what was happening, or both? She wasn't sure. Harold certainly would be against her becoming involved in another extra-curricular crime- solving. He had made that very clear when she told him about finding Shayna's stickpin.

He believed getting involved in another 'out-of-home' activity took time away from him and the kids. He had a valid point. Still, the thought of solving a mystery excited her.

On the other hand, there she was, feeling sorry for herself, sitting in a maternity ward, when real people were becoming ill or dying. I'm selfish, Julia thought. Helping others, that's more important than crying over old infertility problems, though the pain of it all never quite left.

As her mind returned to the present, a proud father carefully pushed his wife and tightly bundled newborn in a wheel chair.

Boy, Julia thought as she watched them almost float on air with the joy of parenthood, if they only knew what being a mom and dad is really like.

She recalled the panic of hearing Jordan's first cries. Was he hungry, have a wet diaper, or was in some discomfort? It took a while for her to discern the subtle differences between 'I want my bottle' and 'I want some attention right now'.

Julia remembered the time she sat in her rocking chair to give Sammy a bottle, when the top fell off and formula spewed all over his face. It was then, after she had cleaned him up and prepared another bottle, this time the right way, she said, "Kid, we're some pair, aren't we. I'm always going to be by your side." She sniffed away a tear. Whatever happened with this school situation, Julia vowed that any decision would favor Sammy, not some faceless bureaucracy.

****

Rose and Devorah were in the hospital room. Rose was holding Tzippi's hand. She looked so small in her bed, everything hospital white except her bright carrot-red hair. At the moment she was sleeping.

Devorah and Julia tiptoed into the hallway. Devorah looked haggard and very sad. Julia told her Rabbi Fine's conclusion. "So you can see, if the rabbi is right, whatever occurred, you weren't responsible for it. Someone or something else was the cause."

"I understand." Devorah was slumped against the wall. "Still, it happened in my house, at my dinner. You can understand."

She was right. Julia hadn't walked in her shoes. She simply hugged Devorah, and went home. It was already two o'clock p.m. Harold was home. Sometimes when he had a night meeting he came home early for a little rest. Julia asked him for Police Chief Scarpelli's home phone number.

"Why do you want to bother the chief, for heaven's sake?" he groused.

She explained the rabbi's conclusions about "the Passover poisonings." Without another word, Harold went to his phone book, copied out the chief's number, and warned, "Julia, this sounds very serious. Please, stay out of it."

There was a rare beseeching quality to his voice. His eyes, behind his glasses, were soft with concern. She wasn't used to this Harold. It seemed as though, all of a sudden, he was seeing her differently. Instead of 'sturdy mom,' his eyes seemed to be seeing 'vulnerable treasure.'

It reminded her how he used to be when they were younger. All those times he gazed at her like she was a rare bird and he was afraid she might fly away. It felt good. Julia experienced an unfamiliar throbbing in her nether parts. What have we lost, she wondered? When did we become cardboard people?

Rather than fall into an existential funk, Julia jumped back to Harold's statement. Stay. Out. Of. It. At least he had prefaced his remark with "please."

"I will if I can," she promised, fingers crossed behind her back. Okay, so I lied, she told herself. While I believe, in general, that couples should share everything with each other, sometimes it's not so terrible to stretch the truth, or maybe tell a little fib. Even Rabbi Fine said that some white lies are excusable in Judaism if they're told to protect someone's feelings.

Harold gave Julia a hard, calculated look. "Don't make me pull rank on you," he said. There was the Mayor Harold Donnelly his employees probably observed when he disagreed with them – a mid-sized, fiftyish man with thinning brown hair turning grey around the sides, owlish wire-framed glasses and a scowl underneath a salt and pepper mustache. It wasn't a pretty sight.

Julia arched her eyebrows. "Rank? I wasn't aware that you had a higher rank than I in our marriage, Harold."

"You know what I mean. You do your thing and I do mine unless we step into the other's territory. Crimes in Crestfall are in my territory."

"I'll take that under consideration," Julia noted, then called the Chief.

Police Chief Anton Scarpelli thought the rabbi's conclusion was a strong possibility. "It's a hospital." he said, "Lots of activities are going on. Unless you're looking for patterns, things can fall through the cracks. I'd like to meet with the rabbi, get the names of the victims he knows about, see if there are any more. This looks like a combination of a Public Health and Police operation. I'll check with the Public Health Department and see if they've been contacted by the hospital. Then we'll analyze and compare the stomach contents, find out if there are any similarities;. After that we'll get going on an investigation and narrow things down. Can both of you be in my office at three o'clock this afternoon?"

He believed me. He really believed me, she thought. On the one hand, I am the mayor's wife. What if he regarded me as some *meshugener* off the street? Second, he can't afford to ignore a possible series of crimes in his town. Some people had already died, and others are still in the hospital. He's got to cover his tail. And third, maybe I am good at this, no matter what anybody thinks. Julia almost felt like dancing around the room until she realized the severity of it all.

All those years of doing research for news articles and editorials was like detecting. Interviewing different people, studying all sides of an issue, then making a final determination of how to solve a problem – it was all very similar. The only difference was that Julia hadn't dealt with crime. Still, she had talked to many people who hadn't wanted to tell her what she needed to know. It was her job to look beyond their words to discover the truth.

And besides, she thought, *who is Harold to pronounce that crime is his "area?"* She didn't recall that particular prohibition in their marriage vows. Julia felt her blood pressure rising. I am not just a household executive, she told herself. I can open my kitchen door, sashay outside, and do whatever I want, she exulted. She caught herself just short of shrieking, "I am woman. Hear me roar!"

****

Rabbi Fine and Julia were ushered into Chief Scarpelli's office by a female officer. A former football jock, the chief's chest was beginning to challenge the buttons on his jacket. His office reminded Julia of a well-used room; an old wooden desk piled with files, blue spiral notebooks entitled five-year plans, crime statistics in surrounding suburbs, and studies on burglaries in the area. The beige walls were filled with photos of the chief standing with a variety of police officials, and one of Harold presenting him with an award the year the department was the first in the state to receive special certification by the federal government. A framed photo of his wife and two handsome teenage boys sat on the desk surrounded by smaller pictures of the boys as they were growing up.

He stood to shake their hands, then invited them to sit in two chairs in front of his desk. Rabbi Fine repeated his suspicions and handed over a list of people who were stricken during or after the Friday night *seder* along with their phone numbers. "If I find out anything else, I'll let you know," he added.

Chief Scarpelli perused the list, then looked at them. He began to lift a finger to his lips, then stopped and pulled at a rubber-band that lay around his wrist. Julia noticed his nails were bitten down. He was probably trying to stop the habit of chewing on his nails. The chief appeared uncomfortable. Clearly, he wanted to say something, but wasn't sure how to do it tactfully.

"Julia, Rabbi," he nodded at them, "what you've brought in could be extremely important, and I want to thank you. In fact, I've already alerted the hospital and they're checking their records for anyone who came in with similar symptoms. They'll make sure to contact the County Public Health Department which will do the analysis and investigation with our help. We're a little behind the eight ball because this has happened during the weekend."

He went on, "You mentioned eight people, three of whom have died. A ninth person was brought into the hospital this morning; couldn't breathe well, glassy-eyed, delirious. The *seder* was held at his house. Maybe he was eating leftovers. I'm hoping it doesn't spread further. But now, you've got to leave this to us."

Julia was caught off guard. Why would the chief say something like that?

He turned to her, "The mayor mentioned how successful you were in locating your friend's missing stickpin." Julia could see that he was trying not to laugh. She had the sudden urge to stick him with that pin, but knew that was an imprudent thought. He snapped the rubber-band again. Julia knew she wasn't going to like what he had to say.

"This is not a stickpin. We're dealing with human lives here. A lot could be at stake. I don't want to trip over either of you if this does, in fact, become a real investigation. Do you understand? I mean, we could possibly be dealing with a serial poisoner. That's not something amateurs ought to be getting into. Right?"

He took a long breath. "You know, I could tell you stories that would curl your toes about regular civilians who stuck their noses in the wrong place."

Without a pause, he went on, "I remember one little old lady who thought her neighbor was killing his wife. Saw him cutting up something through his garage window. It was set pretty high in the wall, and she could only see him lifting up a bloody knife and bringing it down on something."

The chief narrowed his eyes. "Instead of calling the police, she ran into her house, took out her husband's hunting rifle, and raced into the garage to shoot him."

"What happened?" the rabbi asked, taken up by the story. "Well," the chief replied, "turns out that she shot at him and missed. The recoil from the rifle pushed her backwards. She crashed to the cement floor. Gave herself a concussion. She never should have tried to handle the situation by herself."

"What was the man doing?" Julia asked.

"He had caught a deer and was cutting it up into pieces so he could freeze it. He was scared out of his mind when that biddy ran at him with a gun. People need to leave that sort of thing to the professionals," He thumped his pointer finger on his desk. "You never know what could happen. Like now. This situation could be very dangerous." He snapped his wrist rubber-band again.

Julia's head was full of things that she wanted to say. Little old lady, indeed. Biddy? She hadn't heard that word for years. Did he think Julia lacked the ability to assess a dangerous situation? Did he resent the fact that Harold had basically forced him to deal with her? Or, was he actually concerned that something so serious was right on his doorstep? At that moment the junior detective intended to tell Harold exactly what she thought of his misogynistic police chief.

Rabbi Fine sat politely during the chief's little homily. "Did you consider," he suggested softly, "this could be a hate crime against Jews?"

"Looks like it could be," the chief said grimly.

"And," Julia added, "isn't a spate of hate crimes and threats going on in surrounding communities?"

He gave her a dirty look. Of course, he would realize, as wife of the mayor, she would be privy to some of the seamier details of the area.

"No comment." He dismissed her as though she was a reporter seeking news.

"And, pardon me, sir," the rabbi inquired, "will Jewish officers be assigned to this case?"

"No. We don't have any Jewish officers right now." This time an unfortunate finger nail reached Scarpelli's teeth.

"Well, sir," the rabbi said, "at times, our community likes to gather the wagons around."

"What?" The chief's face was becoming flushed. "We like to take care of our own."

"Rabbi, with all due respect, your people are my people." He spread out his muscular arms. "All the people in this town are my people, no matter what religion or ethnicity."

"I don't mean to be impertinent," Rabbi Fine continued. "It's just that Julia and I are known to the Jewish community. There might be a time when we can smooth the way for you, if you know what I mean."

"Smooth the ....." Chief Scarpelli's face was turning an unhealthy shade of red. He was half out of his chair. Julia may have imagined it, but it appeared as though he was counting to ten before saying something he would regret. If Julia were his wife, she'd make sure that he had a stress test as soon as possible.

"Rabbi, I don't want to seem impertinent, either. I would like to make it very clear that any actions by you and Julia in whatever this is will be considered obstruction, not to mention that you could be in grave danger."

By this time they were all standing. The air was charged. The rabbi remained self-contained. Julia could feel her legs shaking from the knees down. She needed to look strong. Remember the chief saying little old lady and biddy, she reminded herself. She still felt like a first grader being disciplined by a stern teacher.

"Julia and I understand completely, Chief Scarpelli, and we thank you for your time and your quick response to our concerns. We won't trouble you anymore," Rabbi Fine said.

They nodded at the chief, then left his office, showing themselves out. *Julia don't speak*, she told herself. She held her breath until they were standing by their cars in the parking lot.

"Don't worry, Julia. No one likes anyone stepping into their territory."

"I just didn't expect him to be so tough on us," she responded.

"It's okay. We won't bother their investigation." The rabbi looked grim. "But there's no reason we can't do our own thing. We simply have to keep it quiet."

"What do you have in mind?" Julia was already envisioning a literal Chinese Wall between Harold and herself in which she wouldn't be able to tell him anything about what she and the rabbi were doing.

"I've come to the conclusion that whatever sickened the victims was a Passover *seder* item that people in our community would buy in one or two specific places in our area which narrows it down to two places, Sophie's Deli and Nate's Nosh. They're the only shopkeepers who serve the more observant Jews if they want kosher products," the rabbi said.

"All of the families who were affected," he continued, looking very serious, "were practicing Jews; observing the rules of *kashrut*. You can get kosher Passover *matzah* at any grocery store. Ditto for macaroons or *matzah* ball soup mix. But for store-made *gefilte fish,* you need to go to those two delis."

"I've got to burst one of your kosher balloons, Rabbi. Devorah's Aunt Sarah made our gefilte fish herself."

"Okay. That's good," he murmured. "Then if I was a betting man, which I am not, I'd go with the chopped liver. Yes," he nodded to himself, "we need to find out if each family had chopped liver and where they bought it."

"That's not going to be easy. How are we going to do that when many of the victims are still in the hospital? And we'll probably run into the police," Julia added.

"You're forgetting something." He smiled. "The *yenta* underground railroad. You and I will discover who went where for Passover with just a few phone calls, the first of which will be to Shayna who always knows whatever goes on in Jewish circles."

Julia hadn't thought of that. He was right. If something happened in Crestfall, or the surrounding towns, Shayna would hear of it first. Her friend was an encyclopedia of Jewish social contacts.

"And I'll also talk to the rabbis who told me about the victims in their congregations. We can get a head start on the police, and ask our friends not to mention our chats. I'm sure they'd rather we get to the bottom of this without the police. And when we reach the point where we need professionals, I have no problem sharing with Chief Scarpelli."

"You know he won't be reciprocating," Julia commented, while getting into her car.

"It's okay. If we can help tie this in a bow more quickly, he'll stop being so critical. Trust me."

Julia did trust Rabbi Fine, though she felt very uneasy. They could be going up against pure evil, and that was no exaggeration. How else could you consider a poisoner who had already sickened at least nine people and actually murdered three of them so far? She shuddered and considered, what am I, a normal suburban mother, getting myself into? What would my family do if something happened to me, particularly the boys? They had already lost one mother, their birth mothers. I couldn't let them lose yet another mother. It would be too cruel.

On the other hand, Julia pondered, why was she classifying herself as a normal suburban mother? Wasn't that what she was trying to get away from? Julia didn't want to desert her family, of course, but would it be so wrong to expand her life a little, through other interests?

A thought streaked through Julia's head. She couldn't catch it, but sensed it was important.

Don't be such a worry wart, she told herself. Rabbi Fine's got a direct line to You-Know-Who. Plus, the thought that's flitting around…it's about the fire. The fire at Sophie's. Why would she have a fire, and now, possibly, a poisoning? Both would shut her down for a while. Might there be another coincidence here? And Julia knew what she and the rabbi thought of coincidences.

Julia was startled to see the similarity between the way the rabbi had worked out chopped liver, and how she had worked out that there must be a connection between Sophie's deli and both incidents. As she cruised into her driveway, there were two distinct tasks to do – contact Shayna and call Rabbi Fine about the fire. Gone was the worry. In its place was a sense of determination.

Shayna did not disappoint. She knew who had gone to three of the *seders* where people had fallen ill. In fact, she had already chatted with guests from two of them.

"The Rosenson's invited the Shulman's because the Shulman's son, Robert, is in Finland for a year. Nadine told me he's doing very well in a big consulting business, and has been assigned to Helsinki until December. His wife Rebecca is very unhappy. She's pregnant and is not looking forward to having a baby outside of the United States."

"That's wonderful, Shayna, but do you know what they had for dinner?"

"Of course. Who do you think you're talking to?"

They went down the list of *seder* menus, even the different kinds of *charoses*. Jews from Europe usually stick to the apple, wine, cinnamon recipe, while those from Spain and Mediterranean countries added dates, raisins and nuts instead.

As Rabbi Fine had thought, all three had served chopped liver as an appetizer, and all three had purchased it from Sophie's. And, of course, the chopped liver at Devorah's was from Sophie's, too. Julia thanked Shayna, said goodbye, then sat in shock. If Shayna was right, Julia had brought poisoned chopped liver into her friend's home. She was responsible for Aunt Tzippi getting ill. She remembered that Tzippi was the one person who ate several crackers' worth of it while they were still in the kitchen. No one in Julia's family would have eaten any. They hated chopped liver. Julia had eaten her fill earlier with the half pound carton she had bought at the same time. She couldn't remember David or Devorah eating any. They were too involved in setting everything up — David pouring the wine for everyone, Devorah preparing the *seder* plate.

How could a shopper purchase two containers of chopped liver, one poisoned and one not? But for fate, Julia could be in the hospital, not Aunt Tzippi. Now she understood Devorah's words when told she wasn't responsible for harming her Aunt. "Devorah, you haven't done anything wrong," Julia had said. "It didn't happen in your house," her friend cried. "You can't possibly understand."

But now she did. Now she was walking in Devorah's shoes, only they were Julia's size ten narrows. She felt sick to her stomach. Terrible. Guilty. But she hadn't known. Can you be guilty of a crime if you don't know you're doing it? That's what she would ask the lawyer when the police dragged her away in handcuffs.

Sammy walked into the kitchen and stared at his mother. "Mom, don't you want to put the phone on the hook? The dial tone is going crazy and no one can make any calls."

Julia looked down. Her hands were in a choke hold around the phone.

"Are you okay?"

"Sure."

Satisfied, he fidgeted, kicked a piece of cereal that was on the floor and asked, "So, what's going to happen tomorrow about school stuff?"

Julia had almost forgotten. She had to flip her brain from chopped liver to Sammy's school conundrum.

"The school's going to send someone to give you some of those standardized tests tomorrow. Then, as they analyze the results and talk to us, they'll send tutors to make sure you don't fall behind in any of your subjects. Does that sound okay?"

"I guess," he seemed fascinated with his bare feet."

"This is really important, Kiddo. You can't fool around on this test. If you score very high, we may have to find a different school that can offer more enriched classes. This could be a good thing for you."

She lifted his chin with a finger. "Do you understand, Sammy?"

"Yeah." One tear rolled down his cheek.

Chopped liver won the poison contest. Shayna had spoken to the third family and discovered that they had served the liver from Sophie's, too.

"They also had an eggplant salad made with chopped eggplant, lemon juice, olive oil, garlic salt and pepper to taste, chopped fresh parsley, and black olives for garnish. I'm going to try to make it as soon as we fly home. Does that help?"

"Except for the eggplant part, which I agree does sound yummy, you came through, as usual."

"So what are you going to do now?" Shayna never took a finger. She always went for the whole hand.

"I'm going to talk to Rabbi Fine, we'll decide on a plan, and we'll get started," Julia said.

"I've got Sophie's phone number and address if you want

"Of course you do." Julia laughed. Shayna was their own Jewish Wikipedia. She imagined Shayna, dressed in another purple moo-moo, reaching into her giant tote, feeling around, and coming up with her thick address book. She called out the numbers in a businesslike tone, gave Julia a huge phone kiss, and announced she was late for a mani-pedi. "The color of choice in Florida is peach, Julia, as if you ever had a pedi." Just before slamming down the phone, Shayna added, "You know, I'm thinking of coming home early. It doesn't feel right to be sitting here by a swimming pool when such bad stuff is happening."

Julia understood. Bad stuff was happening at home, and Shayna wanted to help discover what had happened.

Rabbi Fine was busy. He asked if Julia could make an appointment to see Sophie. She called. Sophie remembered her from the visit with Shayna. She agreed to slip away from the deli and meet at her house at two p.m., the tail end of the lunch crowd. After Julia hung up, she realized Sammy would be home alone while she visited Sophie. He was ten years old. She could leave him without supervision; he knew enough not to answer the door. In fact, he would be perfectly content to sit in bed reading comic books or playing with his action figures. Since they were going to go through this school ordeal, however, Julia didn't want to make life easy for him.

"Sammy, Sweetie, after your testing, I want you to come with me to talk to Sophie, the woman who owns the deli I sometimes buy from. Okay?"

No argument. He'd do anything as long as it wasn't going to school.

Mrs. Finiken arrived promptly at ten a.m. on the dot. She was wearing a sunny yellow sweater set over navy blue slacks. Julia remembered some twenty years ago when her thighs would have fit into those pants — almost. Sammy was already at the dining room table, dressed, breakfasted with eggs and toast, not a sugary cereal, and holding a number two pencil freshly sharpened. Mrs. Finiken delicately sipped green tea with lemon while she gave Sammy the different parts of the timed tests in math, English, social studies and science. In between subjects, she allowed Sammy to stand and take a stretch. She went out of her way to be gentle with him.

At noon, Mrs. Finiken announced that they were done. "Was any of it hard for you?" she asked.

"Some of the math; maybe some of the science, too," he answered.

Oops. Those were his best subjects. Julia hoped it was just his self-deprecation speaking. He had a habit of always under playing his accomplishments.

"I'll be sending someone to come over tomorrow at ten am." She looked at Sammy. "I think you're going to like him. Matt is very casual. His lessons are more like discussions."

Her face clouded over. "I wish real school could be taught that way. Anyway," she brightened, "you'll see. He'll be coming three times a week until we figure this thing out."

Mrs. Finiken told Julia that after the tests were scored, she and other school members would study the results and then they would all get together for a formal ISP, individual student plan.

"Should I bring a lawyer to represent us?" Julia asked. She was a fish out of water here, knowing nothing about any ISPs and what the school would or could do with her son.

Their experiences with Jordan had been simple meetings with his teacher, and sometimes with his teacher and counselor. But those instances were for petty offenses, like smashing his milk carton to make a loud noise at lunch, or not doing his homework. She and Harold were not prepared for big time school problems.

"Goodness, this isn't a trial," Mrs. Finiken smiled. "We'll have a meeting and look at all the possibilities. That's all."

Julia let Sammy relax from the testing and put together a list of questions she intended to ask Sophie. As a junior detective, she imagined herself in a tight red business suit with heels, competently drawing out information from Sophie about the fire, which she was now certain was connected to the food poisonings:

Who stands to gain if anything happens to the deli?

Who was involved in Sophie's life at that time? A boyfriend, any new acquaintance?

Had she started going to any new groups or places like a gym? That sounded ridiculous. What seventy-five year old woman was going to join a gym? On the other hand she reminded herself, seventy-five was the new fifty.

What did the police say after the fire?

What was the insurance situation? Were they still withholding her claim?

How had Sophie been able to reopen without the insurance money?

Did she owe anyone money who wanted it back immediately?

That was only seven questions. Should she ask more? Maybe she should ask Sophie to tell her a little about herself? Where was she from? Were there any ghosts from her past? Or maybe Julia should let Sophie ramble and get more from that?

This was different from Shayna's stickpin "case". Bigger. Far more important. Julia was concerned and excited all at the same time. She also knew it was vital to keep this matter from Harold. He had explicitly made her promise to stay out of it. That meant Sammy had to keep quiet about it, too. Julia wondered how she was going to manage that.

Julia and Sammy were off to Sophie's house at one forty-five. "Kiddo," she started, "I'm going to be talking to Sophie about a fire she had at her store. The police never solved the case."

"Does this have anything to do with the Tzippi thing?"

"Umm," she said.

"Dad told you to stay away from that one." From the mouths of babes.

"How do you always know what's happening in our house?" Julia hadn't thought any kids were around when she and Harold had their whispering match about Chief Scarpelli's warning.

"No one notices a kid," he said seriously. "Sometimes I sit in the kitchen having a snack while you and dad talk in the living room. I hear you even though I can't see you."

A good thing to remember. "The fire, at this point, is not involved in anything else," she said with more decisiveness than she felt. "Still, it's very important that dad not know I'm doing this. Sometimes," Julia turned to look at him, "moms and dads have secrets."

"So this is a secret case you're working on?"

"Yes. A secret case." They were turning onto Sophie's street.

69

"Can I help?" It was obvious that Sammy liked the idea of being in on the secret.

"Sure," Julia said. "We can be partners. You, me and Rabbi Fine. Just don't do anything without talking to me first. Partners have to be straight with each other. Understand?"

"Yeah," he grinned.

My son and I, she thought, undercover detectives. At least Sammy was thinking about something other than school.

Sophie welcomed them into a minuscule living room/dining room that was right out of a dated sitcom. Orange shag carpeting. Lime green chairs and matching couch covered in plastic. Julia hadn't seen anything like it in years. A small coffee table in front of the sofa held tea cups, a plate of what Julia supposed was home-made macaroons, a variety of melons, and cloth napkins.

"I'm not used to having guests so much these days," she fussed.

"Why?" Sammy asked.

"I'll tell you, with all the work in the deli and my husband passing away, these old bones are too tired to…" She stopped herself and peered at Sammy.

"Well, who's this?" Sophie leaned closer to examine him. "A string bean. That's what you are." She looked at Julia accusingly. "Do you feed this child at all?"

"I'm sorry," Julia said, embarrassed for Sammy. "This is my son Sammy. He's home from school today, and I didn't want to leave him."

"And you shouldn't leave him, such a handsome boy." A smiling Sophie drew them into the room and gestured at the sofa. "Sit. Sit and I'll bring out some soda for the boy. I don't expect he'll want any tea," she laughed.

Julia followed her to the kitchen, hoping to help her carry things back to the living room. Sophie opened up an avocado colored refrigerator, brought out a can of Coke, threw some jellied sugar slices that looked like oranges and some chocolate-covered *matzah* on another dish for Sammy, and tut-tutted at the offer to help.

"Old I may be," she said, plowing back into the living room, "but I ain't dead yet."

"Mom," Sammy asked, "can I sit on the floor and play my Nintendo? I won't bother you at all."

"If it's okay with Sophie it's fine with me."

"Wherever you want, young man," Sophie responded. "Just like my Milton," she said wistfully. "That boy never sat on furniture. He preferred breaking it," she said with a shiver.

"What do you mean, Sophie? Was Milton a violent child?" In other words, was he the kind of person who might start a fire out of anger, Julia wanted to ask.

Sophie checked to see that Sammy was off to the other side of the room. She and Julia faced each other on the couch. Then she whispered, "My Milton wasn't such a bad boy." She began picking at a juicy piece of cantaloupe. "He was just a little off, you know? It's not like he meant to destroy things…it's just that he had a little temper. My husband said it was a good thing, because some of the boys at school would make fun of him."

"'Better for him to beat them up before they get to him,' my Al used to say. But every once in a while, he used to push me a little." Sophie looked towards a door that probably led to the basement. "That was after Al died," she admitted, looking sheepish.

"Sophie," Julia tried not to sound judgmental, "does Milton hurt you now?"

"Oh," she appeared to recall an incident, "it's been a while, since before the fire," she said, rushing to assure Julia that it wasn't a big deal.

"Milton and I were arguing about the deli, you know how he wants this pool parlor," she confided. "So we were here in the living room, standing up and talking. I said I wasn't going to give him the deli, he pushed me a little, and I fell back on the couch. That's all." She shrugged.

"He didn't mean to hurt me," Sophie was quick to say.

"Sophie," Julia was very serious. This was a dear woman, and she was beginning to feel that the deli owner was in danger. "Don't you think it's important to go to the police and let them know that sometimes Milton can get violent? Not to get him into trouble, but to start a record of his actions?"

"My son loves me," Sophie huffed. "I don't want no police. Now," she was all business, "tell me why you wanted to see me today."

Julia tactfully tried to explain her visit.

"There've been several cases of food poisoning over the weekend, and from what Rabbi Fine and I can tell, the problem could have come from your deli."

"Who says so?" Sophie sat at attention, ready to attack anyone who would suggest she had intentionally poisoned her customers.

"No one is saying so right now," Julia picked up a macaroon to prove she didn't believe Sophie was guilty of any wrong doing, "but the County Health Department will be taking tests to find out what caused the food poisoning, and where it came from."

The macaroon, made with macadamia nuts, was a slice of heaven. "Sophie, this is utterly delicious."

"Of course, Darling. It's made with my special ingredients. Everyone loves my macaroons."

Julia explained how she and Rabbi Fine had come up with chopped liver as the cause of the food poisoning. Sophie was shaking.

"My chopped liver is the best. Someone must have put something in it," Sophie said bitterly.

"That's why I'm here. Rabbi Fine and I want to beat the police. We want to find out who might want to hurt you or your business."

"I don't got no enemies," Sophie cried, throwing her arms into the air. "I get along with everyone."

"Have you had any problems with anti-Semitic groups?" Julia asked.

"Not to my knowledge. Everyone leaves me alone, I leave everyone alone. That's the way I live," she said.

"I remember when Shayna and I were at your store, you were mentioning some people who wanted you out of business. Tell me about them again."

Sophie went on about her son Milton wanting the deli to become a pool hall, the builder who wanted to buy her block, Nate the deli owner who wanted to buy her deli, too, the mean older man who threatened shop owners, and the deli worker she had fired.

"That's five people already who are suspects in my book," Julia said. "Did anyone new come into your life around that time?"

Sophie made a face, then sighed. "I suppose 'She' did."

"She who?" Julia asked.

"Milton has a girlfriend. For thirty-five years my boy couldn't say nothing to no girl. A long time ago I gave up on having grandchildren. But all of a sudden, this one comes out of nowhere. She's a looker, too. A *shiksa*." Sophie sniffed. "Blond and blue-eyed. She works in some kind of fix-it store downtown. I don't got no reason to say this, but," she leaned and whispered so Sammy couldn't hear, "I think she's a gold- digger." Sophie sat back, folded her arms across her chest and nodded at Julia.

"In fact," she said in a low voice, "she's here now with Milton. He's between jobs," she rolled her eyes. "So any time she's off, they're both over here. I don't know what's going on down there," she pointed to the basement with an ominous look on her face, "but that's the way it is." She shrugged her shoulders.

"Would she have any reason to set the deli on fire?"

"I would say no, but now that you mention it, she showed up just a few weeks before it happened. Milton's in love with her. I'm his mother, so I gotta love him, but I can't understand what she sees in him." Sophie shut her eyes and shook her head.

"Is there anyone from your past who might want to hurt you?"

"The past," Sophie said mournfully. "Everyone from the past is dead from the camps or the Polish ghettos." She patted Julia's hand. "I wish someone from the past was here. It would be a comfort to me…"

The women heard someone stomping up the basement steps. "Ma." It was a pasty-faced man with a very flabby body, the kind that jiggles like Jell-O.

"Ma, look at this…oh," he stopped. "You got company? When do you ever have company?" He eyed Julia suspiciously.

"Today, Mr. Smartypants. Now what is it you want me to see?"

"Uh, it'll keep. I'll be up when your friend leaves." As he turned around, he almost bumped into the woman who had silently walked behind him.

"Hey, you're just like a ghost," he yelled. His hand immediately closed into a fist as though he was going to punch his girlfriend. She didn't give an inch.

"Watch your mouth, Miltie," she warned, "there's a kid here." Her head turned toward Sammy, who was staring open mouthed.

"Besides, Babe," she crooned, "I just wanted to see what your Ma thought about the plans."

Sophie sighed. "What plans?"

"For the pool parlor," the woman said with wide eyes, oozing fake innocence.

"There ain't gonna be any pool parlor while I'm still alive," Sophie snapped.

"We'll see about that," Milton clomped back down the basement stairs; the woman followed.

"You see?" she snarled. "What a *vilde chaya*, a wild animal, that one. She's got my son by the you know whats. Put her on the list," she pointed to Julia's notes.

"What's her name?" Julia asked. "Shirley, Shirley Templar."

"Are you sure? There used to be a movie star called Shirley Temple.

"I don't know from that. All I know is he calls her Shirl all the time."

Julia looked over to Sammy. He had put down his Nintendo and appeared to be sleeping. Usually he was up and ready for any kind of action. This school thing must have tired him out, she thought.

The two women finished shortly after. Sophie gave Julia the names and numbers for the developer and her deli worker.

"That old guy, I don't know nothing about him," she added.

Then Julia remembered something. "Sophie," she said in a low voice, "remember when you showed Shayna and me the cameras at the deli? Did you tell anyone else?"

"No." She repeated the symbolic locking of her lips.

"Do you still have the tapes from maybe Thursday and Friday?"

"Yeah," she said. "It don't erase until a two week loop or something."

"Can we get a copy of those tapes as soon as possible? It could be very important."

"Okay, I guess. I can call Eddy, the boy who set it all up. He can make you a copy."

"Great. And be prepared if the Public Health Department or police come for a visit. The Rabbi and I could be wrong, but you should be ready, and have a lawyer in mind."

"Can't you and the rabbi handle this for me?"

"We can't. In fact, please don't tell anyone we've talked to you. I think that whoever set the fire could also be responsible for poisoning your customers. Someone's trying to put you out of business, and we're going to try to find out who. But we've got to do it all in secret or we'll be in big trouble with the police. Okay?"

She nodded. "Trouble with the police, I understand. I'll have Eddy leave a copy of the tapes in your mailbox," she said. "He won't be able to get them until after we close tonight."

Julia gave Sophie a hug. "We're going to solve this together. Everything's going to be okay." Whatever possessed her to say such a thing, Julia thought. Maybe just being around Rabbi Fine gave her hope.

"From your lips to God's ears," Sophie whispered, shaking with emotion. "Wait," she waved before they were out of the door. She ran into her kitchen and brought out a paper bag with some macaroons in it. "For you," she said, blowing a kiss at Julia.

Sammy followed his mother out of the house.

"Sorry it took so long." Julia apologized. "Glad to see you awake again, Mr. Rip Van Winkle."

"No bigee, Mom. I wasn't asleep, anyway. Hey, did you notice the cool car parked in back of us?"

It was a shiny red Volkswagen convertible with a strange detail on the front passenger door. It appeared to be a voluptuous woman wearing a tool belt. She was bending over, highlighting a very large rear end. Her jeans were worn low, showing the beginning of a crack between her cheeks.

"Neat, isn't it?" Shirley had just walked out of the back door.

"Cool," Sammy said. "What is it?"

Shirley pointed to the decal. "I'm an electrician, see, and you can tell by her belt that she's an electrician from the rear end. She smiled, showing two rows of perfectly white teeth amidst the wad of gum she was currently cracking. "You know the joke about electricians always showing the crack in their pants, so she has a cute crack. And…" She went on.

Julia figured if it took this long to tell a joke, it wasn't worth it.

"See, it says Sweet Cheeks on her back cheeks…" she started laughing. "I had it made special just for me. What do you think?"

"Cool," Sammy repeated. "Really neat." Clearly, she was enjoying Sammy's attention.

"By the way," she lowered her voice, "I apologize for how Milton acted in the house. He needs to be more respectful of his mom and others."

"Thank you," Julia said, offering a treacly smile, "but it's hard to teach an old dog new tricks."

Then, even though it was not her business, Julia asked, "Are you and Milton going steady?"

"Mom," Sammy flinched with embarrassment.

Sweet Cheeks' face went through a variety of emotions. "He wants to tie the knot as soon as possible," she said, "but a girl wants to be sure before she takes that big step. We think it will be very soon. Very soon," her voice took on a different tone. She shuddered briefly, then waved as she got into her car.

"That was gross," Julia said.

"You don't know the half of it," Sammy noted.

"What do you mean?" She wanted to stop the car and listen to him carefully, but Miss Sweet Cheeks was close behind them. "Tell me."

"Well, partner," he said, "that vent I was sitting by goes directly to the basement."

"So?"

"So, when Milton and Sweet Cheeks were in the basement I could hear a lot of what they were saying."

Julia's heart leapt into her throat. What could Sammy been listening to? Was it 'blue' material unfit for her son's ears, or information that could help on the case, or both?

"There's a lot of swears," he warned.

"Without the swears if possible."

"Okay." He turned toward his mother. "They're awful upset about the deli. Milton's got plans for his pool parlor, but his mother isn't interested. Milton told Sweet Cheeks he's got to do something about it or he might miss his big chance. He said he knows a guy who wants to put a big building on that property, and he'll let Milton put his pool parlor there. But Milton has to come up with a way to get Sophie out of the store because the guy is pressuring him. Sweet Cheeks was saying he better hurry up or he'll lose everything. And Mom," he stressed, "Sweet Cheeks wasn't talking very nice to Milton."

"Oh, how do you know?"

Sammy's face reddened. "She told him that he won't be getting any unless he did something soon."

Oh. My. Julia was mortified her son had listened to that conversation. It was, she realized, rather naive of her to think Sammy wouldn't understand that Sweet Cheeks was holding her sexual wiles over Milton. After all, she figured, he probably heard much worse on the playground these days. Julia pushed those thoughts out of her mind with the exception of one new discovery. Sophie was right on. Blondie was a gold-digger.

"And," Sammy added to the collection of fresh information, "Milton told her something big was going to happen any day."

Sammy and Julia got home in time for her to make a family favorite, real macaroni and cheese, not out of a box. Julia used cheddar and American. It created a luscious yellow-orange color. After Sammy set the table, a new rule for those who didn't attend school, Julia called Rabbi Fine and told him about her chat with Sophie and what Sammy heard.

"Hmm," he said after a brief silence. "It seems we have a situation right out of *Pirkei Avot.*"

"What's that?"

"'Sayings of the Father.' It's a volume of the *Mishnah* filled with the rules of Judaism and proper behavior, life lessons I've mentioned in our group. One section notes four types of ownership. Two of those are pertinent here. One kind of person says 'What is mine is mine, and what is yours is yours.' What do you think? Does that sound fair?"

"Absolutely," she responded.

"But, there is another person who says, 'What is mine is mine, and what is yours is mine.' That is a wicked person."

Julia agreed.

"I think," he noted sadly, "perhaps Milton falls into that category. He wants what his mother has. He hasn't made much of himself, so he wants to benefit from others' hard work."

"Sounds right to me," she nibbled on a cheese cube that hadn't made it into the macaroni dish.

"Also, this woman, Shirley you mentioned? Something doesn't ring true. Sophie might be right when she questions why someone like Shirley wants to be with Milton. What I would suggest is that you speak to Milton, try to size him up, and sound him out about her. We might find out something valuable."

"What about you, Rabbi? I thought we were in this together."

"We are, but sometimes things come up in a rabbi's life, deaths, counseling, illness, and I have to attend to those first, but we'll keep in touch. Besides, Milton has already seen you with his mother. You're a familiar face. If you butter him up, he'll probably want to talk to you."

Rabbi Fine might have great confidence in Julia's detecting skills, but she didn't. Still, Julia promised to give it a try. She also made an appointment to see Lester Pintner the builder to get a handle on him. Julia was hoping the wife of the mayor cachet would dispel any questions from him. This was a Harold no-no. He would never approve of her using his mayoral position for any advantage. But sometimes you have to use what you have for the greater good. Helping Sophie and solving the poisoning case was one of those times.

Dinner that night was, for a change, delightful. Though the table was set, Julia had to switch the forks and spoons to different sides of the plate. She did not understand why her sons couldn't remember that forks go on the left over the napkin. She figured it was a genetic thing. When Harold came home from work, a sense of "*Shalom bayit*," peace, nestled over their home. Harold was relaxed. He'd had a good day at the office, Jordan wasn't in any trouble, and they were dealing with Sammy's problem for the moment.

"We just got county funds to redo some of our streets," Harold scooped up a second helping of macaroni. He enjoyed sharing city business with them. Sammy was particularly interested in what was going on in Crestfall.

"Great," Jordan said.

Julia was surprised. Why would he care about street resurfacing?

"Will Delmar Avenue be included?" he asked. Delmar ran alongside one of the nearby parks.

"Yes. Why?"

"So we can skateboard better. Lilac Avenue has so many potholes, you're taking your life in your hands. Of course," Jordan said pointedly, "if I had a car, I wouldn't have to skateboard to get to my friends' houses."

"That's what bikes are for," Julia noted. "And even when you do get your learner's permit, you won't be able to drive unsupervised for a long time."

It was a particularly sore subject. Jordan had "borrowed" Julia's car a few months ago without permission. They had grounded him for two months. He was still too young for a permit. Things had been dicey until lately. Maybe he had calmed down because Sammy was in trouble. Julia found that they frequently went through cycles in which it seemed the boys took turns causing different kinds of mayhem in their house.

"Jordan's right about the skateboards," Sammy noted. He was eating in his favorite position, perched on the arm of his kitchen chair.

"Another small miracle," Julia mumbled between bites, "the boys agreeing on something."

"I took my board out there a couple of weeks ago and hit a pothole. It made a big gash in my knee. Do you want to see the scar?" Sammy raised his leg to share his "war" wound.

"No, Sport, not at the dinner table." Harold patted his mouth with a paper towel napkin. "But," he warned, "Delmar is a busy street. It would be better for you guys to go down the side streets."

"They're not long enough, Dad. Just when you get up enough speed, you're at the corner. Delmar's blocks are longer," Jordan protested while forking up green beans.

"Okay, okay," Harold held up his hands in defeat. "You're 'kid thinking' is right on the button. The adult view, however, is the opposite, and right now, Mom and I win. Side streets for now. Car later."

During a lull in the conversation, Harold looked at Sammy. "Hey Sport, how was the testing today?"

"Not bad." He took a drink of Coke. Julia had lost the battle of no soda during meals. Harold's parents had allowed him to drink sodas with meals when he was a child, and he let the children do the same, much to Julia's dismay. She was a milk and juice proponent. "Tomorrow a tutor's coming for two hours of class," Sammy continued.

Julia crossed her fingers that Sammy had put in a real effort to do well on his tests so they would have a clear picture as to what to do about his problem.

"Two hours with no break?" Jordan was shocked.

"He might stop for a break after each subject," Sammy suggested.

"Jeez, at least we get to walk through the halls between classes. Gets the blood flowing running from one side of the school to the other. I have to run from English to Gym in less than five minutes. That's at least half a mile," Jordan complained. "I don't even get time to go to the john."

Actually, he had a point. Julia remembered her high school days fighting through the advancing hordes every forty-five minutes. It wasn't pretty. There wasn't even enough time for a lipstick check.

Harold turned to her. "What did you and Sammy do today?"

Julia was trying to think how to phrase a response when Sammy jumped in. "Mom and I just hung out together. It was cool."

"Well," Harold beamed, "I hope tomorrow goes well for you, too."

After dinner Julia called Sophie for Milton's number and asked what his favorite dish was.

"Spareribs," she said with distaste. "Pork spareribs. He likes to rub it in my face that being kosher is stupid."

"Thanks."

The plan was to invite Milton to a restaurant that served ribs and ask his advice on the fire. Julia's hope was that he would try to be as helpful as possible, whether he had caused the fire, or not. At ten o'clock he responded to her phone message.

"So you're the lady who was talking to Ma this afternoon?"

"Yes."

"Why d'ya want to talk to me?"

"I'm helping her look into the fire at the deli. There may be some way to make the insurance company pay what they owe her. I could use some advice from you," she said, crossing her fingers this ploy would work.

"You know your mother and her connections better than anyone. Maybe you can give me a lead into who caused the fire if it wasn't faulty wiring."

"I don't know," he said grudgingly. "I'm pretty busy."

"It won't take long," Julia quickly added, "and maybe we can meet at a restaurant, have a meal and talk at the same time. My treat. Everyone's got to eat."

That did the trick.

"You know Bisbees on Drake?" he asked. It was walking distance from his house.

"Yeah. I love the ribs there."

"You like ribs?" His suspicious tone disappeared.

"My favorite meal," She lied. Julia had never enjoyed a meal in which she had to go through half a roll of paper towels to be reasonably non-sticky at the end.

"I don't like the ones with the tart sauce. The sweeter ones go down better with me, you know?"

"Me, too," she agreed.

"And I don't like those stringy ribs some places serve. I like them fat and juicy. Just the way I like my women," he joked.

"Right." Julia almost gagged.

"So, I think I can fit you in about ten am. How's that?"

"Ten a.m.? Isn't that a little early for ribs?"

"Lady, it's always rib time here, heh, heh." He sounded just like a lecherous old man.

"Then ten a.m. it is."

Julia figured the tutor would be with Sammy from ten to noon at least, and she would try to make the meal go fast. The only problem was facing a plate of barbecue ribs and Milton at the same time.

After that gustatory delight, she was looking forward to an appointment with Lester Pintner. Julia figured it was safe taking Sammy to a business office during the day. What could possibly go wrong?

"Tzippi's at home." Devorah sounded so relieved over the phone. "And Rose is staying with her for a few days. The doctors said she was fine, but she's still a little wobbly on her feet."

"Great news. I'll go over to her house and visit soon," Julia said. It was nine o'clock; time to welcome the tutor and dress for her rib date with Milton.

"Do they know yet what caused it?"

"They said sometimes it can take weeks for the blood test analysis. We've got to wait behind all the other cases before they do ours. But for now, the doctor has given her a clean bill of health, *Baruch HaShem*."

"Thank God," Julia repeated. No one else had died as yet. Shayna or the rabbi would have told her. Still, one death was too much. Some victims were still in the hospital. It seemed that those with weak immune systems were hit the worst.

"Mom." Sammy hopped into the kitchen. He was dressed in khaki shorts and a green Ninja Turtle tee shirt, even though it was still quite brisk outside.

"Am I dressed okay for school at home?"

Julia observed that all important parts were covered. He was wearing no socks or proper shoes, but his old fake leather cowboy boots at least matched his pants.

"Fine, Kiddo. Make sure you have a pencil and paper at the ready. Want some breakfast?"

"Can I have my cereal?" he wheedled.

Oh, all right, she told herself. The kid's been through a lot, and we can intersperse junk cereal with real food during the rest of the week. Then she thought, can I go to Bisbees and leave my son with an absolute stranger?

She imagined Shayna, her more relaxed friend saying, "*Check him out. Get his vibe. Worse comes to worse, tell Milton your son is sick and make it for another time.*"

By then it might be too late. Still, she figured a tutor vetted by the school couldn't be too bad a risk. Sammy was running from the kitchen to the dining room, bringing in food and drinks, not unlike his mother when she was preparing the table for her Torah group. The main difference was the choice of food. He had prepared a plate of chocolate chip cookies and half of a cherry pie from last night's dinner along with a bowl of Reeses Pieces. Accompanying that was a half-gallon of milk and a quart of chocolate milk and some paper cups.

"What are you doing?" Julia asked as he whisked by holding real napkins, not their usual paper towels, a knife and forks.

"This is what you do when people come to visit," he said. "Anyway, studying makes me hungry."

The doorbell rang and Sammy zoomed by to open it. Julia and Sammy both faced the chest of a six-foot-five tall string bean with black sunglasses. Some of his blond hair stuck up in the back of his head from a cowlick. He could be Sammy in fifteen years.

As they strained their necks to get a good view of him, his soft voice wafted down, "Hi, I'm Matt from the school. I'm guessing you're Mrs. Donnelly and this is Sammy?"

For some reason his height didn't intimidate Sammy, who led his tutor to the dining room table.

"A perfect place to study," Matt blessed the dining room table. Sitting down he was still taller than Sammy or Julia. "And, wow, what a wonderful spread you have." He pointed to the array of goodies. "Did you do this for me?" He looked at Sammy, who nodded with pride. "Thanks, man," Matt said. "I missed breakfast today." Their relationship appeared to be sealed.

When Sammy was seated by Matt's side, the gentle giant explained that he was scheduled to come by three times a week from ten to noon. He would tutor Sammy in the four major subjects, English, math, social studies and science. They would do two subjects each day and Sammy would get a fifteen minute break.

That sounded fair to Sammy as Julia observed her son's head nodding in the affirmative. She listened for a while as they began an English lesson, and after twenty minutes, felt that it was safe to go out for ribs.

Bisbees was a perfect spot for meeting a stranger. The place was always filled with people, the servers unerringly cheerful, the menu several pages long with notes on what is diet-wise, gluten-free, lite, etc., and the food is fine for a chain restaurant. All in all, a perfect family place. The maître de showed Julia to a table with a view of the door. The room was filled with the sweet aroma of pancakes and syrup, French toast with marmalade, and waffles with strawberry or blueberry topping. Julia was nauseated by the thought of even looking at ribs this early in the day.

Milton must have read somewhere, if he knew how to read at all...Whoops, she thought, that was a cheap shot. Rabbi Fine always reminded the Torah group to watch its snarkiness. Bad thoughts become bad words that, upon being spoken, cannot be recalled. There's a great little story about mean words and feather pillows, but, Julia giggled to herself, while looking around the restaurant, "I digress."

Milton must have read somewhere that being late is fashionable. Twenty minutes after ten Julia was ready to leave when he sauntered in. His body reminded her of a pear. As he approached, she noted that his stylishly white suspenders almost blended into his off-white, needing-to-be-washed tee shirt with a charming "HONK IF YOU LOVE HEAD LICE" emblazoned on it.

"Sorry I'm late," he smirked. "Early business meeting." Right, she commented to herself. He should have met with a washing machine and a bath tub.

"That's perfectly okay," Julia smiled brightly. "Shall we order?"

The waitress who took their order squirmed under the scrutiny of Milton's ogling eyes.

"I'll take your full rib plate," he said without looking at the menu. "And I'll have whatever beer you've got on tap."

"Milton," Julia simpered, "I'm in awe of your ability to eat such a full meal in the morning."

"Makes me more of a man," he beamed.

"Well, I just cannot eat so hearty this early," she said in her best Scarlet O'Hara voice. "I'll have an order of eggs, toast, and orange juice." She imagined the waitress must have been wondering what Milton and a fairly decent looking matron had in common. "I missed breakfast this morning," Julia explained to both of them.

"Now," Milton fixed his beady eyes on her, "what is it that you really want?"

A pang of electric panic ran down Julia's neck.

"All I want is to know more about your mother," she said truthfully. "Maybe something in her past has come back to haunt her."

"Mom doesn't talk much about her past." Milton looked down at his hands. His fingernails were long and dirty. "She told me she came from Poland when she was young. She was married, but lost her parents, sisters and her husband during World War II. Somehow she got here and met my father."

His eyes met Julia's.

She was pretty sure that he was telling the truth.

"They started a small grocery in Crestfall. Mom began adding stuff that she cooked by herself. Pretty soon people were coming in just for her food, so she and dad dumped the store and started the deli. She even makes her own corned beef," he picked up his butter knife and proceeded to clean one of his fingernails. "They used to force me to work there after school and on Sundays. They were always very religious-like. My dad died when I was twelve. Mom sort of fell apart for a while. Then she went back to work until now."

Julia imagined Shayna raging in her ear, "*This one wants a pity party when he has a loaf of rye bread under each arm.*"

"You know," Milton said, anger in his voice, "a kid needs a role model when he's growing up. When my dad went, I didn't have anyone to look up to. I never had a chance to develop to my full potential; always being bossed by my mother." He was full of bitterness. The words "develop to my full potential" must have come from his mother or some other self-help program he had been in. Was he bitter enough to set the deli on fire, Julia wondered?

"I'm so sad you lost your dad," she remarked. "But," Julia brightened, "I hear you've got a great idea now. Tell me about it."

Milton sat up straighter and didn't make a single pass at the waitress as their food came. Instead, he tore a rib off the slab and began eating it before answering.

"This is a once in a lifetime opportunity," he slurred with a full mouth, barbecue sauce ringing his mouth. "A guy comes to me and says he's developing a building in town, see, and he thinks Crestfall needs some entertainment for people in their twenties and thirties. He's got an idea for a modern pool parlor."

Milton threw his meatless rib onto the butter plate and ripped off another. "It's not the old kind of pool hall, you know, where men used to spit into

84

buckets."

What a pleasant thought over a lovely repast, she thought. He went on, excited. "It'll be modern, sleek, and not just for guys." He took a long gulp of beer.

"It's for women, too. And kids. See, he wants a spot for kids to be able to play or watch videos while their parents play pool. There'd be food and drinks, too. He tells me he's been looking for a forward-thinking person — me," he pointed to himself, "to make this thing a winner. And the best part," he said, drinking more beer to help swallow yet another mouthful of meat, "it turns out it's my Ma's building. The one with the deli. Who knew!"

He sat back, pleased as punch. Obviously he couldn't see it. Lester Pintner was using him to get Sophie's deli.

"Sounds exciting," Julia nibbled at the dry toast. It felt ragged as it went down her throat.

"Have you signed a contract or anything yet?" She asked. He sagged, almost put off from snatching another rib.

"No," he said dejectedly.

"Leonard's a handshake kind of guy, and Ma doesn't want to sell. I don't understand her. She's old. She deserves to rest now. I mean, I don't want to run the deli when she gives it up. Besides," his eyes took on a calculating look, "I'll be inheriting it anyway. Why not now? She could give it to me early and I'll sell to Lester, then I'll have the money to invest in the pool hall."

Julia didn't want to confuse the matter with the fact that if Sophie didn't keep the deli open, she wouldn't be earning any money.

"Is this Mr. Pintner helping you out financially?" She asked.

"No." Milton almost threw another rib on the floor. "He won't give me no money. He says he'll take care of everything, though, if I only get Ma to sell the deli to him."

A mental genius Milton was not. Even Sammy would be suspicious of this plan.

"Hmmm," Julia feigned looking troubled. It wasn't difficult. "I just don't understand."

"Understand what?" He ordered a can of Pepsi.

"Well, Sweet Cheeks said something big was going to happen any day."

"What?" He was surprised. "You know Sweet Cheeks?"

"I met her yesterday at your house, remember? We met on the street by our cars as we were both leaving. She said you and she were thinking about getting married very soon. You were just waiting for something big that was going to happen any day."

His eyes suddenly teared up. He spoke yearningly. "You say she wants to get married?"

"I guess all that's stopping the two of you is something that's going to happen."

Julia dropped her voice. Milton's shirt and face were awash in barbecue sauce. His napkin, however, was pristine.

"What's your secret?"

"My secret?" He seemed confused.

"What are you waiting for before getting married? A catch like her isn't going to wait very long."

"I, uh," he stammered, peering around to make sure no one else was listening, "it's a secret. That's why she doesn't know it either. It's a real secret." He nodded solemnly and made the sign of a key in a lock, just as his mother had done when she had shown Shayna and Julia the cameras.

Was this the arsonist who had flummoxed the fire inspectors? Was this a man who could work out a way to poison and kill? Was he playing her, she wondered?

Milton had finished his meal. Julia couldn't finish hers. His final gesture was to crush his Pepsi can and belch.

"Well," she grabbed her purse, "I wish you two kids luck on your secret."

As Julia stood up, a thought occurred to her. How did Milton and Sweet Cheeks find each other? She suspected that more than love at first sight was involved here.

"Milton," She sat down again. "Just how did you and Sweet Cheeks first meet?" People in general, she knew, loved nothing better than to share their love origin stories. She was positive Milton would be very proud of his tale.

"It was pure luck," he beamed, with pieces of ribs still stuck in his teeth.

Julia wasn't so sure.

"You know that comic book store in downtown Crestfall by the bus stop? I was in there, looking at the latest DC comics, when damned if this beautiful girl doesn't bump into me."

"Really?" She was all ears.

"Shirl was into a Wonder Woman and wasn't looking where she was walking. I'm more into the Batman and Superman series. Anyway, just like in the movies, she bumped into me, and we just started talking right that minute. Then we went to the little coffee shop that's on the corner, and we talked for hours."

"About what?"

"About everything," his words seemed to fly. "We're almost twins. Her father died when she was young, too. And her mother used to boss her around something terrible. When her dad was alive, he tried to…to…you know what to her."

Milton looked shamefaced.

"Couldn't she tell someone?" Julia asked.

"Her mother wouldn't believe her. She became even meaner and threatened to kick Shirley out of the house if she didn't shut up about it."

He stared down. "Her childhood was worse than mine."

"Does she come from here?" Julia wanted to know.

"Naw. She ran away as soon as she could and never looked back. I think she's from somewhere out west, one of those states with a population of three."

"Ah," was all she could come up with.

"You're very lucky to have met your *b'shert*, your soul mate," Julia said. "Treasure her while you can," which, she figured, probably wouldn't be too much longer.

As Julia left, Milton reached out. She thought he was going to shake her hand. Instead, he grabbed her wrist and held it tightly. For such a flabby looking man, he had a very strong grip.

"Nice talking to ya," he said, giving her a Clint Eastwood eye squint. "Just make sure you don't give my ma any ideas about keeping the deli. Understand?"

He squeezed harder.

"I have no idea what you're talking about," She said with gritted teeth as he let go and she made a beeline to her car.

Yessir, Julia noted, as she rubbed her now greasy wrist, we're certainly going to keep that one on the suspect list.

****

Matt and Sammy were having a companionable conversation when Julia returned home.

"How did it go, guys?" she asked after calming down from breakfast with Milton.

"You've got an awfully bright kid, here. We were able to cover more than I had on my schedule for today. Sammy gets it the first time around, but," he hurriedly added, "I make all my students re-explain what we've just been through. He could be teaching me."

87

Clearly Matt was taken by Sammy. He collected his books and papers. "Sammy has some work to do in math and a brief paragraph to write for English. It was nice meeting both of you. See you tomorrow." He pointed to Sammy who looked sorry to see him go.

"Man, that was spectacular," Sammy beamed. It appeared that suddenly, her balking son was high on school. "That guy really gets it. None of the stupid review crap we get every day. You learn it; you show that you know it, and you go on from there. Why can't all teachers be like that?"

"That's just the way public education should work," Julia threw up her arms in frustration. She didn't understand why schools hadn't figured out how to meet a child's individual needs.

"I can't wait for tomorrow. If we finish math quickly, Matt's going to show me algebra," he said adoringly.

Harold would never believe this.

"So, partner," he asked, stretching his hands high so that he looked like one very tall lower-case letter I, "Are we working on our case today?"

"I have a meeting at two. Do you want to have some lunch, take a short rest, and come with? I don't want to interrupt your homework."

"It's nothing I can't do in an hour," he rolled his eyes. "Will your appointment take long?"

"I doubt it." Julia was opening a can of tuna for tuna salad, but was having difficulty, as usual, fitting the lid of the can onto the electric can opener. They had always used a manual opener until she cut her hand wrestling with the dulled instrument and a can of Starfish chunky. Jordan and two of his horrified friends watched as she threw a rag around her bleeding hand and ran around the neighborhood looking for Harold to drive her to the emergency room. He was forever walking the dog and getting into deep street-side discussions with neighbors.

"I'm not even sure what I'm going to say. Maybe you can sit in the office with me for good luck."

A large, brown brick, shoe box. That's what came to mind when they arrived at Lester Pintner's building. If this was an example of one of his developments, he had little to add to Crestfall's architecture. Whenever their family took long weekend jaunts, Harold always had Julia shoot photos of interesting outdoor art or striking buildings. Then he'd research the artists or building designers to see if there was some way to bring them to Crestfall. This building was an eyesore. No personality. No panache. Julia hoped Lester had more to offer.

Armed with his trusty Nintendo, Sammy accompanied his mother into the darkened anteroom where a bland-faced receptionist spoke into a phone to announce their arrival. Pintner came out to greet them, arm extended to shake their hands.

"I assume this isn't Mr. Donnelly," he chuckled, vigorously shaking Sammy's whole body.

"I'm Sammy. She's my mom. Pleased to meet you, sir."

"Oh, starting our political correctness early aren't we? Getting ready to take your father's mantle?" He laughed a little too heartily.

First of all, Julia wondered who the young man was standing beside her. What a change from the boy who usually ran around the house dressed in a swim suit and a red cape. She wondered what other secrets he was keeping. Second, it was obvious that Pintner knew who Julia was.

"Come in." He placed his hands on their backs and steered them into his office like a mother hen.

"Wow." Sammy's eyes almost popped out of his face. Julia's, too. It was as though they had entered an urban rain forest. Green potted palm trees and what appeared to be tropical plants adorned the huge room. Vines and ivies hung from containers attached to the ceilings. Metal tubing with pin point holes must have been Pintner's misting system. She could envision little monkeys swinging across the back wall. Sammy approached the colorful array as if he were in some magic wonderland.

Julia loved watching her son's excitement as he stepped into a new environment. His enthusiasm belied the problems he had been having at school. But, while he showed amazement as he inhaled the musky aroma of damp earth, she was reminded of the Garden of Eden, and wondered where the snake was lurking, and if it would strike.

"Are these alive?" Sammy asked. It was apparent to her that his hands

89

were aching to touch the leaves and fronds.

"Sure." Pintner opened a desk drawer to pull out several laminated pages with photos and most likely information about each plant.

"Here," he gave the pages to Sammy. "See if you can identify some of them. And be careful, I've got a mister that spritzes my babies several times a day. You might get wet. Look," he turned a switch on the door they entered, and a soft shower wafted over the foliage.

"Geez."

Sammy was entranced.

"Is it okay to look, Mom?"

"Go for it, Kiddo. Nothing can ruin your outfit."

Sammy skipped over to the window to examine a particularly interesting specimen. Lester led Julia to what one would call a conversational arrangement of chairs away from his desk and his jungle. There was also an architectural rendering of a building placed on an easel.

It reminded her of tall, skinny coffin made of black glass. She shivered imagining being in an elevator in such a claustrophobic edifice.

"So, Mrs. Donnelly, what can I do for you?"

"I'm interested in architecture."

"Really?"

"Yes. In fact, when my family and I take trips, we look for interesting buildings, ideas that might fit in our town."

"A very enterprising way to think about Crestfall."

"It's our home. We want it to look nice."

"I completely agree with you," he nodded sagely. The conversation stalled. What to say, Julia wondered. Perhaps I should ask him if he'd poisoned any chopped liver recently.

"Is this building we're in one of yours?" she asked.

"He made a face. This is temporary headquarters. I have something much grander in mind."

"What might that be?"

"Do you know the block at Granville and Central?"

That was Sophie's block.

"Yes."

"I'm expecting to buy everyone out, tear the whole thing down, and put up what I call my masterpiece."

"You talk about it as if it was a skyscraper."

"It will be high," he said, standing up and walking to the rendering. He looked at it lovingly. Clearly he was enamored by his creation. Julia was still seeing a coffin, but now she noticed small, slit-like windows that brought to mind medieval castles where warriors shot arrows at invaders through similar slits, rather than a homey atmosphere.

"There are height restrictions."

"Pffft," he blew through his lips. "A mere zoning variance. I hope your husband will take pity on me. This could be a very notable edifice for Crestfall."

"Do you own the block now?"

"Not yet," he said uncomfortably, "but I anticipate I'll have it all, soon."

"How does a developer do that?"

"Well," he sat down again and steepled his fingers, "I simply buy up all the individual stores and buildings. If you know the area, you have to admit it's an eyesore for this town." He leaned toward her and spoke confidentially, "You have to understand, these are very old shops in a gentrifying neighborhood. Sooner than later they'll have to go. I'm hoping for sooner." He smiled like a contented cat, or was it rat?

"So what's keeping you?"

He frowned. His furry black eyebrows reminded Julia of caterpillars. "My lawyers are working things out. We've given these people more than fair market offers on their stores. Some have accepted; some are still holding out. Do you know there was a fire a few months ago in the deli? It's called Celia's or something? The mayor should shut it down. I heard they cook their meat in a filthy roach-infested basement. The county health department ought to investigate."

"I heard she rebuilt the basement."

"I heard her insurance company won't pay out on the policy. They think she set the fire."

"What else have you heard?" she asked as Sammy ran toward them.

"Is this right?" he asked excitedly, and pointed to a plant on the back wall. "Is that really a Venus flytrap?"

Pintner was delighted to see a fellow enthusiast.

"Do you mind?" he asked. "This will only take a moment."

He rose, put his hand on Sammy's shoulder and the two approached the plant. Pintner was about Harold's height, five foot ten, wearing a store-bought suit. He didn't act like a bully, if you don't mind someone who ousts shopkeepers who've been eking out a slim living for years. Of course, he had lawyers and the old man to do his scut work.

"Mom, you should come and see," Sammy called.

"I think I'll sit this one out." Still, Julia got up and hovered in the background to make sure her son didn't lose a finger or get bitten. Sammy was a willing student, absorbing all the knowledge about Venus flytraps that Pintner was sharing.

"It's probably time for a feeding." He looked down at the plant. Its red, lip-like leaves had cream colored hairs sticking up on the edges. Julia was reminded of the witch in Hansel and Gretel trying to convince the little girl to check the oven. "Come here, my pretty; just lean in a little more..."

"Mom, Mom, can I feed the flytrap? Mr. Pintner says I can."

How can you say no to such an experience? Julia was nauseous again. Twice in one day.

She remembered the fateful time when the boys announced that Cujo, their precious newt, had gotten out of a makeshift container when they were washing his cage. Each boy accused the other of being responsible for the crime. For three days Julia was afraid to sleep, scared the newt would crawl across her face in the dark. To the boys' chagrin, and her secret pleasure, they discovered the poor creature dead in the clothes hamper. How he got there is still a mystery. Just the thought of being suffocated by boys' dirty laundry still made Julia shudder.

Pintner brought out a large mason jar with grasshoppers jumping over each other, trying to escape.

"Take one," Lester instructed. Sammy stuck his hand in and brought up a squirming victim.

"Now, hold it over the leaf and drop it in."

Julia was too sickened to watch the process and instead, examined her shoes. She knew it was over when Sammy said, "Cool."

"Can I do it again?"

Pintner took one look at Julia and said, "Perhaps another time. I don't think this is your mother's thing."

"Can I at least look around for a little, Mom?" her youngest child pleaded. He was in jungle heaven.

"Okay. Maybe five minutes or so." Pintner and Julia sat down again.

"What's your plan for redevelopment?" she asked.

He smiled, leaned forward in his chair and went into a well-practiced sales pitch. "I envision a fifteen story glass and steel building, commercial on the bottom, condos on top. We'll cater to the young professional who needs a one or two bedroom home. Thanks to your husband bringing new business to town, there's more demand for housing."

Forget the fact that such a monstrosity would definitely not fit in with the surrounding neighborhood, she thought.

He took a breath. "Stores on the bottom will cater to the condo owners. A cleaners, a Starbucks or similar coffee shop, a small cafe."

"What about a pool hall?"

"A pool hall?" he said sharply. "Who told you that?"

She grappled for something intelligent to say. "It's my older son. He's always complaining that Crestfall's boring; that it needs a place where teens and adults can do something like," Julia shrugged, "playing pool. He says other towns have them."

"There definitely will not be a pool hall in this building." Pintner scowled with disgust. "This will be high class, all the way."

"Well," Julia gathered up her purse, "it certainly sounds fascinating."

"Where do you get your grasshoppers?" Sammy asked. "I could maybe help you find some," he gushed hopefully.

"I get them from an online plant supply house. They also sell chocolate grasshoppers and recently started a grasshopper flour business. You can ask your Mom to bake you a grasshopper cake."

Oh joy. Julia pictured herself measuring out one cup of grasshopper, adding water and a little bit of baking powder. One insect cake coming up. But, she also considered, if you can order grasshoppers online, maybe you can also order the chopped liver poisoning, too. Something to tell Chief Scarpelli about. Julia wanted to leave Pintner's office as soon as possible. Maybe it was her imagination, but she began to feel as though little spiders were creeping up her legs. Julia almost dragged her reluctant son out of there.

"Come back any time," Pintner offered, as they left the building. "I'm always delighted to talk with a fellow plantsman."

"What a plantsman?," Sammy asked.

Julia could almost see the wheels in Sammy's head churning.

Pintner smiled, and looked at Sammy. "A plantsman is a person who loves plants, like a really good gardener."

"Oh," Sammy said, "like a horticulturalist?"

Pintner showed no surprise that a ten year old would use that term. On the other hand, Julia did.

"Where did you pick up that word?" she asked.

"Oh, sometimes when I'm bored in school I pick up the dictionary and read through the alphabet. I was just going through the letter 'h' a few weeks ago."

"A horticulturalist is a professional plant person. I'm more of an amateur," Pintner said with modesty. "But I really mean it, Sammy. If you ever want to visit again, I've got lots of fascinating vegetation for you to see."

"I will," Sammy called as they walked out.

"That was fantastic, Mom." He hopped in the passenger side of the car.

"I'm glad you were entertained."

"Are you mad at me?" Her son, the empath. He could always sense when someone was at odds with themselves.

"No, Kiddo. I'm not really comfortable among carnivorous plants. The whole set-up felt creepy to me."

They were about to turn left at a busy intersection when Sammy announced, "I saw something."

"What? What did you see?" *Probably a dead mouse being eaten by a snake*, she thought.

"Right after we came in, I went to the window to look at plants?"

For some reason, so many people end their sentences with a question mark. It drove Julia crazy.

"Yes?"

"I saw Sweet Cheeks' car zoom by."

"You're kidding." Julia almost plowed into a car turning in the opposite direction. How was Sweet Cheeks involved with Pintner?

"Why do you suppose she was there?" Julia wondered aloud.

"Maybe she likes plants?" Sammy offered. She had to turn her head to look at him. He was giggling.

"Made you laugh," he teased. Julia giggled, too. Sammy's mood was infectious. It felt good to share a positive moment with him.

"Well, I found out something, too," she shared. After all, they were partners.

"What?"

"Mr. Pintner has no intention of putting a pool hall in his new building."

"No."

"Yes. Everyone's lying. Milton swears he's got an agreement with Mr. Pintner to run the pool hall. Pintner says there won't be one. Milton thinks he and Sweet Cheeks are going to get married, but she was threatening him down in the basement. And now, you see her around Pintner's office. What does it all mean? And the horrible old man and the owner of Nate's Nosh are still on the list to interview. I don't think we're getting anywhere."

Julia hit the steering wheel with both hands, realizing she was giving her son a front row seat to adult frustration.

"You'll find the answer, Mom," Sammy said softly. "Remember what you always tell Jordan and me? Stop. Count to ten, and then start all over again."

Julia almost cried. This special child had really listened to her words, and he had complete confidence in her. She couldn't let him down.

After dinner, Harold and the boys drifted to their individual pursuits. Harold was watching the news shows in the family room. Jordan was on his computer emailing friends about girls, no doubt. Sammy was finishing his English paragraph or reading Freud, for all she knew. Julia called Rabbi Fine to share the day's activities.

"Milton," Rabbi Fine said with a sigh, "is a *shnook*. No good will come to him. All he can see is how everyone else has something and he has nothing. It doesn't occur to him that he has to work for what he wants.

"As for Shirley Sweet Cheeks," he continued, "we may need help from the police on her. She's willing to put a lot of effort into something, but it's not sincere. I'm afraid that she's in for disappointment, too."

"What about her connection to Pintner?"

"You and I both believe that her fortuitous meeting with Milton had to be a set-up, Wonder Woman notwithstanding. So who was responsible? Who told her to do it?"

Julia could picture him *davening* by the phone as he processed all the information.

"Could it be Pintner?" She asked.

"If so, why?" the Rabbi asked rhetorically.

She loved it when he asked questions like this. It forced her to think analytically, something mothers who fold tee shirts and wash sticky kitchen floors don't do every day.

"If Pintner can't get the store from Sophie, he'll bamboozle it away from Milton. He might have added Sweet Cheeks to the equation to pressure a lovesick Milton to act more quickly or she'll leave him," Julia suggested.

"That's possible, but what's in it for Sweet Cheeks?" "Maybe Pintner's offered her money," she added, "or maybe they're having an affair."

Wonders of wonders, even in this vile situation, she was enjoying herself. It was almost like creating an outline for writing a book. Should the villainess simply be greedy, or have an affair with the main bad guy?

"And," the rabbi went on, "maybe he has no intention of getting serious with her and is simply using her as a ploy to get the deli.

"This Pintner," the rabbi mused, "he reminds me of the prophet Ezekiel when he explained the great sins of Sodom and Gomorrah."

Julia wasn't familiar with Ezekiel. Another sign that her Judaic knowledge was ten ounces short of a pound.

"Ezekiel," he explained, "one of our major prophets, said that the people of Sodom and Gomorrah were punished because they were arrogant, overfed, and unconcerned. They did not help the poor and needy. And compared to Abraham and Sarah who welcomed the three angels who visited them, the inhabitants of Sodom and Gomorrah were inhospitable to strangers."

"So, how does this relate to Pintner?" Rabbi Fine asked. "He has a lack of empathy. Even if he follows the law to a "t" in Sophie's case, he's hurting those in need of making a simple living. Pintner may not even be aware that he's being cruel. He wants what he wants, and he will have it at any cost."

"What about progress?" Julia was playing devil's advocate. "If every Sophie and every shoemaker stayed in their decrepit shops, the cities could crumble."

"There's always a kinder way," Rabbi Fine insisted. "But he's offered them above market price."

"Maybe he's done it in an insulting, arrogant fashion that only invites trouble."

The rabbi sounded very sad. Julia was sad, too. It seemed like they were running in circles.

"Julia." His voice picked up some enthusiasm, "I have a quote for you. Are you listening?"

Without waiting for an answer he recited, "Rabbi Tarfon said, 'The day is short, and there is much to be done. It is not your responsibility to complete all the work. However, you are not free to give up trying to do it.'"

That was it in a nutshell. They had to go on. Someone had to be on Sophie's side.

"Do you understand why what we're doing is crucial?" he asked.

"Yes, partner. As Harold and I tell the boys after a bad day, 'there's always tomorrow.'"

They decided to discuss their next two interviews, the old man who terrorized the shoemaker, and Nate from Nate's Nosh, the next day at Julia's house while Sammy and Matt studied.

Normally Orthodox men do not go into the home of a woman outside of his family if no one else is present, but Sammy and the tutor would be there. Julia hung up the phone and stretched. She was tired. It was time to call it a day.

Almost.

"Julia," Harold ambled into the kitchen looking for a cookie. "Who was that on the phone?"

"Just Rabbi Fine."

He leaned on the wall, hands in his pocket, going for a relaxed look. Julia wasn't fooled. After all their years of marriage, she detected a hint of skepticism in his eyes.

"Do you have a separate Torah session going? It seems like you two have been on the phone a lot since the *seder*. You're not investigating the case, are you?"

"The food poisoning?" Eyes wide open and innocent. "No, of course not. But I never said I wouldn't check out Sophie's fire. The insurance company won't do anything unless she can prove it was a spontaneous fire or that someone else beside her committed arson. And the fire department hasn't found anything definitive yet."

Harold seemed satisfied. Julia could practically hear his brain working. 'Julia isn't going to be able to do anything more than the fire inspectors. Let her play detective with the rabbi.'

'It'll give her something to do with her spare time.' As if, Julia responded to his unspoken thoughts, she had any time to spare.

Chapter Sixteen: Wednesday

The house was jumping Wednesday morning. Matt and Sammy were deep into photosynthesis while Rabbi Fine and Julia talked about means, motive and opportunity. Part of her wished she was back in fifth grade science with Sammy, because she and the rabbi were facing some pretty large holes in the investigation.

So far, they had some idea of where three subjects stood as to motive. Milton wanted his mother's store to create a pool parlor. If Sweet Cheeks was, indeed, in love with Milton, and Julia didn't even think so for a second, then perhaps she had helped him set the deli on fire. They still had a question mark as to what her relationship was with Pintner, if one existed. And, Pintner wanted Sophie out of the deli so he could tear everything down and build his masterpiece.

Means. Who had the knowledge or ability to commit the crime? Milton didn't strike them as being able to start a fire that would successfully puzzle fire inspectors. Sweet Cheeks, on the other hand, was an electrician, and would have the knowledge to commit arson.

Pintner didn't have to start the fire himself. He could simply hire someone to do it for him — possibly the old man.

The black hole was opportunity. Where were they at the time of the fire? That was a matter for the police. They could check phone records, look into credit cards, talk to neighbors. At this point, there was little more the rabbi and Julia could do with their three suspects than wait for more information to drop.

"You know," Julia said, thoughtfully, "there's one more person or persons we haven't put on our suspect list."

"Who?"

"The people who are calling in bomb scares. Maybe they already hit Crestfall with the fire at Sophie's and we didn't even know it."

"Wow." The rabbi started *davening* unconsciously. A whole new food group of suspects. Terrorists or simply hater wannabes.

"You've certainly opened up the field," he said. "But how are we going to find any information on them? The police haven't found anyone yet."

"I've got a crazy idea," Julia said, finishing up her cup of tea. She walked into the dining room and asked to talk to Matt for a second. She assured Sammy that it had nothing to do with him.

Matt self-consciously came into the kitchen and joined her and Rabbi

Fine.

"Matt," Julia began, "you're young."

He nodded, puzzled. A pink blush rose from his neck to his cheeks.

"You know lots of different kinds of people that the rabbi and I don't have any knowledge about."

He nodded again.

"There isn't any other way to ask this, and please," Julia stressed, "please don't think this has anything to do with you. We love you, Matt."

Matt looked confused.

"Matt, do you know of anyone, or maybe a group of kids, who hate Jews?"

His eyebrows almost jumped off of his head. "Why would...?"

"Matt," she repeated, "I think the world of you. Someone is doing bad things in the surrounding towns, and the rabbi and I are trying to catch them, but we have no connections. I thought you might know someone who knows someone..."

"Oh." He looked relieved. "You mean the Blades, a gang around here."

"The who?"

"The Blades. It's short for Switchblades."

Julia felt a tremor of fear running down her back.

"You've got your goths, the kids who wear black all the time, the skinheads who generally hate Jews, etc., and you have the Blades. They hate Jews, too, and they're really bad guys. In order to get into their group, you have to do something obscene."

"What's obscene?" Rabbi Fine asked softly.

Matt thought. "Like beating up people, knifing them, pipe bombing places"

"What about calling in bomb scares?" Julia wanted to know.

"Yes," he nodded. "Especially things that screw with the police."

It felt right. They could be looking for a Blade.

"How could we find one?" Julia asked. It was frightening just to consider the prospect of walking up to someone who wanted to see her not exist.

"I'm not saying I'm friends with any Blades, or any skinheads for that matter, but," Matt had absently put a macaroon into his mouth. He just breathed in the whole thing at once. Julia imagined what his mother's grocery bill must have looked like while he was growing up. "The thing is, my former college roommate had a brother who once was a Blade. I could call him and see if I can make a connection for you."

"That would be great, Matt." Julia pumped his hand which was the size of a Labradoodle puppy. "We'd like to set up a meeting as soon as possible."

Matt stood. His head almost touched the kitchen ceiling. He ambled back out to the dining room. Soon he and Sammy were deep into school work again.

"That was progress," Julia noted.

"Yes," he agreed, "unless we're dealing with real terrorists, and I have my own sources to that end."

Julia looked at the rabbi cockeyed. What was she missing here?

"I just thought of something," the rabbi almost jumped up from the kitchen chair. They were drinking tea out of styrofoam paper cups. Though far from being kosher, Julia was making baby steps to keep kosher for herself. When Rabbi Fine and the Torah group met at her house, they snacked off of a large supply of pretty paper plates and generic styrofoam cups.

Also on hand was a new tea pot that she used only for them. "We've been talking to everyone, but we haven't looked at the fire records at all."

"Are they available to the public?"

"There's only one way to find out. Let's go to the fire department." He took a last gulp of tea and stood up.

"Wait," Julia said. "Before we run off, let's talk strategy on our last two subjects. We might as well have a clear picture of all of our suspects before checking the fire records. I can call Chief Grenschler any time. We know each other."

Rabbi Fine sat down again.

"Would you like another macaroon?" Julia offered that Shayna had decided to fly back from Florida. She and Julia had stopped off at Sophie's deli the day before. The store was almost empty. Sophie looked terrible with red, puffy eyes and a pallid face. After handing them the box of airy kosher mounds, she told them there already were rumors that her chopped liver was responsible for the recent illnesses. Business had been down Monday and Tuesday.

"I can't even give my food away," she complained. "No one's said nothing to me yet." She sighed. "I suppose I should be happy for that, but the rumor mill, it's killing me."

Back in Julia's kitchen, Rabbi Fine moved the box of macaroons away. "No, thank you. Wherever I go, people say 'take a little taste, that's all.' A little taste here, another taste there, and all of a sudden you're talking extra pounds and I can't button my pants." He gave a self-deprecating laugh, then settled down.

"Okay. So how do you think we should handle the old man? Do you know anything about him? Where he lives? Where he hangs out?"

"All I know from Sophie is that he lurks," Julia answered.

"Lurks?" The rabbi was confused.

"Yes. He isn't in any particular spot at any given time. He appears unexpectedly, does something obnoxious, then disappears. There's no way to know."

"Sometimes," the rabbi ruminated, stroking his beard, "having only one person to question someone is the right thing to do. Other times," he scratched his neck, "for the sake of safety, it's better for two. I think that in this case, you and I should track him down and have a little civil chat."

Julia agreed, purposely pushing away any thought of danger.

"And, as for Nate, that one I think I can handle alone," he said.

It was fine with Julia. It was about 10:30 in the morning. Since Matt and Sammy were still studying, she and Rabbi Fine drove in separate cars to Sophie's deli. The shoe repair shop next door was still open. For the first time they noticed that other shops on the block were vacant. Some had metal gates up and were closed permanently. A few had wooden boards nailed over broken windows. They were closed, too. Maybe, Julia thought, the old man is doing his lurking in a closed building.

It was a beautiful beginning of an April day. The sun was out. It was crisp but not cool. Nothing bad ever happens on a lovely day like this; Julia repeated that mantra as she parked behind the rabbi's car. First they went into Sophie's deli. No customers. The counter workers were standing around, chatting in low voices.

"Is Sophie here?" Rabbi Fine asked.

"She left for a while," a woman in an apron told them. "We don't know when she'll be back. Are you interested in buying something today?"

They shook their heads.

The rabbi cleared his throat. "Did the old man come by yet?"

Everyone knew who they were talking about.

"Yeah," answered a baker by the look of his matzah meal sprinkled apron, "he already made an entrance. When we showed up for work this morning, cigar ashes covered the whole floor."

"Can't the police help you with that?" Julia asked.

"No," a young Latino girl said. "The man, he always gone before we see him do it. Then, after the police go, he comes back in and he say 'have a good day.'"

"What direction did he go?" Rabbi Fine asked.

They inclined their heads toward the shoe repair shop. "Thank you." Their echoing feet left a sad tattoo as they exited the empty store.

The owner of the shoe repair shop was sitting on a short stool behind his counter when Julia and Rabbi Fine came in. He was staring out into space.

"Excuse me," the rabbi began, then stopped when they saw tears running down the man's face.

"Oh, I'm so sorry for disturbing you," Rabbi Fine strode to the man's side. "Can I help you? Here's a handkerchief. Do you have a teapot here? If you can't find one, Julia, go next door and bring some tea back for us."

As she walked to the rear of the store in search of a tea pot, Julia saw several tall shelves turned over, shoes and purses scattered everywhere, their identifying tags torn up. She nixed the teapot and immediately ran to Sophie's for tea and Passover mandel bread, similar to a biscotti. By the time she returned, the owner was speaking to the rabbi in a raspy voice.

"You break your back year after year to make a living for your family, and what do you get?" he said bitterly, tearing open a sugar packet and emptying it into the tea.

"Did the old guy do this?"

"Who else?" the man said. "This is what it looked like when I came in this morning."

The rabbi nodded to Julia. "We're about twenty minutes too late."

"I can't take this anymore," the owner cried. "First there were offers to buy the store. I didn't want to sell. Then there were threats — let us buy the store or you'll be sorry. Next came the dirty tricks. Mail ripped up. Bags of shit put in front of the door. After that dead rats. One day I found a snake. The police do nothing. I know who did this. They say they need more proof. I tell them, when you see my dead body lying on the floor, will that be enough?

"My wife used to help me here every day. Now she's afraid. My helper quit last week. What am I going to do?"

His whole body was shaking. The rabbi looked very concerned. "Do you have anyone to call?" he asked.

"No one will come. They're all scared. I'm alone."

The storekeeper looked up as though seeing them for the first time. "You know," he whispered, "this used to be a good neighborhood. We all came here around the same time, right after World War II. We were young servicemen coming to start new businesses; refugees like my wife Chloe and me starting a new life. She and I met in the displacement camps in France. It was a real United Nations in this area. And all everyone wanted to do was to be an American, work hard, raise a family, have a decent place to live." He smiled wanly.

"What happened?" Julia asked.

The man shrugged. "We got old. People moved away for better housing and schools. The buildings weren't so new and shiny. But," he wagged a shaking finger at me, "it was still home for Chloe and me. Until this man, this developer and his goon came around."

"That would be Lester Pintner and the old guy?" the rabbi asked.

The man nodded.

"Now most of the stores on this square block have closed, or the owners are shaking in their boots. Where am I going to go?" He raised his arms in supplication. "Even if they pay me for this place, I'm too tired to start all over again." The tears started flowing again.

The rabbi took off his jacket, threw it on the counter, rolled up his sleeves and turned to Julia.

"Can you spare an hour?" he asked.

"Sure." Julia put her purse behind the counter. She and the rabbi both marched to the rear of the store and began to push the shelves upright. A minute later the owner joined them.

"My name is Albert," he introduced himself, as all three heaved up another shelf.

At the end of an hour, they were all sweating like pigs. There were still pairs of shoes to be sorted, but they had made a lot of progress.

"Listen, Albert," Rabbi Fine said grimly, "I know some young men who can spend time with you. If the old guy comes around while they're here, they'll make sure he doesn't bother you again. How about it?"

"Rabbi, at this point I'll give anything a chance." Albert wiped his forehead with his shirt sleeve.

"Good, my friend." The rabbi patted Albert on the back. "Have some faith."

Julia looked at her watch. It was past time to go home. "How are we going to find him?" she asked.

"He'll find us," the rabbi said complacently.

"How?" She didn't want to find this man standing on her doorstep.

"I gave Albert my phone number to give to him. And we'll leave my number at Sophie's. He'll call. He'll want to know why we're looking for him. Don't worry so much, Julia."

Warning bells rang in Julia's head. This is getting a little too close to home. Harold will be furious. She could be putting the boys in danger, she thought.

"Go home to Sammy. Take a break. We'll see the old guy when we see him. I'll pay a visit to Nate's Nosh later after I get cleaned up," the rabbi said.

His shirt was smeared with dust, his tie undone, and his yarmulke askew. Julia suspected that she looked the same, too. "Who are the young men who can stay with Albert?" Julia asked.

The rabbi's face darkened. "Better you shouldn't know." Julia realized that the rabbi's life wasn't all cherries and cream. There must be another side of him that the Torah group and perhaps the *Kollel* didn't know. She unlocked her car. It was just after noon and she wanted to be home before Sammy was alone too long.

"Will I see you tonight at Torah group?" Rabbi Fine asked.

"Tonight is Wednesday. Group is tomorrow night, isn't it?"

"Normally, but tomorrow night is a holiday, the end of Passover. We have a festive dinner and people don't drive, so rather than miss a night of Torah, we agreed to study one night earlier."

Julia had forgotten, as usual. There were so many festivals and holidays she didn't know about.

"I'm not sure I'll be there, Rabbi. Today has been rather tiring, and it's not even noon yet."

"Come," he said. "I promise it will be calming. You'll be surrounded by friends. We'll be learning together. How bad can that be?"

Hearing him say it that way, Julia decided it would be a good idea to go to class. She could use an island of calm within the stormy seas around her.

105

Lilah's house was like a Greek haven; bright and roomy, done in tones of white and Aegean blue. The floors, covered with tasteful pastel rugs, were a bleached off white color. Coral shells and sea urchins lay out in lovely patterns on coffee tables that one might see in *Architectural Digest.* Fresh flowers adorned several vases. It felt like a beautiful mansion on the sea. So different from Julia's cluttered rooms. And yet Lilah would give it all up in a second if she could bring a child into the world.

Tonight her dining room table held large plates of perfectly cut melon, as well as oranges. With no children to preoccupy her time, Lilah had cut the oranges into thin circular slices, halved them, and then, separated a small bit of the orange from its peel on each side. It made eating the juicy fruit a far neater affair.

Everyone came bustling in. Faigie, looking more positive at each meeting, Devorah, looking a little disheveled, Malka, Bubbe, and Chava, Shayna, and Julia.

"I can't remember what I was going to say," Bubbe complained.

"You'll remember later, Bubbe," Chava soothed.

"Yeah, later at two in the morning." Bubbe grumbled. When she saw Julia she came to her side of the table and pinched her cheeks.

"How's my best girl," she chirped.

"Fine, Bubbe."

Julia had taken a quick bath, washed her hair, changed into clean clothes and still had time to make a meat loaf dinner, and catch up on the day's news with Harold and the kids.

Unfortunately, her muscles were beginning to seize up from the morning's effort with Albert the shoemaker.

Rabbi Fine ran in as the women were filling their plates with fruit. He looked at his watch and said with surprise, "Amazing, I'm actually on time." Everyone sat. Just before he began to speak, Faigie interrupted. "Rabbi, you said you'd look into Nate's Nosh and let us know if everything's on the up and up."

"Well, it just so happens that I paid Nate a visit today, and I was planning to talk to you about it later. Will that be okay? The lesson first, then Nate? That's why we're here, isn't it?"

Faigie nodded. Everyone settled down again. Julia's mind wandered. When did he have time between helping Albert, dinner, and class? What is it with men? Are they always so capable of compartmentalizing? Helping Albert clean up his store had almost finished her for the day.

The rabbi was talking about Ruth and Naomi. Julia knew that story. Naomi's husband Elimelech, an Israelite, decided to leave their home in Bethlehem with their two sons, Mahlon and Chilion. It occurred to Julia that she never knew why they had left but she didn't have to wonder for long because Lilah wanted to know the same thing.

"Most people simply accept the premise that they left because there was a famine in the land," the rabbi intoned, "but the *midrash,* rabbinic commentary on Torah, suggests that while Elimelech was a well-to-do man, the people around him weren't doing very well. The burden of taking care of so many of his neighbors was too much for him. He chose, instead, to move to Moab with his family."

"So, when you say the burden of caring for his neighbors was too great," Malka commented dryly, you really mean the guy didn't want to share his riches anymore?"

"That's right," the rabbi said. "Basically, he was an unfeeling man, selfish. He desired to maintain his own wealth while others suffered. And what happened?"

"Karma," Bubbe broke in.

"Exactly," the Rabbi agreed, "He died."

"But his sons lived," Lilah noted.

"They did live, and both married. Mahlon married Ruth, and Chilion married Oprah," Devorah, the Torah group savant added.

"And then?" the rabbi asked.

"Karma," Bubbe shouted. "I'm right, aren't I?"

"Yes, Bubbe," Malka whispered, then tried to shush her grandmother.

"Stop with the shushing, already. I'm awake, I'm participating, I'm answering questions right. What more do you want from me?" she huffed.

Malka raised her hands in frustration and fell back in her chair in defeat.

Rabbi Fine smiled. "Bubbe's right on the nickel. Both sons died after ten years."

"Why did it take so long?" Lilah asked.

"Do we understand God's ways?" Rabbi Fine was being rhetorical. "Perhaps it took ten years for Naomi's cousin Boaz to be in a position to marry. Some say he never married before meeting Ruth. Others say he was a widower."

Faigie interrupted, "Please, tell us about Ruth and Naomi, that's my favorite part."

She sounded like a child asking a parent to recite an often told tale.

Rabbi Fine took on his sing-song voice. "After Naomi's two sons died, she decided to return to Bethlehem. She told her two daughters-in-law to go back to their own families and remarry. Oprah left, but Ruth said—

They could hear Faigie's voice fervently reciting, "Whither though goest, I will go, and whither thou lodgest, I will lodge. Thy people shall be my people, and thy God my God. Where thou diest, will I die, and there will I be buried"

The women sat quietly, touched by the simple yearning in Faigie's voice. She ached to have a connection like that to someone, perhaps her husband, who was still trying to keep their marriage together.

"Such loyalty. Such love," Faigie remarked when she was finished. "And she was rewarded with Boaz."

"Right," said Rabbi Fine. "Ruth returned with Naomi to Bethlehem. Boaz was a rich man who owned fields of barley. In those days, it was a biblical commandment to leave a corner of each field for the poor. During harvest time, those in need would go and pick up the fallen stalks. Ruth, now a poor widow, was among them

Devorah, usually quiet, jumped in. "That traditional practice was called *gleaning.* Naomi told her cousin of Ruth's loyalty, and when Boaz saw Ruth in the fields, he was taken with her. In the end, they married in what was called a *levirate* marriage."

"What's a lever marriage?" Bubbe asked. "I never heard of a marriage with levers. Maybe a Jacuzzi or one of those sex toys, but never levers. I'm sure of that."

Chava turned pink. Malka put her hand over her mouth.

"*Levirate,* Bubbe." The rabbi was always very patient with her. "I'll give you the official version from Deuteronomy, and then we'll see how this affects our story. The *Torah* tells us that if there are brothers, and one of them dies and has no child, then the wife of the dead brother should not marry a stranger. Her husband's brother should take her as a wife and perform the duty of *Yibum.* 'And it shall be that her firstborn child will have the name of the dead brother, so that his name may not be wiped out from Israel.'"

Rabbi Fine continued, "Now, if there is no brother, the next closest relative has a special *mitzvah* to marry the widow. Their first son fills the void of the dead brother, inheriting his estate and his portion of the Land of Israel. The relative thus "redeems" the name and memory of the dead man who otherwise would have no lasting remnant in this world."

"Boaz was Naomi's cousin, so he could marry Ruth and, if they had a son, would continue the family line for Naomi's deceased son Mahlon. What Boaz did was considered a sacrifice, because he didn't create an heir for himself, rather one for Mahlon."

"Good heavens, I'm glad that doesn't still apply today. My bachelor brother-in-law is an idiot," Lilah said, then put her hand over her mouth in embarrassment. The words had slipped out before she realized it.

Ignoring her comment, Rabbi Fine continued, "Boaz gladly followed the laws of the Torah and helped the less fortunate through *gleaning,* offering a portion of his harvest to the poor. That, by the way, is related to the notion of tithing, giving a tenth of your profits. In fact, the term *maaser* means taking a tenth."

"I know that if you're at a wedding in Israel, there's usually a table set aside for the poor," Chava offered.

"Even today, at a kosher store you'll see a person go up to the proprietor and ask for food, and he'll usually receive a meal. It's considered a *mitzvah,* an obligatory good deed."

"That's what I couldn't remember," Bubbe shouted, rising from her chair.

"What?" Chava helped her to sit down again.

"Remember I told you that I thought Nate had a heavy thumb on his scales? Well, the other day I saw a man dressed in a black suit, wearing a fedora, you know, a *yeshiva bucher,* a Torah student, go up to Nate in the store. He asks for some food."

"I was with you," Malka interrupted. "Nate brought out some soup and bread."

"Yeah, but did you hear what he told him? You were too busy looking in the dessert section."

"What did he say?" Chava asked.

"Right after he gave the man some soup, Nate said, in a *farshtinkener* voice that he thought no one could hear, but I got great ears." She pulled off a hearing aid and held it up as proof of her excellent hearing skills. "He said, 'Why come here to beg? Why don't you go and get a job?' In my opinion," Bubbe said, "that isn't a *mitzvah.* If you do something good, but with a hard heart, it can't be a *mitzvah,* can it?"

"No." Rabbi Fine's face looked troubled.

"I was just there today," he told us. "Nate seemed like a nice guy. I said that my Torah group was interested in his deli, and he showed me around. He's kind of interesting. First he studied at a Yeshiva in Israel. Then he came back to the States, and went to college majoring in chemistry. After he graduated, he worked in restaurants starting as a fry cook, gradually improving his skills. About five years ago he decided that he wanted to have his own Jewish deli and prepare the food he enjoyed as a boy. He saved his money. Finally, about a year ago, he started Nate's Nosh."

"A regular Horatio Alger Hiss, he is," Bubbe said. "I still don't trust him."

"He has a *mashgiach*," Rabbi Fine added.

"What's that?" Yet another new term Julia didn't know.

"A *mashgiach* is someone who watches over a kosher restaurant to make sure everything is done properly. Like making sure the owner doesn't use non-kosher products. Nate's *mashgiach* was there when I stopped in. He gave me his card. I think I'll call him just to see how Nate is really doing."

The women talked amongst themselves. Rabbi Fine whispered to Julia, "He seemed like an okay guy, but I don't like Bubbe's comments. She may be old, but she's sharp as a tack. If he really treated that gentleman poorly, it doesn't speak well of him. I'll let you know what more I find out."

By that time, Nate's deli seemed more interesting to the group than the story of Ruth.

Just before class ended, Malka asked, "Is there anything more on the anti-Semitic acts in the surrounding towns?"

Julia looked at the rabbi. She didn't know what to say, considering that they were trying to make an appointment with a Jew-hater as soon as possible. Rabbi Fine, in his wisdom, said, "I haven't heard anything from rabbis in the surrounding towns. For now, we wait."

They all said their goodbyes, and Julia went home for another hot bath and some aspirin.

The next time she and the rabbi came upon a clean-up project, she was going to volunteer Sammy and Jordan to do the job.

"I have two new things to tell you." It was Rabbi Fine breaking the Thursday afternoon quiet of the Donnelly household.

"And I've got news for you, too," Julia added.

"Tell me."

"Matt called. He talked to his old roommate who talked to his brother. The brother cleaned up his act. He's working as a camp counselor at the Park District, but the brother contacted another member of his old group, and he's agreed to meet with us someplace where no one will be able to see us. He's going to get in touch with me tomorrow."

"Great, I think. We've got to be very careful with this one, Julia. This gang is brutal. Even though they might be anywhere from their teens to their twenties, their fists hurt, just the same."

She shuddered.

"Now, let me give you my good news. The old man called."

"Aha. The game is afoot," Julia joked. A good night's sleep had improved her disposition from yesterday. Also, she and Sammy had made a quick visit to Tzippi's house after lunch. They brought flowers that Sammy had picked out from the florist. Tzippi was up and about, fussing over them, putting on the tea kettle, serving home-made cookies someone had brought. They paused to say a grateful prayer that Tzippi and all the other victims except for the three poor people who had died, were back at home.

"Julia," he chided, "this is not a laughing matter."

"I'm sorry, Rabbi." Truth be told, she was full of vinegar, ready to whip the world into shape. "What did he sound like?"

"He sounded like Clint Eastwood in a Dirty Harry movie. Low key threatening."

"Is he going to meet with us?"

"Yes," Rabbi Fine said. "He's puzzled why a housewife and a rabbi are interested in him."

Julia's hackles rose. A housewife he called me, she inwardly boiled. A pox on that man. I'm so much more that an ironer of clothes and bandager of cut knees. She felt the heat of anger swelling inside of her. I'm a detective, too, you old goat. Maybe finding a stick pin or a stolen relic isn't going to change the world, but it's detective work, and I did it. The word detective rolled seductively over her tongue and it felt good.

"When does he want to meet?" Now, faced with the reality of seeing the mean man face to face, Julia was beginning to feel a little tense.

"Are you free today at three p.m.?"

She'd have to leave Sammy alone for an hour or so, but he could handle it. He'd been working with Matt and studying enthusiastically. Sammy'll be okay, she convinced herself.

Actually, she admitted, he'd be thrilled that his mom considered him old enough to take care of himself with no one around.

"Okay. Where are we going?" She asked.

Rabbi Fine mentioned a bar Julia had never heard of, which was no surprise. Even when she was single, bar-hopping was not on her dance card.

One, she didn't drink more than a glass or two of wine on holidays and possibly when visiting at someone's house for dinner, and two, bars are depressing. She was more of a coffee shop woman.

"I'll pick you up," Rabbi Fine said.

That was chivalrous and daring. It was sweet that the rabbi didn't want Julia to drive to the bar alone, but he was going against Orthodox practice by being in a car with a woman who wasn't a member of his family. Still, knowing who they were going to meet, she was very happy to have company.

The rabbi's old silver Chevrolet was comforting to her. It was filled with papers on the seats and on the floor. There were announcements and programs for Jewish classes that he or the *Kollel* he belonged to were offering. The *Kollel*, which paid Rabbi Fine a small stipend for teaching Torah in the community, was a group that supported Orthodox Judaism. It sent out several rabbis to nearby towns. They did not proselytize, though if they could convince people to be more observant, that would be considered a success. Rather, they wanted to educate people to what lessons the Torah contained. Under a collection of brochures was a car seat, reminding her that Rabbi Fine was a father, too, although he rarely mentioned his wife and child.

They drove to a run-down section of town and stopped by a bar that looked closed on the outside. Inside they were hit with the sharp, stale odor of beer and cigarettes with an understated soupçon of urine, even though Crestfall had passed a no smoking ordinance two years ago. It was dark, better not to see the dirty floor and dingy walls covered with old posters touting different brands of liquor. At a table in the rear sat a sixtyish looking man dressed in black. He raised his hand signaling that he was waiting for them. As he stood, Julia realized that this man was elderly in age only. He was about six feet tall, thin, but sturdy. His arms, in a well-fitting, long sleeved black tee shirt, looked wiry, with the possibility of strength. His face, however, was frightening; a dark six o'clock shadow at one p.m., a mouth that curled down, and haunting black eyes that looked like pieces of coal. Julia would not want to meet this man in an alley. In fact, she didn't want to meet this man anywhere, including now. What, she thought, were they getting themselves into?

"Sit," the man said. It was more like a command.

Surprisingly, the rabbi gave Julia's back a little shove, and the two of them slowly walked over and sat opposite him in a booth that offered more stuffing than the fake leather covering.

"So," he was gauging them. "What do you want from me?"

Rabbi Fine took the lead. "As you know, I'm Rabbi Fine and this is Julia. And, " he asked, "what's your name?"

After a few seconds hesitation he replied, "You can call me Jin."

"Jin?" The rabbi looked confused.

"Yeah. Like a genie except with a 'J'. I make things happen," he said and chuckled.

"Well, Jin, we've been looking into some happenings at Sophie's Deli and her neighbor Albert. They're pretty upset. Do you know anything about that?"

Jin breathed in and let out a sigh. "They should have sold their stores like the others. They were…talked to."

"But they don't want to sell," Julia said, forgetting that she was scared of this man. "All they want is to keep doing what they've done for years. They're too old to start all over again."

"Progress, lady. Things change. Sometimes you've got to push people into the future."

"Does that include terrorizing senior citizens?" Rabbi Fine asked.

"Whatever." Jin checked his fingernails. They were well manicured. Except for his face, he didn't look like a rough sort of person.

"How are you related to this development? Do you work for Lester Pintner?" Julia asked.

"Lester," he said, making it sound like an unpleasant hiss. "He's nothing but a little pissant."

"Then," the rabbi jumped in, "why are you helping him out?"

"Helping him?" Jin's laugh was mirthless. "I'm trying to help myself."

"How so?" Rabbi Fine leaned forward. He was going into rabbi mode, one where there was no judgment, only the ear of a neutral person.

Jin hunched forward. "Want to hear a story?"

"Sure," they said at the same time.

Jin suddenly moved his hand to his pockets. Julia was afraid he was reaching for a gun or a knife. She gripped the edge of the table. It was sticky with…she didn't even want to think what made it gooey. Perhaps some Ajax cleanser would wipe it all away. She felt like the Martha Stewart of dive bars. This guy wouldn't try anything in public, would he? Though a dark bar with no customers and a bartender who was engrossed in a baseball game on TV wasn't exactly a public place.

Instead of a weapon, Jin pulled out a scuffed black leather wallet and shuffled through various cards until he found what he was looking for.

"Check this out," he said, pushing over the photo. It was a picture of a man and a young boy, possibly around fourteen. They were both smiling, leaning against the side of a sleek green car. Julia didn't know the make. It wasn't important. What was important was who the two were.

The man was Jin, some thirty years younger. The teenager looked as if he could be Lester Pintner.

"Is that you and Lester?" Julia asked.

Jin nodded.

"Are you his father?" Rabbi Fine queried.

Jin nodded again.

"So, you're working for your son?" the rabbi continued.

A look of distaste transformed Jin's face from threatening to hateful.

He spat out his words slowly and full of disdain.

"I do not work for Lester Pintner."

"Then what is your connection?" Julia wondered aloud.

"I work against him." Jin answered.

Both the rabbi and Julia were confused. How could Jin be working against his son if he was threatening people to leave so the square block could be developed?

"I am Lester's father. Gave him a good life, especially while my wife Eloise was alive. We lived in an old bungalow, but I kept it in tip-top shape. I was a developer-builder. I'd identify places that would be ideal for a building, find investors, then create a place that would make people feel at home. You check out my buildings from ten to twenty years ago. They're still standing, fitting in with their neighborhoods, filling a community need.

"Then, I began to have health problems. Eloise passed, and I didn't take care of myself. Didn't have anyone cooking for me anymore, forcing me to take a rest and enjoy life. I brought Lester in to teach him the ropes. I knew I wouldn't live forever, and I wanted to leave my son something. Lester hadn't found himself yet. He was in his twenties, just floating around different jobs. When he joined the business, he blossomed. We had a good relationship. I loved him. He loved me. I thought.

"Cut to the chase," he said, "I had a stroke. Lost the use of the left side of my body. Affected my brain. I was a mess for a long time. While I was in rehab, learning how to eat and walk again, what does my dear son do but take over the company. While I was ill, he brought papers to the rehab center for me to sign. I had no idea what I was doing. He did. When I was well enough to know what was what, I discovered that I had signed away my business."

Julia couldn't believe someone could be so mean as to steal a man's livelihood right out from under his father. Lester had been so charming to her and Sammy. But, as Harold always says, you never know who a person really is. When he first entered politics, Harold warned that she shouldn't trust people completely; that they might want to be her friend simply because that would get them close to the seat of power. She thought he was nuts, until one of their so-called friends betrayed Harold and ran against him.

Julia had shared so many confidences with that person. She was hurt. It took a long time to lessen the pain of a lost friendship. The experience made her cynical. Harold and Julia tended to be friends with people they knew before politics, and were acquaintances with everyone else. But Lester doing such a thing to his father? Unforgivable.

"More than that," Jin continued, "I found out that he had been quietly working against my interests for a few years before the stroke, trying to undermine my authority. I would order first class materials, then he'd change the orders for second class materials and put the difference in cost in his own pockets.

"I thought my world had ended," he muttered, talking more to himself than to them. "Something happened to me during the stroke. My left side had been affected, but so had my brain, the way I thought. Instead of being the man I used to be, living a good, honest life, I was different. I didn't care about being decent, especially after what Lester had done to me."

He looked both of them straight in the eyes. Julia felt as though she was looking down two empty holes.

"I decided to destroy my son."

"Destroy?" the rabbi asked, "as in murder?"

"No." Jin's grin was as creepy as a horror movie just before the vampire is about to pounce upon an innocent maiden.

"I expect to destroy what's most important to him. His business. My business."

"If you do that, you'll have nothing left?" Rabbi Fine offered.

"That's exactly what I have now," Jin said. "Nothing. But at least it will be on my terms. Besides, I had a separate account from the business. Investments. They'll keep me going till I take over again."

"How does all of this relate to Sophie and Albert?" Julia was confused.

"Can't be helped. I have to create a record of him using unsavory tactics to oust people from his projects."

"These are innocent people," Rabbi Fine's hand slapped the table. "Why should they suffer for you?"

"Hey, you're a rabbi. You know that people suffer all the time for no reason. Think about Job. Why did your God choose to make his life miserable? Bad stuff happens to good people. That's just the way it is."

Julia glanced at the rabbi. He was building up steam and could explode any moment. There we were, sitting across the table from someone who could probably take them both down at the same time. Julia was no fighter, and the rabbi was a little soft around his middle. They needed to move this along fast. "Why is it important to make their lives miserable?" she asked Jin.

"I still know people in my old business," he said. "I've seen the plans for this cockamamie building he wants to put up. It's a disaster. Lester has the creative ability of a skunk-weed. He's in debt up to his ears. He doesn't have the business sense that I had. If this project doesn't go through, the company may go bankrupt.

"I'm going to send a tip to the media that bad things are going on with Lester's project. When the papers start looking at his finances and find out he's terrorizing store owners to leave, there might be even be a public outcry to dump him.

"I want the mayor of Crestfall and the board of trustees to see what kind of operator he is. If they have a brain in their heads they won't accept this project. I'm sure the mayor's already heard some stories. Sophie's Deli and the shoe repair will be the *coup d'gras*."

Julia didn't say a word. She was praying he didn't know that she was the mayor's wife. That could lead to additional problems.

Jin put the photo back into his wallet, than shoved the wallet back into his pants.

"No mayor wants a developer with neighborhood problems. It's not good for politics," he noted.

"Did you start the fire in Sophie's Deli?" the rabbi asked.

"No." Jin answered without pause. "I do psychological terror, nothing like setting fires. It's too dangerous, could leave clues. I don't intend to spend time in jail."

"Would you give people food poisoning to shut Sophie's down?" Julia asked.

"That's above my pay grade." Jin's smile reminded her of a hungry hyena, an evil-eyed hunk of danger. "I have no desire to physically hurt anyone other than my son."

Jin pointed his finger at Rabbi Fine and Julia. "That could change, however, if you give me any more trouble."

He slid out of the booth and began walking out of the bar. As he reached the door, he turned in their direction to offer his final statement.

"You really shouldn't leave Sammy alone, Julia. A ten-year-old boy could get into a lot of trouble on his own."

Julia shrank against the wall. Rabbi Fine slid out of the booth and jumped up. By that time Jin was already out the door. They ran outside, but he was gone.

"Get in the car," the rabbi ordered. He drove like a maniac to Julia's house. She called the home line, but no one answered. They ran from the car to the house. Julia fumbled with her keys to unlock the door.

"Sammy," she shouted. "Sammy, where are you?"

There was no answer. They checked each room. No Sammy. Julia was getting a little hysterical, when she looked outside. There was Sammy, making holes in the dirt near their garden. She and Rabbi Fine almost fell through the back door into the back yard.

Sammy looked up when he saw his mother's shoes.

"Hi, Mom. I'm trying an experiment. See, I'm planting peach pits, cherry pits and apple seeds to see if they'll grow into trees. Then we won't have to buy them from the store, and maybe we can sell the rest to the neighbors."

Julia pulled the earplugs out of his ears.

"Earth to Sammy," she said. "Didn't you hear the phone?"

"No. I've been out here digging and planting and looking for spiders and grasshoppers. Maybe we can take these to Lester's for his Venus flytrap."

Sammy proudly picked up a mason jar with two forlorn spiders and one nervous grasshopper in it.

"I used a nail and the hammer to make holes so they can breathe until we go to Lester's again. Is it okay that I used Dad's tools? I didn't break anything."

Sammy could see that Julia was stressed, but he didn't understand why. He was beginning to get anxious. She realized she was pushing her anxiety on him. It wasn't fair. Julia took a calming breath and tried to be as gentle as possible.

"Do me a favor, Kiddo. Go into the house now. You didn't do anything wrong."

A confused Sammy went inside. Julia and the rabbi followed. They both dropped into the kitchen chairs.

"Take a slow breath," he said.

"I can't," she protested.

"We fell for it."

"Fell for what?" she asked, exhausted now that she knew Sammy was safe.

"That's what he does, terrify people. He didn't have to lift a hand, and he made us go crazy."

"He's evil," Julia, unable to sit still, opened the refrigerator, her hands were shaking. "Do you want some freshly-squeezed lemonade?"

"No thanks. I have to pick up my daughter from child care and help my wife get ready for the holiday tonight."

"Call me if you can, and we'll talk." Julia took a sip of lemonade.

"I won't be able to. Tonight begins the last two days of Passover. We'll be having big dinners and spending the days in prayer and meditation. I'll call you right after Shabbat ends to touch bases. And don't let Sammy out of your sight," the rabbi reminded me.

Julia sank into the chair again. The lemonade felt soothing as it slid down her throat. What a sad situation between a father and a son. She wondered if meeting Jin helped them out at all.

Harold came home that night looking worried.

"What's up?" Julia asked. She was broiling skirt steaks for dinner. The boys loved them. Thin strips of meat, no difficult fork and knife choreography which sometimes ended with a thick sirloin hitting the floor. Meat, veggies, and a tomato and lettuce salad. In her culinary opinion, that qualified as a fair meal. Julia was still shaken by Jin's threat. She hoped that would be the end of it.

Harold put his briefcase on a kitchen chair and loosened his tie. He stared at her.

"Bad news?" she asked.

"You knew," he said. "You and that rabbi were right all the time."

"Right about what?" Her heart was palpitating.

"It definitely was food poisoning. Chief Scarpelli's been working with the hospital and calling people back for blood and urine tests and questioning all week. I didn't want to tell you because it's not really your business, but you're the one who started the whole thing."

Finally, he was giving her some credit. A left handed compliment, but credit, at least.

"What caused it?" she asked.

Harold sighed. "We don't know. If Scarpelli goes the traditional way, he'll send everything to the county lab."

"How long for them to analyze everything?"

"That's the problem. They're so backed up it could take more than a month to get the results if we're lucky."

"If it's attempted poisoning, that time delay throws off the entire investigation." Julia threw down the dish cloth she was holding.

"Except for one thing." Harold's face lightened. "What if the mayor of the town in question had an emergency fund that could cover the cost of going to a private lab, and that lab could do an analysis in four work days?"

Julia almost yelled hooray. "Would you?" she asked.

"I would, I could, and I did earlier today." He smiled, delighted to have surprised his wife. Rare was the time that the mayor used his authority to promote one of Julia's ideas.

"I can't believe it." Julia was euphoric. Some men give their wives jewelry to make them happy. All it took for her was a few urine tests! Then she calmed down. "Why did you decide to do that?"

"Well," he sat at his usual place for dinner, "the chief began following up on your list of names not because you're my wife," Harold made it a point to say, "but because it was possible that numbers of people were suffering from food poisoning, and three people died."

That means the chief took her seriously, she thought. If he believed she was a ditz he would have disregarded the whole thing.

Harold removed his glasses and was massaging the top of his nose. "First he called the hospital. A nurse who had put in a double shift over Friday night to Saturday afternoon told him that she had noticed an unusual number of people coming in with similar symptoms — fast heart rate, confusion, hallucinations, nausea…There are more symptoms, but I don't remember them all. Anyway, she made sure the other nurses in the emergency room took blood and urine samples when more victims came in. She was thrilled when Chief Scarpelli contacted her. It meant that she wouldn't have to argue with any docs who wouldn't want to take the time to check out her theory.

"Then, from Monday through today his detectives have been calling everyone who went to the *seders* the victims attended."

He put his elbows on the table and laid his chin on his hands. "It's amazing what the police do in cases like this, really painstaking work. They have to interview every guest, ask each of them what they ate, in addition to what went into their stomachs three days previous to the *seder*. Then, they discount everything that doesn't match, and eventually winnow it down to the one food everyone ate that caused the trouble."

Should I tell him the Rabbi and I already knew that information, she asked herself? No. It's enough for me to know the rabbi and I are still way ahead of the police. And it appears we're on the right track.

Harold sat up straight and sniffed. "What's for dinner?"

"Skirt steaks. Everything will be ready in about five minutes." Julia could hear the sizzle of the meat finishing in the broiler.

"Great. I could eat a pig." He flinched playfully. "Sorry, I shouldn't have said pig. It isn't kosher. I will correct the record and say I could eat a cow." He stood up to go upstairs and get into more comfortable clothes, and hugged me. Why couldn't every day be like this, she thought?

While in his arms, and things were going so peachy keen, she decided to push her luck. "Harold?" She could still smell the soap from his morning shower. For some reason, it always caused an extra thrum in her heart.

"Yes?" They were still in an embrace. In fact, they were doing his version of the two-step, moving from side to side without ever lifting a shoe.

"Umm, have you learned anything more about the anti-Semitic crimes going down in the area towns?"

He pulled back his head and looked her in the eyes.

"Now why in the world would you bring that up when we're having a moment here?"

He was hurt. She couldn't blame him. She tried to make lemonade out of a lemon.

"I was feeling so good in your arms, and I was thinking that it is so wonderful to have you as my husband. Then I thought I couldn't bear to live without you, and I started thinking of things that could take you away from me, and the anti-Semitic gangs just popped into my mind."

Did he believe her? Could she sell him a bridge in Brooklyn? Julia wasn't sure, but he seemed mollified. He dropped his arms and they separated, but not in an unfriendly way. He spoke to her as he would speak to an equal who wanted some inside information.

"We've got nothing. The chief isn't thinking terrorists, the kind we see in movies. We're looking at crimes against Jews in the past few months, trying to see if there's any pattern."

Julia interrupted. "I think the fire at Sophie's Deli might qualify as one example. It just happened about four months ago."

"I'll tell Scarpelli about it," Harold said. He scratched the back of his head.

120

"We can't get a bead on who's doing this. If it's kids, they'd probably leave clues, but these threats haven't given us anything to work with, especially since the crimes are happening in different towns. We've got them there, though, because our task forces are working together."

He began walking up the stairs.

"Sooner or later, someone's going to make a mistake, and then we'll get them. We've just got to be patient and alert."

Patient and alert. That's what she'd be. Little did Harold know that his wife might be meeting with one of the bad guys."

"Hey," he asked, "did the Chief have anyone call you today? We haven't been questioned yet."

"I don't know. I was out for a while today. I'll check for messages right now."

Harold made it halfway up the stairs when he yelled down, "Hey, Julia, don't we have that school thing tomorrow morning with Mrs. What's-her-face?"

"Yes. Eight a.m. in the principal's office."

"That's what I thought."

Of course Julia was the one who knew when and where their meeting would be. Harold ceded all responsibility when it came to "home situations." In addition to being the bad mom to his good dad when the boys got into tussles, Julia was also the social secretary, though she didn't consider this "social."

Sammy's test results were in, and the tutor had assessed where he was in his school work. Harold and Julia expected the principal, counselor and Sammy's teacher to inform them how they were going to address their son's problems.

Julia picked up the phone and heard a pulsed buzzing. She had been so spooked by Jin and Sammy she had forgotten to check for messages. That's a no-no in the house of the mayor. It was a given for Julia to check the phone when she returned from being out. There could be a call from an angry constituent or some important elected official. Missing something like that could cause Harold a bushel full of trouble. Once, when Julia was out, and Harold was in the shower, their congressman called to speak to him. Jordan was about four at the time. The congressman said, 'Is your daddy home?' Jordan said, 'Yes,' and slammed down the phone.

Today, there were two messages. One was from Shayna; the second was from the chief.

Julia called him immediately.

"Mrs. Donnelly," he said, "we haven't had an opportunity to interview you and your family yet. Can you come in tomorrow after school and bring the kids."

"I can," she responded, "but I know what everyone ate at the *seder*. It's a mother's special super-power. Besides, no one from our family got ill. Can I come without the kids?"

"Fine," the chief said. "But your entire family has to be tested at the hospital. If the mayor hasn't already told you, as soon as we get your samples, everyone who attended the affected *seders* will have been tested. We should have the results sometime next week."

Julia was caught between a rock and a hard place. Should she tell the chief she and the Rabbi believed they knew which food was poisoned, or leave well enough alone. Four days was still a lot of time to wait. She still had no idea if there was a criminal on the loose, or if the chopped liver was simply bad from the beginning. It could still be sitting in unsuspecting people's refrigerators, waiting to be eaten.

"Chief, I've got a question for you. Can you determine from the tests what specific food caused the outbreak?"

"At this point we're not sure. There's the matter of people using sugar, drinking similar wine, eating some of the same foods. Why?" His voice changed. "Do you know something I don't know? I told you and the rabbi to stay out of this."

"We did, sort of. We haven't personally gone around questioning *seder* guests."

Julia didn't mention Shayna, their secret weapon.

"I think it's doubly important you come to the station tomorrow. And bring that rabbi, too."

The chief's attitude seemed to have soured from the beginning of their conversation. Julia wasn't looking forward to seeing him, especially since Rabbi Fine wouldn't be available to share the blame with her. At least Sophie had saved her chopped liver, and Julia had asked Devorah to save hers rather than throw it out.

Just before dinner Julia slipped into her bedroom for privacy and called Shayna.

"What took you so long?" Her friend was irritated. Usually they talked at least once a day, and it had been several hours since Shayna had left her message. "I was hoping you could come over for tea and talk earlier. Now it's too late. Our holiday dinner is starting."

"I'm sorry. I've been busy."

"Busy with what?"

Shayna always knew when something was wrong. First, Julia swore her to secrecy. Then she told her everything that had happened.

"This is getting very scary. Maybe you and the rabbi should stop."

"Are my ears hearing right? Is this really my friend Shayna who always pushes me to investigate cases, or is this a wrong number?"

"I'm not kidding, Julia. There may be a poisoner out there, and you were just threatened by a nutty old man. Did you tell Harold about him?"

"Not yet. Rabbi Fine and I didn't have a chance to discuss it. He had to pick up his daughter at daycare."

"Listen to me. This is dealing with real criminals. As much as I believe in you, you're not equipped. Remember, when we took self-defense, you sprained your ankle? And that was before class began."

"In my defense, I didn't see the basket of dirty towels before I tripped over it."

"But then you fell over the garbage can and broke your glasses. We missed the all-important eye-poke lesson and neck lunge. I had to go back myself and learn it without you."

"Self-defense wasn't exactly my cup of tea." Julia leaned back on her pillow.

"I've had my ear to the grindstone," Shayna continued. "I've heard that the police went to everyone who hosted the *seders* and took away all their leftovers. I suppose it'll be like that CSI program where everyone wears lab coats and drops roast chicken into different colored chemicals."

Oh dear. They must have done that at Devorah's house. Why hadn't she called about it?

"Shayna," Julia felt miserable thinking of Devorah opening her refrigerator to strangers. "I think I'll pass on tea."

"Come over to my house for dessert later." Her best friend used her most convincing voice. "I might be able to stimulate your little grey cells, as Hercule Poirot says."

"I can't," Julia said. "I'm pooped. Besides, Harold and I have to be at the school early to meet with Mrs. Finiken. Sammy's test results are in, and we're meeting with the administration to discuss them."

Shayna the indefatigable accepted defeat on the dessert front. "Mark my words, Julia, the kid probably aced the tests. The school doesn't know what to do with him. These days, it's the smart ones who are ignored. I bet they suggest a private school. Goodbye $20,000 a year."

"I'm sure that won't happen. He's smart, but he's no genius. The school ought to be able to give him enrichment assignments to keep him busy."

Shayna snickered. "My friend, busy means busy-work to the average teacher. They don't have time for the kids who're a little different from the norm."

"Well," Julia said, "we'll find out tomorrow."

"Call me after *yontif* unless you want to come over here and talk. You know, in some ways it's easier that you're not as observant as I am. You can drive while I obey religious restrictions and stay around the house. I'm not complaining, mind you. Sol and I have chosen this way of life, but sometimes it's hard."

Julia almost felt guilty. There are 613 *mitzvot,* and she, who wanted to be more religious, was disregarding the *mitzvot* against driving and talking on the phone on *Shabbat* and other holidays. What kind of Jew was she going to be?

"I'll send you a smoke signal to let you know," she said ruefully. Julia hung up, served a perfectly cooked dinner and found a book that required no serious thought whatsoever. The only thing that cracked that perfection was the uncertainty the next day would bring for Sammy.

Of course, Sammy hadn't done anything wrong, as opposed to the meetings they used to have with Jordan at the John F. Funchion elementary school. Still, sitting in the principal's office, Julia felt as though she was guilty of something. Harold was reading a position paper on the decreasing space for garbage dumps. He wasn't bothered by this meeting.

"Look, Julia," he told her before they walked in, "there's nothing we can do now. We'll just sit down and hear what they have to say."

Schools never change, Julia thought as she looked around slowly. The room divider that comes up to your chest separating you from everyone who works in the office. The clock on the wall, always brown wood surrounding a round face. The secretary always looks like she's guarding Fort Knox. No one gets by her. Even the chairs are the same, uncomfortable, set back in a line against the wall like you're the victims of a sit-down firing squad.

A bit too late Julia came to the realization that if she was feeling this way, what must be going through Sammy's head. He had been reluctant to come with them this morning until they promised he wouldn't have to go into a classroom.

"How are you, Kiddo?"

"Bummed," he mumbled, slumping in his chair.

"Can you offer me any other thoughts in greater detail?"

"Mom," he put down the papers he was reading (he was beginning to remind her of Harold), "you know I don't like to be in a classroom. You know I don't like to be in school. I feel bad vibes when I'm here."

He returned to whatever he was doing.

The receptionist gave Harold and Julia a saccharine smile and told them to go right in.

Who knew how many people could sit around one small conference table? Julia counted eight before sitting down. Eight of them. Harold, herself, and Sammy. Not in the least daunting to a ten year old boy.

"Mr. and Mrs. Donnelly, we've brought together a working group of our people to give you a clear explanation of what we have here. Sammy," The principal looked at the child for the first time, "could you please go back out to the office. We'll call you in when we're ready."

To say that Julia and Harold felt outnumbered would be an understatement. Julia wondered how Harold was doing. He was used to attending large meetings, but usually the power was on his side.

It took a few minutes for introductions. She could not remember a single name except for Mrs. Finiken, who looked like a skinny spoke in a much bigger wheel.

The main points boiled down to three major statements. One, Sammy had done extremely well on his tests, better than before. That, Mrs. Finiken explained, was likely because he was being watched and couldn't daydream. Two, according to his tutor, Sammy could understand concepts immediately. His ability to pick up new material was exceptional. Three, the school had accelerated classes aimed at Sammy's level, but he tested far above what they offered.

Harold cleared his throat, then spoke. "It's my understanding that by law, public schools are supposed to teach all children whatever their level."

"In principle," the principal said, "that is true. But when you have twenty-five children in each class with one teacher and, hopefully, one aide, the goal is to try to keep the slower students up to grade level."

Julia's mind wandered for a moment. She remembered when she first learned to spell principal by learning that principal 'the person' was your pal. She did not think that was the case in this situation.

"So what do you do with the more advanced students?" Her husband asked.

"We have pull-out classes in which the brighter students go to a separate room for more advanced math and English, but I'm afraid that Sammy's reaction to those classes is the same as when he's in with the rest of his class." That was Sammy's teacher.

"And what is his reaction?" Julia could see that Harold was becoming irritated.

"I'll give you an example," his teacher offered. "I'm at the front of the class. I ask a question. I know Sammy has the answer, but he doesn't raise his hand."

"What's wrong with that?" Harold was bristling.

"Instead of answering the question, he whispers the answer to the girl who sits in front of him. I'm positive there's no way she would know the answer without his help. That's how he reacts — as a ghost student."

She continued, "And then he zones out. Looks out the window. Keeps his eyes open but I know he's lost somewhere in his head. This happens in the accelerated classes, too. We can't seem to keep his attention because he's bored."

"Of course he's bored. You're not challenging him. It's your job."

Harold had high expectations of all public servants, from garbage collectors to principals. He believed, and rightly so in a perfect world, that anyone paid by the public should serve the public. It seemed as though my husband was about to enter his "high dudgeon" zone, a rarely seen, not pretty sight.

The principal intervened before Harold lost his temper. "We've discussed Sammy's situation. He's a good boy. Never bothers anyone. He's helpful, but our school is not working for him."

The principal took a deep breath. Julia knew what he was going to say next would be akin to sucking a sour lemon. "We all agree that you should consider enrolling your son in a different school, one that caters to extra bright children. We have a list of private schools, some local and some boarding schools that would better meet his needs. Mrs. Finiken will be more than pleased to help give you an idea of what each of these schools could offer Sammy."

He was finished. The meeting was over, in his opinion. People started rustling their papers, preparing to get up. Harold stood before anyone else.

"Excuse me," he said.

People looked up at him. Harold is not one to be toyed with.

"This is not over. Federal law requires that you meet my son's needs. If you don't, you are required to come up with a plan to do so. And if that plan includes sending my son to another school, this school district is responsible for paying for it."

There was an intake of breath.

"If you think you can overwhelm us by bringing in a roomful of people to talk high-falutin' educational theory, you're wrong. You have a fiduciary responsibility to educate my son, the same as, for example, any other child with special needs, and at our next meeting, our lawyers will be sitting beside us."

He turned to the principal. "I suggest you continue sending a tutor to our house until this matter is settled." He then gently put his hand on Julia's back and they left the room.

"Well, I think that went well," she said, trying to regain a regular heartbeat.

"I had our corporation counsel check out federal law yesterday. This school has to meet Sammy's needs or pay for another option. You can be sure we won't be paying for this out of our pockets."

Harold was on a high.

Julia was just hanging on. How was this going to affect Sammy? The family?

Sammy stood up as they walked out.

"How did it go?" he asked.

"Okay, Sport," Harold clapped Sammy on the back. "Seems you've been keeping a secret from Mom and me."

"You mean the smart thing?"

"Yep," Harold said as they strode out of the office.

"I just didn't want anyone to notice me," Sammy shrugged.

"What do you mean?" Julia asked.

"I don't know."

Hmm. She tried to use Rabbi Fine's method of figuring things out during the ride home.

Why does someone want to remain unnoticed Julia asked herself? You don't want to be noticed because you've done something wrong, or you feel you don't believe you have earned that notice. Positing that Sammy hadn't done anything wrong, she was left with his not wanting to be noticed because he didn't deserve the attention or didn't want the attention.

Now why didn't he want to be noticed? He was a good boy from a good family.

Julia looked out the window and an idea hit her between the eyes. They weren't his first family. His first family didn't, or couldn't, take care of him so they gave him away. Did he do something as an infant that caused his birth parents to give him away? Did he cry too much? Keep them up at night demanding to be fed? Was he ugly in their eyes? Of course, as an adult, these reasons were bogus, but to a child, they could mean a lot.

They passed a playground with kids running around at recess as Julia continued her train of thought. But why did he say that everything was Harold's fault? Did he hate his father? Had Harold done something unforgivable to hurt Sammy? No. She knew her husband loved Sammy with all his heart. But, as Shayna said, Harold was the mayor. Could that position cause Sammy anxiety? Of course, she realized. Clear as day. Being the son of the mayor meant that he would be noticed, that people would expect him to act in a certain way. And if he did get noticed, maybe he would be thrown away again, just like someone else, ten years ago, had thrown him out.

Oh God. Julia tried not to cry as the realization came over her. No matter how much she and Harold told both boys they loved them more than life itself, both children had a dirty little secret. Their birth parents hadn't wanted them. Julia thought Harold and she had been so smart to let the kids know they were adopted from the very beginning. Maybe it had backfired for Sammy. Maybe letting him know in his very formative years, that his birth parents had rejected him, now caused him to believe he wasn't worthy of love.

Memories came back to her, talking to Sammy about why his birth parents may have given him up. He had been found in a college town. Perhaps they were students and didn't even know how to take care of a baby. He had said, "Mom, you and dad are my parents. You're there when I'm sick. You and dad love me. I don't need anything else."

But maybe he did.

Was it too late for a psychologist to help him? Was there too much harm already done? Why was she running around trying to solve this stupid crime when her son needed help?

Talk about low self-esteem.

Julia felt like a total failure. While she and Harold had spent so much time with Jordan and his antics, Sammy had always been the quiet one. The good one who never caused any trouble. And all the while he had been suffering. Alone.

Julia would tell Harold about this brainstorm, of course, but she wondered what difference they could make at this point. She vowed to spend more time with Sammy, try to see things from his point of view and act accordingly.

At peace with herself, at least for the moment, Julia asked her son what he was reading.

"Oh, just some stuff about Mr. Pintner's plants," he said, keeping his eyes peeled on the page.

It was going to take a lot to break into Sammy's inner workings, she realized.

128

Crash. The sound of a breaking window. The tinkle of little pieces of glass falling on an uncarpeted floor. Like raindrops.

"Mom," Sammy came running in, dressed in his swimming trunks and, for some unknown reason, swimming flippers. "Did you hear that? I think someone threw something at our house."

It was Saturday morning, about nine a.m. Harold was already out at some meeting. Jordan was sleeping. No one was awake except Sammy and Julia. She ran downstairs and checked the windows. Sammy, sans swimming fins, shadowed her holding a baseball bat. Everything was in place. They raced down to the basement area. In the laundry room, on the floor next to the washing machine, was a rock the size of a hand surrounded by shards of glass from a nearby window.

"Don't touch it." She held her hand against Sammy's chest the way a parent holds a hand across a child in the car at a sudden stop no matter how old that child is. "You're barefoot." Julia yelled, even though he was right beside her.

"So are you," he pointed out.

"Yes, but I'm taller." Julia leaned over and picked up the offending gristly rock. There was a note rubber-banded around it. The fact that the rubber band was red disturbed her.

MEET ME BEHIND SMITH'S FISH MARKET AT 8 P.M. COME ALONE and signed with a crudely drawn picture of a knife.

"What does it say?" Sammy was jumping up and down trying to read it.

"It says to meet this person behind Smith's Fish Market at eight p.m. tonight."

"Does it have anything to do with the fire at Sophie's Deli?"

"It might."

"Does it have anything to do with the rumors that gangs are putting bombs in buildings?"

"It might."

"Don't you think it's dangerous?" Sammy absently put a finger up his nose.

"Hey, let's go upstairs and put on shoes. We've got to sweep this up and get the window fixed before Dad sees it."

"Is this still a secret?"

"Yes," Julia said, prodding him upstairs in front of her. She really had no idea of what to do. She couldn't get in touch with the rabbi. He was involved in Passover festivities and Shabbat observances so he wouldn't be answering his phone. But, Julia thought, she could go over to Shayna's house. Shayna'd have some suggestions. She always had suggestions.

Julia swept up the glass and threw it in the garbage. She gave Sammy the job of measuring the window and calling Pete's Window World to get it repaired as soon as possible. She couldn't count the number of times they'd called Pete because some baseball or frisbee had smashed through a window or someone was locked out of the house and needed to break the window in the back door to open it from the inside.

In the meantime, Julia got dressed and waited until she knew that Sol and Shayna would be back from the synagogue and finished eating their *Shabbat* lunch. She drove over to her friend's house. When Shayna opened the door, her eyes grew large with surprise. Julia never interrupted her on *Shabbat* unless Shayna had invited her over.

"What's wrong?" Shayna asked.

"I didn't say a word." Her friend responded.

"I can see it in your face."

"I need your advice," Julia began.

"Shoot."

Shoot was not the right word to use just then. After swearing Shayna to secrecy, Julia told her about the list of suspects for Sophie's fire. When she got to the Blades and the lovely rock someone had heaved in the basement, Shayna stopped her.

"Julia, you know, this is madness."

"It may be madness, but it could help solve some crimes. What if this is a series of crimes committed by a group that hates Jews? Isn't it our duty to find that out? What if they set Sophie's Deli on fire? Didn't you want me to look into that before? What if they poisoned the Passover food? Are we supposed to sit around and wait for someone to stumble over them?

"What would Moses do?" Julia asked her friend. "He killed the slave master to save a slave he didn't even know. We know Tzippi. You know just about everyone else who got sick and those poor people who died."

"Julia, you know this could be a trick to get you alone. They could do heavens knows what to you."

"Isn't that a risk someone has to take?"

"Someone, yes, but not you."

"If not me, who else?"

"It could be very dangerous," Shayna warned.

"Hey, walking across the street can be dangerous," Julia countered, recalling that she had said the same thing to Harold not too long ago. "When it's your time, it's your time." Her father, *alev ha shalom*, had always said that until he died peacefully in his sleep.

Another hesitation. So rare for Shayna to be speechless. Then she said, "Alright. So I'll go with you."

"That's your advice?"

"You would prefer I suggest you email Superman to assist you? Calling the police could ruin what you need to accomplish. By the way, what is it exactly that you think you're going to accomplish?"

Now Julia was at a loss for words.

She and Rabbi Fine had thought it important to meet with a Blade, but they hadn't actually decided what to talk about. Perhaps now was a good time to prepare some questions. Julia assured Shayna that she would have a fine list of questions to discuss with the little gang-banger, and made arrangements to meet at seven at their favorite coffee shop.

They hugged, and Julia drove back home. Sammy accosted her at the door.

"What are you going to do?"

"Shayna and I are going to meet him later tonight after *Shabbat* is over,"

Julia said blithely, like it was every day that she met a Blade.

"What if something happens?" His forehead was pursed with concern.

"What could happen?" she answered, pushing a feeling of dread behind a sense of wellbeing.

"They could come in a gang and beat you up. Even if one guy comes, he could beat you up. He could have karate moves." Sammy punched his foot out in a threatening fashion. "He could have a gun, even a small one leaves a hole in you. He could have a knife or just a baseball bat, Mom. There's lots that one person can do. You're not into this kind of stuff. Even Jordan isn't into this stuff."

"Sammy, I can't make you not worry, but I have a good feeling about this. The guy we're going to meet knows that Matt's roommate's brother knows that we're meeting. If anything happens, the police will go straight to him. It's my insurance policy."

"Can I go, too? You always say no one notices me."

"No." Julia watched his pleading eyes. "I need you here to keep Dad occupied. Maybe you can get him to play a game of chess or something. I don't figure on being gone too long. Shayna's going to tell Sol that she and I are going out for coffee. I'm telling Dad that I'm going out to coffee with Shayna. Jordan's used that one on us before. I don't know why I'm giving away my secret detective tricks to you." It felt very odd discussing this with a ten-year-old.

"It's because we're partners," Sammy said. "I'll do my job with Dad. You just stay safe."

He came toward her and enveloped his mother in his arms. Sometimes a ten-year-old is all one needs to feel strong.

****

"You know you're crazy, don't you?"

Shayna was still none too pleased with the decision to meet with the Blade.

Julia sighed, actually agreeing with her friend when they met in the Coffee Shoppe parking lot. Shayna was going to follow her to the site an hour early to scope it out and make sure they found a good place to stand. At least that's what the TV cops always did.

"Take some kind of weapon, like the baseball bat you have in your trunk. You've got to have something to defend yourself if it goes bad," Shayna whispered.

"I have faith," Julia told her.

"What's wrong with you, Julia Donnelly? Have the Torah classes gone to your head? Is your brain cooked? You know, it's one thing to believe in God, another to disregard any pretense of safety."

"It'll all work out," Julia soothed, though in her heart, she knew Shayna was right. Julia had gone bonkers. On the other hand, she felt as though God was with her. She knew if she ever said anything like that to Harold he would mock her, but it was true. Julia either was completely off her rocker, or faith was leading her.

Shayna and Julia were taking separate cars in case something happened to one of them. Julia was thinking that one of the gang could take the air out of her tires, but Shayna's car would be a few blocks away, and they could run for it if

131

necessary.

Sure, an inner voice sneered. You're a forty something; she's at least forty pounds overweight, and you're going to outrun these mamzers? As if.

They parked Shayna's car about two blocks away from their target site. Then Julia drove where the gang banger had instructed them to park, behind a dark factory building. They had arrived an hour ahead of their meeting to scope out the area. Julia's hands were sweating against the paper on which she had written the questions she was going to put to the gang member. Stupid, stupid me, she thought, realizing it would be dark and she wouldn't be able to read her list without a flashlight, which she had forgotten to bring. She hadn't noticed her friend's choice of outfit until Shayna got out of the car modeling an actual trench coat with a belt, just like the detectives in the old movies. Julia was moved to ask if she knew where the Maltese Falcon was, but held her tongue.

"Why are you dressed like that?"

"Clothes make the man, as the saying goes," Shayna said archly.

They walked quietly behind Smith's Fish Market. Smith, or whoever had owned the place, had gone out of business a long time ago. The aroma of rotten fish, however, lived on. Shayna and Julia found an old garbage bin, and with a little bit of effort, stood behind it. They had a good view of each end of the building. It was dark. Cold. Creepy. Julia thought of all those horror films with the music pulsing, getting louder and louder, letting the audience know the monster or the mad scientist would soon be there, unbeknownst to the innocent heroes. Then she was overcome with laughter. That's what happened when she was uncomfortable or afraid. It was an unfortunate idiosyncrasy. She was caught mid-giggle when they heard, "You're early." A deep voice pierced the crisp April air. Julia pictured a six-foot giant covered in tattoos. This might not have been such a good idea, she told herself.

So now you admit you're a *putz*, Julia shrieked to herself. *Run now.*

Running is difficult when your feet are glued to the ground in fear.

Shayna looked to the left. Julia looked to the right. No one.

"I'm always early." Julia forced herself to sound natural, though her voice may have been a few octaves higher than usual. "Where are you?" She asked.

"Never mind. I thought I told you to come alone."

She cleared her throat. "This is alone. Shayna is my best friend. I hide nothing from her. Besides, what are two older women going to do to a Blade?"

"Good point," he said. "I'll be right down."

Of course, she almost slapped her head. He'd been on the roof the whole time, probably laughing his *tuchus* off.

Shayna was unusually quiet, clinging to Julia's right arm. Good thing that I'm left handed, she thought, though she didn't know what she'd do with her left hand anyway.

Well, she decided, the die is cast. We're here. He's here, and now we'll see what's what.

They heard a scuffling sound on the left side of the alley.

"It's him," Shayna whispered.

"Good guess," Julia tried not to giggle.

A five-foot tall creature dressed in what looked like a neoprene wetsuit came into view. Its head was completely covered in black. There were holes for eyes, nose, and mouth.

"Hello," Julia said. Sticking out her hand to shake his seemed like overkill, excuse the pun.

"I hate you," he responded in disgust.

"Why?" Julia was puzzled. She didn't know this person. At least she didn't think so. She was relieved that his voice belied his height.

"You're a Jew, aren't you? Both of you?"

"Yes." They stood straighter. "We are. So what? We've never done anything to you."

"You people own the banks, the entertainment industry. You've taken over the government. You're trying to control the world."

"Boy, are you misinformed," Shayna said.

"It doesn't matter," he sneered. "The Blades will rid this town of all of you, one by one, and we'll take back our country." Julia was actually hoping that someone had turned on the Batman light to tell Batman they could use some help. Seriously, it felt like her heart was in her throat. What can anyone do when faced with such illogical hate?

"That's fine," she answered, "though people like you have been threatening Jews for hundreds if not thousands of years, and yet we're still around. But that's not why I'm here."

This was a teenager, of that she was sure. Probably a loner, a pimply-faced loser who nobody ever listened to. Julia moved from behind the garbage bin closer to him. Shayna shuffled beside her.

"Stop right there, Ladies."

Julia did. So did Shayna. She wasn't going to push her luck, which she was sincerely depending on at that point.

"Why do you want to talk to me?"

"Is your group responsible for the bomb scares around our neighboring towns?"

"I wish we were," he said, "but no."

"Did your group try to burn down Sophie's Deli a few months ago?"

"No," he said. "but she's on our list. Why are you asking?"

"Because the police are looking for who's responsible, and we are, too."

He moved closer to them. Shayna was gripping her arm as tightly as a vice. They were now facing the creature head on.

"The cops are hassling us about this stuff," he said. "They're driving us crazy. We hate Jews, but we do other stuff, too." He tossed out a list of the gang's additional activities including robbery, shakedowns, stealing cars – Julia stopped listening after he mentioned maiming. "But," he continued, "when we do something, we take responsibility for it. You know, like leaving a sign that it's the Blades."

"You mean like a rock thrown through a window with a note?"

"Yeah, like that," he nodded.

There was so much she wanted to say to this kid. She had more questions. She wanted to change his mind about Jewish people, but Julia was realistic. This kid was reciting a litany of things he was taught by rote. He had been indoctrinated. She wouldn't be able to unteach him in one meeting. That is, if she survived it.

133

"What's your name?" Julia asked.

"Black Slash," he responded with a flourish.

"Listen Black Slash," she said, "I have a deal for you."

"You can't do anything for me, but we can do things to you," he said menacingly.

At that moment, he was joined by three identical black-garbed creatures in back of him, and three behind the women.

Shayna gasped. The air grew colder. This could be bad, Julia's mind registered. "Very bad."

"What kind of deal do you have, Lady?" asked the tallest creature. He approached them, took out a knife from what might have been a slit in his costume, and flicked it. It was a very long switchblade. Julia recognized it immediately. Jordan had come across one and had brought it home. It went out in the garbage as soon as she and Harold saw it.

Lazily, he and the point of his blade ambled toward Julia. She was afraid. She had no idea who this new person was, though she suspected he was the leader of the Blades. There was a dark aura about him. It seemed that the knife was a part of his body, and he would use it at the slightest provocation. Shayna stiffened beside her. Julia was stuck in place, too, staring at the blade. Still, she forced herself to speak.

"Here's my deal," she said, trying to speak with a shred of confidence. After all, did Moses show fear when he tried to convince Pharaoh to let the Jewish people go? What about *Nachshon*, the first person who was brave enough to step into the *Sea of Reeds* when God parted the waters? Moses commanded them to walk across the sea. *Nachshon* jumped in first. Now it was Julia's turn.

"I can keep the police off of your back as far as these bomb threats."

"How?" He laughed. It wasn't a good laugh. It was more like a derisive grunt.

"If you help us find out who's responsible for these crimes, they'll leave you alone."

"We don't know who's doing it."

She felt stronger. "Do you mean to tell me that the Blades can't find out who's calling in bomb threats and leaving fake bombs around? I thought you guys had your finger on the pulse of everything bad that happens in this area."

Perhaps the head Blade took that as an impudent statement. The point of his knife grazed Julia's neck. She could feel it pushing in ever so softly. It was a delicate movement with the threat of terrible danger. Julia stopped breathing; pretended she was a statue. Sweat gushed from every pore. They stood there motionless, the leader, the knife, and Julia. It could have been five seconds. It could have been an hour. She heard a whimper in the night. Did it come from Shayna or herself? She didn't know. Suddenly he pulled back his switchblade, raised it into the air, and walked backward far enough so that Shayna and Julia couldn't hear what was being said. Everyone gathered around him.

"We could run away now. They're in an intense huddle," Shayna whispered.

"No. We came here to do a job, and I have a feeling they're going to help us."

The group dispersed to their original positions, three in front, three in back, and Black Slash.

Their leader approached Julia again and stopped about three feet away. Out came the knife. He clicked it toward her. Again, she held her breath. A mental photo of Sammy, Jordan, and Harold, without her, jumped into her mind. Why was she missing from the portrait, she wondered? Another click brought her back to the present, and he put his switchblade away. Julia felt like collapsing in a shapeless lump. But she didn't.

"We've decided we have a common goal," he said. "Kind of the enemy of my enemy is my friend."

"Well said," Julia responded, in spite of herself.

"Give us a few days, and we'll get back to you."

"And," she requested, "this time, could we dispense with the rock through the window? You made your point. How about a letter or a phone call. That'll work just as well."

"Don't push it, Mrs. Mayor," the leader said menacingly. He put his hand up to his head in an informal salute.

"Go," he commanded. "Black Slash will escort you to your car. Drive your friend to hers, and don't come back here again."

"Don't worry," Shayna said, her voice trembling. They marched to Julia's car in silence. When the women opened their doors, Black Slash saluted and disappeared into the night. That's when Julia's blood pressure dropped back to normal. She drove Shayna to her car, met at the Coffee Shoppe, and stumbled into their favorite booth.

Julia checked her watch. Twenty-five minutes. That's all the time it had taken from leaving the restaurant parking lot, having the 'meeting' and returning again. It felt more like twenty years. Shayna was still trembling, but not so much as to affect her appetite. She ordered a banana split with whipped cream and a cherry, and ate it like she was a steam shovel.

"Oh my God," she whispered. "Did that just happen? Did we actually meet up with a real gang?"

"Yup," Julia nursed her hot chocolate.

"You were stupendous," she *kvelled.* "Weren't you scared for your life when he put that knife to your throat?"

"Yup."

"Do you think we actually have a deal with them?"

"Yup," she said.

"Can you say anything other than yup?" Shayna was a little irritated that Julia wasn't as excited as she was.

"Hold that thought." She phoned Sammy. "Hi, Partner. Just wanted to report in. I'm fine and will be home as soon as I finish my hot chocolate. Did you and Dad play chess?"

"I won three games. Now Dad's reading next year's budget. You're sure you're okay?"

"I'm double sure. Do you want me to bring you a chocolate cake donut?"

"Yes, please," he said. Her son, the polite one.

She hung up, happy to be able to report that her expected demise was greatly exaggerated.

135

"Weren't you scared?" Shayna asked.

"I almost wet myself when he pointed that knife at me." It was amazing to talk about it now that it was over.

"I may have," Shayna admitted, shame-faced, "but it all worked out."

"Maybe," Julia said.

"Maybe what?"

"It'll all work out if they find out who's sending in the bomb threats, and that means that they aren't suspects in Sophie's crimes. I don't think they're sophisticated enough to pull off the food poisoning. It's too subtle for them."

"You might be right," she agreed, wiping her face with a napkin. An entire banana split eaten, and Julia was still on her hot chocolate.

"Well," she took a final swig, "a good night's work. Tomorrow's another day."

"Keep me in the loop," Shayna gave Julia a big hug, and they both drove off to their homes.

The phone rang much later that Saturday night. It was just past 11:30 and Harold and Julia were in bed. Her sons must have had a special power to reach phones before anyone else. There she was in her bedroom reaching for the darned thing, and Jordan answered it first. It was Rabbi Fine. Jordan was disappointed it wasn't for him. He yelled, "MOM" at the top of his lungs, even though she was in the next room.

"I'm sorry for calling so late," he apologized, "but I had a feeling we needed to talk."

Julia got out of bed and walked to the living room. "Boy, are you ever right." She said, "We haven't had time to talk about Nate and the old man."

"I can't get a reading on Nate," he answered between crunches of something.

"What are you eating?"

"Celery with peanut butter," he said glumly. "Myra wants me to lose some weight. This is her idea of a healthy snack."

"Why is Nathan a blank to you?"

"He seems normal."

"Normal?"

"Yes. He made Sophie an offer about eight months ago, but she said no, so he put all of his money into Nate's Nosh. He tells me business is good, but he still wants to expand by buying Sophie's Deli. He'd like to continue using her name. And to tell you the truth, it's not such a terrible idea."

"But she doesn't want to sell."

"I'm not sure she really understands what he wants to do. He'd like to have Sophie's Deli as a brand because of her good reputation. He thinks using her name could boost business. And, he'd like to keep her on, maybe as a manager. He wants to make a deal where she could continue working, just not as hard as she does now."

"Why does he need the deli on her site? It's in a run-down area," Julia asked.

"An area, he tells me, that's ripe for gentrification. He says he has an investor who's willing to go in with him if he can get Sophie's store."

"Any idea who the investor is?"

"He didn't say."

Probably Lester Pintner, she thought. Mr. Pintner's fingers were in an awful lot of pies trying to get Sophie out of her deli.

"What about the rumors he cuts corners?" she asked.

"I still have to have a sit down with the *mashgiach* who watches his store. But I can do that tomorrow. You know in Israel, Sunday is called *Yom Rishon*. That means day one. It's the beginning of the week, so the *mashgiach* will be working," the rabbi said.

"Any new thoughts about Jin?" Just saying his name made her shudder.

"I think he's capable of doing great harm, but his main goal is to destroy his son. I don't believe he'd poison people to get Lester in trouble, but I could be wrong," the rabbi said.

"Listen," Julia was a little concerned about telling Rabbi Fine about her experience with the gang. "I have a story for you, but you might get upset. The thing is, I'm okay now." She confessed to the rabbi about meeting the Blades. He got very angry.

"Do you realize how dangerous that was? Why didn't you tell me? I could have sent along protection."

"First of all, you were observing the last day of Passover as well as Shabbat. Secondly, he said to come alone."

"So you took Shayna?" He was disgusted. Julia had never heard Rabbi Fine use that tone of voice before. She wondered what other sides he had that she didn't know about.

"I don't want you to think that I have an army at my fingertips, but Jews must always be prepared for anything. So, I know a few people, and my people wouldn't have been seen. They don't wear neoprene suits, but they've been trained to blend in with the night or whatever is around. That leader wouldn't have gotten near you with his knife, and I'll wager there would have been several black eyes to match their outfits, and maybe some broken arms. Promise me, Julia, never do that again."

She promised, this time without crossing her fingers. She knew she'd been lucky, and didn't intend to push that luck.

"Still," he said, "I feel the same as you. I don't think the Blades are responsible for the poisonings. Other things," he mumbled under his breath, "but not this. I hope they find out who's doing the bomb threats so some good can come out of your experience. But. Do. Not. Do. Anything. Like. That. Again."

Rabbi Fine gave Julia a telephone number. "If something like this ever happens again, call that number. Don't ask for names. Just tell the person who answers what the situation is and mention my name. That's all you need to do, and they'll help you. Understand?"

His words came out like strong, marching warriors, not at all like her kind, sweet Rabbi Fine. Julia meekly agreed. Then she remembered something else.

"Oh, by the way, can you come with me to meet with Chief Scarpelli at 1 p.m. tomorrow? When I explained that you couldn't talk to him until after Saturday night, he said he wanted to see both of us on Sunday."

"I promised my wife we'd spend the afternoon together. If we make it quick, one o'clock will work.

"Great. I'll see you then.'

"God willing," Rabbi Fine said. "And if we're lucky, he won't arrest us for obstruction."

The phone rang at 6:00 a.m. on Sunday morning. It was Black Slash.

"Who's calling so early?" Harold mumbled into his pillow.

"Oh, just one of the Torah group women. She needs to ask me a question," she said, walking into their bathroom and shutting the door.

"Hey," Black Slash said.

"You couldn't call later?"

"Nope. Something bad is going down tonight. I wanted to tell you about it because it's those kids who're calling in the bomb threats."

Julia was completely awake.

"Who are they?"

"Do you got a pencil or something?"

She found her purple eyeliner pencil. "Shoot."

"Albert Ribble and Ozzie Walker. They're bad guy wannabees," he said with disgust, "students at Crestfall High School."

"And what are their plans for tonight?"

"You know the Jewish Cemetery along Golf Road?"

She did. It's where her mother and father were buried.

"They plan to kick down gravestones and throw black paint on them."

She felt sick.

"Are we cool now?" he asked.

"Yeah, we're cool," she answered. "I'll call the police and tell them the Blades aren't responsible for the bomb threats or the poisonings."

Julia didn't want to end their call just then. She wanted to say something that would express to Black Slash that Jews weren't all bad.

"Listen," she said, "I want to thank you and your gang for coming through. You're a scary bunch, but you kept your word, and I appreciate that."

He seemed surprised. Didn't know what to say.

"Tell your leader that one day I'd like to meet him without the suit and just hang out. You, too."

"Okay," he said, the surprise evident in his voice. "Good doing business with you, too. Don't forget to tell the cops."

"I'll do it today. I've got an appointment with the police chief this afternoon. Bye Slash. Take care."

"You, too, Mrs. Mayor."

He hung up. Maybe she had touched an unused decent synapse in his brain. It was 6:30 a.m. Still time to get some zzz's before meeting Rabbi Fine and the Chief.

****

Did you talk to the *mashgiach*?" Rabbi Fine and Julia were standing by their cars in the police station parking lot.

"No. Didn't have time. When I told my wife about our meeting at 1:00 p.m., she insisted that I stay home for the morning, too."

"I understand," Julia said.

"You do?"

"Sure. Rabbis, mayors, doctors, they're always on call. If I didn't put my foot down, Harold could be out at some meeting every night of the week. It's the wives who have to fill in the vacuum, watch the kids, settle fights, help them with their homework."

"You do understand," he marveled. "I should have thought of that."

"In fact," she continued, "when we adopted the kids, we agreed that no matter what, we'd both be home for dinners. After dinner we could go to events, but at dinnertime, every seat around the table would be filled."

"A good plan if you can keep it," Rabbi Fine sighed. "Unfortunately, sickness and death don't take time out for meals."

A policeman took them up to the chief's office. Chief Scarpelli was wearing his uniform today. He stood when they entered.

"Well, if it isn't Nancy Drew and Andy Hardy," His arms were crossed over his chest, his comments delivered snidely.

"Not so," the Rabbi twinkled. "We're a bit older than they were."

"So," they all sat down, the chief behind his big desk, "how did you really find out what happened at all those *seders?*"

The Rabbi explained that some Jewish communities are very insular. "Everybody knows everyone's business," he said.

"All of the tests haven't come back yet. Do you two know what caused the poisoning?"

Rabbi Fine cleared his throat. He and Julia had decided to tell Chief Scarpelli what they suspected.

"It might be the chopped liver," the Rabbi ventured.

"The chopped liver?"

"Yes," Julia said.

"Based on what?"

"Based on who ate what at our *seder*, then following up with the other *seders.*"

"I thought you said you didn't go around questioning the guests," the chief was beginning to get irritated.

"We didn't," Rabbi Fine stated. "Julia knew who ate the chopped liver at her *seder*. The woman who had the most had to be rushed to the hospital before dinner was over. A source (they had decided not to tell the chief about Shayna), told us what was served at the other *seders.* Everyone had chopped liver on their menus."

"Who eats chopped liver?" The chief had a look of distaste on his face.

"Jews," the Rabbi and Julia chanted together.

"I think with a little more grinding, other people call it pâté," she noted.

"Oh, that," the chief said. "I don't like pâté, either. "Are you pretty sure it's the liver?" the chief asked.

"Based on our premise, yes," the Rabbi answered.

"Okay, then."

Chief Scarpelli picked up his phone. "Detective Evans, tell the lab to try the chopped liver immediately."

Julia was astounded. No arguments. No doubts. The chief believed them.

"Now," he continued, "what are your thoughts on the cause?"

"The cause?" I asked.

"Yes. How did the liver come to be poisoned?"

Rabbi Fine was ready for this one.

"Julia and I believe that the poisonings are connected to another crime that has not yet been solved. We've been giving that crime our attention."

"Which crime?" The chief was beginning to gnaw on a cuticle.

"The arson at Sophie's Deli," Julia said. "We believe that someone tried to burn her out first, and when she reopened, they tried poison."

The chief picked up the phone again. "Evans, check the liver. Find out where it was purchased in each case. Then get me the files on the Sophie's Deli fire a few months ago. You can get the files now. The fire department is never closed. Thanks." He hung up.

"I'm not saying you junior G-men are right, but I'll accept leads from anyone. Even you."

He squinted at them.

"Do you have anything more to tell me?"

"We've found several people of interest." Julia tried to use her best TV detective show terms.

"Yeah? Who?" The chief was holding a pen in his hand, beating out a strange rhythm on his desk.

"First of all," Julia said, "we think they're all connected to Sophie's Deli."

The rabbi noted that each person had a reason to want Sophie to sell her business.

"And," Julia added, "there might even be a conspiracy to close her down."

"Now you've got a conspiracy?" Chief Scarpelli looked amused.

"There's the son Milton, his girlfriend Sweet Cheeks and Lester Pintner, the developer. They all want Sophie out so the building can go up," she counted off on her fingers.

"And," the Rabbi mentioned, "Nate from Nate's Nosh also wants to reopen Sophie's Deli in Pintner's building."

Julia jumped in, "I'll bet the nameless investor Nate was talking about is Pintner himself."

"Don't forget the guy from the deli that Sophie fired. He threatened her," The rabbi reminded her.

"What about Pintner's father?" the chief asked.

"An enigma," Rabbi Fine said, "but you should talk to Sophie's crew and to Albert the shoe repair man. Maybe they can tell you something you can use against him. He's terrorizing them, but they say the police aren't doing anything."

The chief 's hand pounded his desk. "You know, there's a little thing called proof that we need before doing anything. I'm told this guy is never seen when the act occurs."

"But he always comes around later to taunt them," Rabbi Fine said. "What if you could assign someone to tail him?"

"That's the TV shows talking," the chief groused. "Our force is just big enough to handle the domestic disputes and teenage graffiti problems around here. Now if your husband were to stick a hand into his magic pocket and pull out some cash for another one or two policemen, I'd be able to run a tail."

"In the meantime," the chief said, "I don't want the two of you mixed up in this anymore. You were lucky this Jin guy didn't harm Sammy."

It was clear their meeting was over.

"Please, don't tell Harold," Julia almost begged. "That was told to you in confidence."

"I'll respect that," the chief said as he shook our hands. "But if this is all connected, you're dealing with dangerous people."

"Oh," she said, "talking about dangerous people, we have some information for you."

"What?" His tone suggested that he didn't really want to hear anything else from her.

Julia cleared her throat. "I have some information about the bomb threats and a crime that may occur tonight."

"A crime?" His eyes opened wide in surprise, then became slitted with suspicion.

"A crime."

The chief started snapping the rubber band that was still around his wrist. "How did you get this information?"

"A phone call early this morning."

"Who called you?"

"A source," she said, like any journalist.

"Tell. Me." It was clear Chief Scarpelli was not in the mood to play games. She gave him the information, the boys' names, high school, and the cemetery they were going to deface that evening. She hoped it was reliable. If it was wrong, Julia was in deep trouble, but she believed that Black Slash was telling the truth.

"And by the way," Julia ended, "my source is from the Blades. He gave me the information so you and your force would stop trying to put these crimes on them."

The Chief was close to blowing his cool. "Your source is from the Blades, and I'm supposed to believe them? Do you know what that blasted group is capable of? Just to get in, a prospective member has to commit a crime, preferably with a switchblade."

Julia felt a familiar shiver run down her back. Thank heavens none of the guys had to prove themselves last night. That knife could have done some real damage. She did feel ashamed to be defending such an odious group, but, as the leader had said, 'The enemy of my enemy is my friend.'

"If those two names pan out; if you can catch these kids in the act tonight, will you leave the Blades alone, just for this situation?"

"You're going to get yourself seriously hurt hanging around people like that, Mrs. Donnelly." The chief was barely civil.

"Rabbi, I suggest you take this woman out of here and give her a talking to."

The meeting definitely was over.

Back in the parking lot, Rabbi Fine and Julia started laughing. Apparently he suffered the same embarrassing habit of laughing in the face of danger.

"It's nerves." He took a breath to try and stop the giggling.

"He believed us," she gasped between chortles. "Don't you think he took us seriously?"

"I do. What I don't know is what action he'll take."

"Are you suggesting that we keep looking into Sophie's fire and the possible connection to the poisoning?"

"I'm not sure right now." He looked at his watch and stopped laughing. "1:30. I've got to get home. Let's think about this before we do anything else. And," he added, "stay away from those Blade people. They may not have committed our crimes, but that doesn't mean we won't meet up with them again. Really, Julia, don't get into any more trouble."

That was fine with her. Julia wanted to get back to her regular life of driving one son to baseball practice and trying to get the other one to play outside. In addition, she and Harold were facing a pretty important challenge with Sammy. She had looked at Mrs. Finiken's packet of information on other schools that Sammy could attend. One, a math and science academy, was a three hour drive away. He'd have to leave home. Julia wanted him to be educated in an environment that met his needs, but she didn't want to send her son to a boarding school.

At home, Harold grilled Julia on what had gone on at the meeting. She told him almost everything, emphasizing that she and Rabbi Fine thought their information was helping the investigation of two cases. She knew he didn't like her being involved in his area of the universe. The police, the fire department, public works, all of them were in his bailiwick. Even if Julia was being helpful, he was worried that someone would resent her participation. Pleased that the chief wasn't angry at her, she kind of glossed over the Blade part. Then Harold put down his reading material and surprised her. In the spirit of family togetherness, he suggested that they all go out and play miniature golf. Jordan groaned, of course. What would happen if any of his friends saw him going anywhere with his parents? How embarrassing. Sammy, as usual, was happy to go. He liked to hit the ball based upon angles that only he understood.

Lucky for them, Jordan was always up for a little competition, just like his father. The two played as though it was the Masters Tournament. Sammy and his mother followed behind, actually enjoying the one-upmanship between father and elder son. They didn't care about scores, they were there for the enjoyment of being out on a lovely afternoon. April was being its usual self, one day cold, and the next day like spring. At one point, Sammy actually got a hole in one when he played one of his angles and went right through the windmill door at the perfect time. Jordan expressed a few choice words as his ball, hit with brute force, struck the windmill and flew into the next hole's water trap.

They finished the game as Julia figured they would, with Jordan and Harold a point apart. She didn't know if Harold had tried to lose, or if Jordan actually won. There always comes a time when sons overtake their fathers in strength and agility. She wasn't sure they were there yet, for Harold's sake. Though Julia usually played to win, this time she wanted to let Sammy get the better of her. Their scores were close, but he bested his mother by three points. His face was flushed with the thrill of triumph, confident that his theory of angles had saved the day. After a decent dinner at a restaurant that didn't throw food at you as soon as you entered the door, they returned home, tired, but happy. Julia wondered what the new week would bring for all of them.

Two things happened on Monday. First thing in the morning, Harold called to say that the police caught the culprits who were phoning in bomb threats and leaving fake bombs around.

They found out from an informant, Chief Scarpelli had told him. Two kids from the same high school Jordan went to. Then, in the afternoon, Harold called from work to tell her that not only was chopped liver the guilty culprit in the Passover poisoning case, but everyone had bought theirs from Sophie's Deli. This was one time she was not happy to be right. As mayor of Crestfall, Harold had used his authority to close Sophie's Deli until they could identify what specifically was wrong with the liver. He said it could take the lab a few more days to narrow down the cause.

If, for example, a bacteria had caused the liver to go bad, Sophie would have to professionally clean her equipment and utensils, throw away all the ingredients she had used to make it, and clean any area the ingredients had been stored. That would take time and expense.

It was also possible that one of her workers could have inadvertently passed the bacteria on, in which case everyone connected to the making and packaging of the liver would have to be tested. All of this, Harold explained, would cost Sophie a bundle, and then she still wouldn't be able to open until the county health department certified she had fully addressed the problem.

Julia wasn't so sure that bacteria was the culprit. If it had been, she would have expected more people to fall ill. Sophie's chopped liver usually flew off of her refrigerated shelves. Julia recalled there were several containers of liver lined up when she made her purchase, so why didn't she get sick from eating the half pound container she had bought for herself? None of this made sense unless someone had intentionally poisoned the liver. Who could be so evil, she wondered?

Julia sat and thought of all the things they knew about the two crimes, the arson and the poisoning. She and Rabbi Fine had interviewed five suspects, but couldn't determine who was guilty. What had they missed? Even though her head was filled with images of Milton, Sweet Cheeks, Lester Pintner, Jin, and Nate, though she hadn't met him, there was something niggling at her.

She called Shayna for a pep talk, and got a stern talking to instead.

"Stop thinking, already, your brain is too full," Shayna warned. "Get rid of everything you know. Think of what you don't know."

"How did you come up with that?" Julia asked, feeling a headache coming on.

"It made sense at the time," Shayna retorted. "You're the detective, not me." And she hung up.

Maybe she's right, Julia thought. That niggling thing was getting closer to the surface of her consciousness when the phone rang. It was Rabbi Fine.

"You know what we haven't done yet?" he asked. "We never looked at the fire records."

"You're right," That was one of the thoughts she hadn't been able to grasp. "But how are we supposed to find anything when the fire inspector still hasn't determined if it was arson?

"Maybe we know more now that he did then. We should read the records and look at the photos."

Julia agreed half-heartedly. She always told the kids, attitude is everything. If you're negative about something, there's no way you're going to succeed. She decided she should listen to herself more often. Julia called the fire chief. He was confused as to why she was interested in Sophie's case, but he agreed to give her copies of what he had. "It's all a matter of public record," he said. "The only problem is the case isn't solved." He laughed. "If you find out who done it, let us know."

Julia planned to pick up the records later in the day. There was another thought she couldn't catch. She felt like a scientist trotting through a field of poppies with a net on the trail of a beautiful butterfly. The image was so clear, the sun in the sky, the bright red poppies, a monarch butterfly just ahead of the net. It was pretty as a picture, she thought.

Pictures. That was it. Sophie had given her a copy of the security camera tapes and she hadn't had time to look at them yet. What an idiot she was. Maybe someone had pranced through the store with a sign saying, 'Look at me. I'm putting poisoned chopped liver into the refrigerated section.' It couldn't be that easy, could it? Anyway, the police had the tapes, too. As far as Julia knew, they hadn't reported anything suspicious on them. If they had, Harold might have told her.

She felt a prickle of excitement at the back of her neck. Maybe she and the rabbi could see something with fresh eyes without actually getting in contact with any of the suspects.

It was 2:00 p.m. Julia asked Sammy to come with her to the fire department. She didn't want to leave him alone until this case was solved.

Chief Grenchler's office was in Crestfall's largest fire station, a massive red brick building. The town had two stations. One of the first things Harold had done after becoming mayor was to pass a bond issue to build a bigger, more modern fire facility. The huge garage door was open, and Sammy was awed by the majesty of three hulking fire engines, one of which was being washed when they walked by. A receptionist led them to the chief's office on the second floor. He was one of Julia's favorite people, always taking the time to lend an ear to anyone who came up to him. Framed photos on his desk showed a more slimmed down version of the paunchy, grey-haired man who stood to welcome them. He came around his desk and made a point of shaking Sammy's hand.

"Have you ever had been to a fire station?" he asked.

"I did a long time ago when I was in the first grade, but I was just a kid then," he responded.

Chief Grenchler coughed to mask his smile, and asked Sammy if he'd like a tour. Julia's son, interested in all things, nodded quickly.

"Well, after your mom and I are finished, if it's okay with her, we'll give you the grand tour."

Another educational experience, she thought. Being schooled at home did offer unique opportunities.

Chief Grenchler handed her a folder.

"This is everything I've got."

She removed a thin collection of papers and photos.

146

"What's this one?" She asked, pointing to one picture. The debris from the fire made it difficult to understand what she was seeing.

"That's a shot of the vats Sophie uses to make her corned beef. Each vat is connected to a long pipe which is also connected to a large container of propane gas. That's how the gas fuels the fire that cooks the meat."

"Was the fire caused by a ruptured gas pipe?" Julia asked.

"We don't think so. If you look carefully, you'll see that all the pipes look to be in one piece, all connected."

Sammy's finger traced the pipe connections.

"Was the fire started by a spark from the cooking vats?" Julia's son was, after all, her partner.

"We don't think so," the chief said. "Normally, that could be a cause, but according to Sophie, she and her staff cook during the day; the fire occurred at night when the gas was supposed to be turned off."

"So no one was around." Julia wanted to be certain.

"That's what Sophie says."

She was getting an uncomfortable feeling that the chief didn't completely trust Sophie.

"Then, what do you think caused it?" Sammy asked.

"Had to be something that went wrong with the electrical wiring. There are lots of ways that can happen. A frayed extension cord on the floor by a rug. It gets hot in the basement when they're cooking. Our department had visited Sophie's before on an anonymous phone tip not too long before the fire. The unidentified caller said that she was using old fans to cool things off instead of an air conditioner. We gave her a warning to get rid of those old monstrosities. It looked like they came from the 1950s. Apparently she didn't get around to doing that."

Sammy pulled on Julia's blouse sleeve. "But if no one is around, and the electricity's off, how could the frayed cord start the fire?"

"Smart kid," the chief nodded. "No power on, nothing to spark the cord, unless someone lit a match or held a lighter to it." His eyes became slits.

"Actually, we did find a V burn pattern on the wall by the junction box. That tells us the fire could have started there, but because of the damage, it's not clear how, short of arson, that it was the point of origin."

He began to sound more business-like. "The fire inspector checked for fingerprints, but there are so many different people who had access to the basement, nothing panned out. There were no clues. We talked to witnesses nearby. No one had seen anybody going into the store, and for good reason. We figure the fire started sometime around 3:00 a.m."

"Any suspects?"

The chief stared at Julia. "Why the sudden interest in this case?"

Julia decided to be completely honest with him. She explained that just a few months after the fire, Sophie was now embroiled in another big problem and was forced to close down again. "I don't believe in coincidences, Chief," Julia said, and explained that she was trying to help Sophie out.

"Do you suspect Sophie of doing this?" Julia asked.

"Doesn't matter what I think. The fire inspector considers this to be a suspicious fire, and the insurance agency hasn't paid out any money. The case is still open, but we're not making any progress on it. If you've got any new ideas, we're always here to listen."

He turned to Sammy. "So, do you want to see how a fire department runs?" Sammy's smile nearly cracked his face.

Chief Grenchler took them through the station, introduced Sammy to the firemen who were sitting around the kitchen table. He showed them the room where firemen could sleep, and their emergency call center. He even let Sammy sit in the driver's seat of one of the monster trucks. Her son was ecstatic. On the drive home, Sammy was talking a mile a minute on what they had seen, how becoming a fireman might supplant his desire to be an astronaut. Julia fixed him a peanut butter and jelly snack, and sat down in the kitchen with the fire material.

It occurred to her that after studying the photos and written report, she might benefit from a trip to Sophie's basement. It was a silly thought, because Sophie had redone the basement and nothing was left from the fire, but it might help put things in perspective.

Julia called Sophie to ask if she could borrow her key to visit the basement the next day.

The deli owner agreed, though she couldn't understand what could be gained from it. Then she proceeded to sob her way through the fifteen minute call. Julia told her that a report on the liver was expected in a few days. If it was poison, that would let her off the hook, to which she replied, 'Who would want to shop in a store where someone poisoned the food? I wouldn't.' Julia also told her about their visit to the fire department.

"If I can offer them an additional suspect, anything, I know Chief Grenchler will have his people look into it."

"Thank you, Julia," she said, "you're such a *mensch*, but I think it's over now. A person can only take so much. In a day or two when I'm feeling a little better, I've decided to sell. If I'm careful and put my money in safe investments, maybe I can string things out for a few years. Who knows, maybe I'll be lucky and die before the money runs out."

"Stop that kind of thinking, Sophie" was all she could say. "Just be a little more patient. I think we're getting close. The liver analysis will lead the way to whoever is doing this to you. Do you want them to win? If you sell the store, you'll be playing right into their hands."

"I don't know," she sounded like a broken person. She sighed. "We'll see."

"What about Milton?"

"Milton's a man now. He'll have to do for himself. Maybe the girl will take care of him."

Julia very much doubted that.

"I'll be over for the key at about two tomorrow. Will that be okay?"

"What else would I be doing?" she said, and began to cry again.

Chapter Twenty-Five: Sophie's Basement

It didn't occur to Julia to call Rabbi Fine about going to Sophie's basement. It seemed like a harmless activity. It wasn't as though she was keeping a secret. She did tell Shayna earlier that morning while Matt was tutoring Sammy.

"It's not a bad idea," Shayna said between bites of toast smothered, Julia imagined, with butter and strawberry jelly. Shayna was on a new diet, she told her. Toast and tea for breakfast, plain tuna fish for lunch, and a normal dinner.

Unfortunately, Shayna's version of toast was to slather lots of fattening things on it. This would be, yet again, another failed attempt to carve a few inches from her very generous curves. She had been dieting in some form or another since they had first met twenty years ago.

"It's not that you'll find a clue or anything, but it might nudge your brain toward something."

"I'm glad you have such confidence in me." Julia was crunching, too. Sammy's sugary cereal had opened its caloric arms to her that morning.

"You're going at two, so give me a call when you get back."

"Will do," she promised. Julia cleared off the kitchen table, put the dirty dishes and utensils in the dishwasher, then cleaned the table and swept. While doing these mindless chores, she pondered why the machine was called a dishwasher when it required that she pre-clean those little nuggets of food that harden onto plates and pans. Some days, it seemed as though she worked harder than the darned machine. Not for the first time did Julia question what she was doing in this kitchen day after day after day instead of something more productive. Then, after enough self-flagellation, she tried to make sense of the fire packet.

There were photos of grayish, incomprehensible shapes melted and broken by the fire.

She identified the wall with the junction box, whatever that was, a photo of the back door and one of the front of the store. The report, itself, seemed as though it was written in a different language. She didn't lose heart, however. Like any naive beginner, she held onto hope.

Julia put her cell phone in the bedroom charger and got dressed in a pair of blue slacks and a white top with pink flowers that went over the pants. She had gained a few pounds (ten) and didn't want anyone to focus on her protruding stomach. In fact, Julia had three wardrobes. One that she usually wore, another for those times when somehow her body expanded, and a smaller collection of clothes that she would never, ever, fit into, but hadn't been able to resist their sale prices.

"Do these pants make me look fat?" she would periodically ask Harold.

As any husband with an ounce of self-realization, Harold always responded, "Dear, you are beautiful in anything you wear."

It's hard to get irritated with someone who says that.

A few errands while Matt was still around, a few more housework tasks, and it was almost 2 p.m.

Time to make the donuts, Julia announced to Sammy. It was a phrase from an old television ad that she could never get out of her head. Sammy took it to heart.

"Could we stop off at Dunkin' Donut?" he begged. "Please."

Why not? It was three or four hours before dinner. They deserved something to keep them going. Armed with a chocolate éclair for her and a donut with sprinkles for Sammy, they stopped off at Sophie's. Rather than get caught in another session about her troubles, Sammy knocked on the door to get her key.

The deli was just ten minutes away. Albert's store had wooden plywood over the front window. Someone, no, she thought, Jin, must have broken it. They parked the car in the back of the deli to reduce any attention to themselves. Julia unlocked the store door and they stepped into darkness. Sophie had told them where the light switch was or they would have missed it completely. It was spooky, a dark, deserted building. Julia was reminded of a number of horror movies and regretted not calling Rabbi Fine to come along. They slowly walked down a steep flight of stairs into a large room. Just as Chief Grenchler had described, they noted the three large cooking vats. They were empty now. A sharp, gassy odor cut through the air. This must be the way a vacant basement smells, Julia remembered thinking. A new junction box was on a concrete wall by the stairs. The floor, also concrete, was cluttered with cardboard boxes, some full, many empty. An air conditioning window unit adorned another wall. Several folding chairs looked as if a small audience had just left. An old card table sat forlornly in another corner.

"Here it is, Kiddo."

"Yup," Sammy agreed. He walked the perimeter of the room, then zeroed in on the vats.

"Remember those from the picture?" she asked.

"Yup," Sammy said. His brow was wrinkled.

Julia stood there. No revelations popping into her head.

"Um, Mom?"

"Yes?" Sammy interrupted her lack of thoughts.

"Didn't the chief say that the long rod was connected to each vat?"

"Yes." Her eyes took in the starkness of their surroundings. She could hear the hum of the fluorescent lights lined up like soldiers above them.

"Um, Mom?"

"Yes, what is it Sammy?" She might have snapped at him. It was so hard to think of something important and come up with nothing.

"I think there's something wrong with these."

"Hmmm?"

Julia walked over to her son. They stood together, looking at the middle vat. Sammy was right. She stooped down to take a better look. Yes, someone had, indeed, sawed the little connecting rods right off of the longer one. Did a fine job of it, too, she thought.

"I agree," she said. "They do seem to be broken."

"Well, isn't that bad, I mean, couldn't gas come out of there?"

"Right. That is, if the gas was turned on."

"Mom," he said again, this time more urgently, "I think it is on."

"No one's cooking. Why would the gas be on now?"

Of course it's on you twit, a little voice roared in her head. *It's the reason*

150

for the gassy odor.

Click!

That's when the lights went off. Total darkness. A bit too late, Julia realized that they were standing in a pitch dark room filling up with gas.

"We've got to get to the stairs," She told Sammy calmly.

He took her hand and they lurched their way through full and empty cartons until they reached a wall. Sammy led the way to the stairs. They scrambled up, but something was preventing them from getting out. Julia and Sammy pushed and shoved, but her son's beanpole frame and her unexercised body were no match for whatever was jamming them in.

"Let's go back down. There's got to be another entry into the store."

Holding hands, they crept down the stairs.

"I saw something before," Sammy said. "A big gray square door in the wall."

"A door to get out?"

"No, smaller than a regular door."

She wondered what it could be.

"Do you think they carry everything upstairs?" Sammy asked. "I once saw this movie where they had this thing called a dumb something. You opened a door, and it was like an elevator."

"A dumb waiter." That's what it must be. Julia felt like a dumb mother. She idly wondered when the gas would knock them out.

"Can you find it now, Sammy?"

"Sure," he said. Suddenly Julia saw a pinpoint of light.

"I always carry around this keychain flashlight," Sammy announced.

"Why? You don't even have a key to the house?"

"What if the electricity goes off and I have to pee at night? Jordan keeps turning off the nightlight to scare me."

The light picked up the door. They maneuvered their way over and opened it, but couldn't get it to work.

"It probably needs electricity to run," Sammy guessed.

Julia felt lightheaded. They had to find a way out. If only they could contact someone. Wait, she could call Harold. Julia reached into her purse for the phone. It wasn't there. She pictured the last time she had held it, and clearly envisioned it sitting on the bedside table, safely charging away.

Idiot, she thought. *Never go anywhere without it again. That's if we ever get out of here.*

She swore she would get Sammy a phone after this. He'd never forget to bring it with him, and it would be charged. This child was always prepared. He even picked out his clothes every school night and then he'd lie down on them to make sure the outfit felt right.

Think, Julia said to herself. *What do you know? What did you learn from that nice Chief Grenchler? When Sophie redid the basement, what was different?* It dawned on Julia. *Sophie bought an air conditioner.*

Julia shouted to Sammy, "Find the air conditioning."

He used his keychain light to locate the air conditioner. It was above her head. How was she going to get it down? Darkness plays tricks on you. So does propane gas. Her mind was speeding at the rate of molasses. Everything she did was in slow motion. Julia dragged one of the folding chairs to just below the unit. She got on the chair. Sammy held on to keep it from tipping over. She had to raise her arms high to reach the unit, which was firmly in place. She tried pushing it from side to side. It wouldn't budge. Where was bad workmanship when you really needed it?

Julia tentatively tried to shimmy it out. Unfortunately, the chair didn't appreciate that effort and promptly gave way. There she was, hanging onto the blasted unit.

"Sammy," Julia grunted, "It's not so far from the ground. I'm too heavy for you, but if you can catch hold of one leg and guide me down, maybe the fall won't be so bad."

She let go and dropped about two feet to the ground. Without Sammy to lessen the fall, she might have sprained an ankle.

"Wait here." Sammy sprang away with his little penlight. Julia heard him dragging something.

"Here's the card table. I'm bringing another chair. You can step from that to the table. It'll give you more height," he said.

Just what she wanted to do in the dark, she told herself. Still, Julia didn't know what damage long term inhaling of gas could do. Would it knock them out? She remembered reading articles about depressed women putting their heads into gas ovens to commit suicide. Sammy deserved more than that.

Julia got up on the new chair and gingerly mounted the table. It held. She was up higher than she had been on the chair. Then she had a new thought. Instead of using brute force, of which she had very little, Julia would remove the grout that she had felt before. The grout had been applied to keep the air conditioner in the wall. With the help of Sammy's penlight Julia was able to find her key chain which had a small Swiss Army knife with a nail file, flat screw driver, and teeny scissors.

Very carefully, she began to chip away. The grout began falling out. It seemed interminable, but Julia was able to remove it from the bottom and one side. The unit seemed to wiggle a little. She imagined feeling fresh spring air seeping through. Was it for real, or was the gas fooling with her mind? Nevertheless, flushed with success, Julia moved to work on the other side, stabbing away, forgetting that the card table might resist any further motion. It did. The legs collapsed. Julia hit the ground hard. She felt a burst of pain, then nothing else.

The next thing she remembered was waking up in a hospital bed with an oxygen mask on her face.

"What?" was all she could say. Without glasses, she could barely make out a face hovering above. Julia knew that face, she told herself. It looks a little like Harold.

"Julia, Julia," a voice was saying. She tried to get up. A creature wearing white took her hand. "Lie back," it said. "You've been hurt."

Sometime later, Julia opened her eyes again. The oxygen mask was off. This time she was certain Harold was lurking nearby.

"Sammy?"

"No, it's Harold, Sweetheart."

Julia knew then she must be in heaven. Harold had never called her sweetheart.

"Is Sammy okay?" She croaked.

Harold took a breath. "He was trying to catch you when the table fell, and one of his arms is broken."

"What kind of a mother breaks her son's arm," Julia sobbed.

"Don't worry. It's a clean break, and it's not his writing hand. If we ever find him a school to go to, kids will be scrambling to sign his cast. They're keeping him overnight, just in case, but he's already been out of bed trying to see you."

"He had a penlight keychain," she said. "We need to get him a phone."

"Sure," Harold said.

Julia fell back to sleep.

The third time Julia awoke, she tried to move again. She felt awful, as though her back was on fire.

"What happened?"

"You've got a fractured coccyx, a torn ligament in your knee, and a concussion, as well as a few bruised ribs." Harold said.

"A coccyx? What's a coccyx?" She giggled. What a silly word. Then Julia tried to sit up, and nothing seemed very funny anymore. Everything hurt. Especially her coccyx.

"It's your tailbone," he grimaced as he heard her painful gasps. Julia needed to talk to a nurse about pain pills fast.

"Are you sure Sammy's alright?"

"Yes. He's here. I'll let him and Jordan see you and then we have some talking to do."

Sammy looked so pale when he came to the side of her bed. He seemed self-conscious about his cast. It was lime green.

"Mom, can you come home soon?"

"My hero," She announced to anyone in the room. "Kiddo, I wouldn't have made it if it wasn't for you." She tried to give him a kiss, but when she moved her head, his face got very fuzzy.

"He really was a hero," Harold said quietly. "Sammy, tell Mom what happened after she fell."

Sammy looked down at the floor. He didn't want to talk about it. Jordan stepped up to bat. It was one of those very rare times when he lauded his younger brother.

"See, when you fell, you were out like a light. Sammy had to do something. He used his pen light to find the dummy waiter. He got in and checked out the ceiling. It had screws holding the wood on. He used something from your Swiss knife, unscrewed the screws and was able to take some of the ceiling down. Then he climbed up the cable like we do on the ropes in gym, and with his bare hands and fingernails, manhandled the door open on the first floor."

Jordan took a breath. "I can't believe he climbed that cable. Sammy hates heights. Anyway, once he got out he was in Sophie's kitchen. He ran to the front door and escaped.

"Rabbi Fine was just driving up then. They called 911, managed to get the back door open, and ran downstairs to stay with you until the EMT's came.

"You were a hot mess," he added.

"That's enough, now," Harold stopped Jordan. "What remains to be said is that the rabbi turned off the gas, the EMTs took you upstairs on a gurney, and gave both you and Sammy oxygen. For the moment, both of you are safe and sound."

Harold looked at Julia with hooded eyes. She knew there was a lot more he wanted to say.

Jordan actually gave her a kiss. "Mom, you've got to stop trying to be macho. Besides, Dad can't cook for shit."

They usually didn't allow the kids to use curse words, but it brought just the right tone to the discussion.

"You guys, I'll be home as soon as they let me. Maybe tomorrow?"

Harold shook his head.

"The day after?"

"Let's see how you feel," he said. "Boys, give me and your mother some privacy for a minute. I'll be right out."

"Now tell me what you were trying to accomplish."

Gone was the tender tone.

"I didn't think there was any harm in going to Sophie's basement to look around, get a feel for the scene of the arson."

"You didn't think at all, Julia. We could have lost you and Sammy." He took off his glasses and wiped away tears.

"What did happen? Why was the rabbi there?"

"You can thank your friend, Shayna."

"Shayna?"

"She said you told her that you were going to go to the deli around two and would call her back when you returned. By three she hadn't heard from you and she started worrying.

"She was afraid to call me because she knew you weren't exactly sharing the whole story with me, so she called Rabbi Fine." Harold took time to give Julia an irked look, then continued.

"He drove over and saw Sammy reeling out onto the street. Someone had tied rope onto the back door and a nearby telephone pole making it impossible for anyone to get out of the basement. Nine-one-one was there in minutes. The rabbi had already pulled the air conditioner out of the window so fresh air could come in.

"Julia, you have to promise me to never do something like that again." He put his hand on her shoulder. "I don't know what I'd do without you."

He was crying full out. She had never seen her husband express such deep emotion before, even when they saw their children for the first time.

Julia started crying, too. Harold bent over me and kissed her on the lips. Then he stood up.

"There's someone here to see you," he said. "I'll come by tomorrow morning. I'm taking some time off work to make sure you and Sammy are alright."

He kissed her on the forehead and walked out.

Oh God, Julia thought, I must really be in bad shape for Harold to take a few days off. Nothing could make that man stay home, even when he had pneumonia. She was beginning to feel very sorry for herself when the door opened again, and Rabbi Fine walked in.

What was it about him that filled her with hope? He looked more disheveled than usual, his yarmulke askew, his tie at half mast, white shirt wrinkled and partly out, and yet suddenly Julia was at peace.

"How do you feel?" he asked.

"Like I look," she said.

"Then you must be in pretty bad shape." he smiled.

"I guess I have you to thank for saving me."

"Thank Shayna and Sammy. I'm just an afterthought."

"Do the police have any idea who did this?"

"Not yet."

"What about Sophie's cameras."

"She turned them off when she closed up." His usually sunny mien turned grim.

"Do you think it was Jin?"

"I'm not sure. What do you think?"

"I've got nothing, except a headache," she said. "Where are we now? Have the lab results come in?"

"The only lab results you should be concerned with are yours, Julia."

"We can't stop," She tried to get up but the pain was horrible. "Remember what Rabbi Tarfon said, 'We have to try to do the job'."

"Yes," he agreed, "but he also said that one might not finish the job. It may be we're at that point."

"But I believe we've learned something from this latest episode," I said.

"Other than almost losing you and Sammy, what can you possibly know?"

"That's the point. There were only two people who knew that I was planning to be at the deli, Shayna and Sophie."

"There's no reason why Sophie would hurt you. We've been trying to help her."

Rabbi Fine dragged a heavy lounge chair closer to the bed.

"That's the point. I called her at home. It's possible she wasn't alone."

"You mean Milton?"

"Maybe. Or possibly Milton and Sweet Cheeks."

155

"*Baruch HaShem.* This is big. Very big. I'm going to talk to Chief Scarpelli right now."

"Rabbi," Julia asked. It hurt so much to talk, even to breathe. "Could you please stay a moment and pray with me? I know the prayer for lighting Shabbat candles, but that's about all. Is there something we can say?"

"There is one thing we recite for people who are ill that would fit this situation. Moses said it when his sister Miriam was sick. '*El nah refah nah lah,* God please heal her.' You know, there are no instructions to communicate with HaShem. Some use music. Others recite psalms. But we can just be together and talk to Him in our own thoughts. That's prayer, too."

And that's what they did until Julia fell into a deep and calming sleep.

****

Julia did not see fuzzy faces when she awoke the next day. Nor did she see two-headed people. It appeared the effects of the concussion were waning, but pain was ever present. It hurt to breathe, even though she acknowledged the practice as a necessity.

"Take deep breaths," the nurse had said.

"It hurts too much. What about little shallow ones," Julia countered.

Try arguing with a nurse.

"You need to breathe deeply so your lungs work properly. You don't want to develop pneumonia and end up coughing your guts out."

This woman could have been a drill sergeant in another life. She was a vision of sturdiness in her peach colored jacket and pants. Julia was not moved by the little spotted giraffe attached to her stethoscope. The nurse, who reminded Julia of Nurse Rachett, a frightening character in the absurdist book *One Flew Over the Cuckoo's Nest*, explained that there were some children on their floor. She raised the hospital bed to a sitting position. Julia sat there for a few moments. Nothing earthshaking occurred except that her bottom half felt like there were a thousand needles sticking her at the same time. Then Nurse Rachett commanded Julia to dangle her legs over the edge of the bed. After that, she quickly placed Julia's arms around her shoulders and pulled her off the bed. Julia almost fainted from the knee and back pain, but at least she was standing, and then she was falling, almost taking Nurse Rachett along for the ride. She hadn't really been aware of the extra pain from the torn knee ligament until she put weight on it.

They danced around and almost fell into the lounge chair, whereupon the nurse got up. Julia stayed, and later someone brought ice for every part of her body. By the time Harold and the kids came by after school, she had periodically been sitting on a special donut pillow with a hole in the center, lying down, and staggering a few feet at a time with crutches. A new nurse had informed her that it was important to move around regularly, but then, there should be periods of quiet rest. Julia opted for more periods of rest than moving around, but unfortunately the nurse outvoted her. Besides, she had a mustache, and Julia realized she could take her with one finger. How will any of this work at home? She wondered between bouts of pain.

"I bring good news." Harold and the boys burst in with flowers and balloons. Julia would have laughed, but it hurt too much. "You're going home tomorrow."

Great, she thought excitedly, which quickly turned into fear. How was she going to take care of herself? Who was going to do the cooking, the housework?

"We've got everything planned." Harold was on a roll. "Each Torah group member has volunteered a day of prepared meals, and the boys and I will be responsible for keeping the house clean. Your job is to get well."

He and the kids looked so hopeful. Julia started crying again. Everyone's faces fell. This was a workable plan, she imagined Harold thinking, "What's wrong with her?" the boys asked.

"These are tears of relief, guys. I'm so impressed I don't have to worry about anything."

Harold asked the boys for a moment alone with her.

"It's going to be alright, Julia. Trust me."

She always had. She knew after the first date that Harold Donnelly would never let her down. He had looked like a straight shooter from the first moment she had met him, in a church of all places, where she was covering a congressman meeting with parishioners who were concerned about Social Security issues. Harold had been the congressman's aide.

"And," he went on, "I have some other news you'll want to know. The police brought in Milton and Shirley for questioning. Shirley insists that Milton committed the arson and then tried to get rid of you and Sammy. Milton says he didn't do it. He's so broken up by what his true love is saying about him that Chief Scarpelli has him on a suicide watch."

Harold sat in the lounge chair by the bed. "What's most interesting to the police is that Shirley, aka Sweet Cheeks, was with Milton when you called. They could have heard Sophie talking to you or picked up the phone to listen in. Also," he was really getting into this, "there is no Shirley. The police took her fingerprints and discovered her real name is Coralee Binks, and three different police departments have been trying to locate her for bunco schemes. It seems she finds patsies, swindles money from them and then leaves town."

Good for our side, Julia thought.

"Right now she's in custody with a $100,000 bond, and nobody's banging down the doors to pay her bail."

Harold took a breath.

"Why did she pick Milton to swindle? He doesn't have two dimes to rub against each other."

"Maybe she somehow found out that he wanted his mother's store, and she could wheedle the money out of him."

"Or," Julia countered, remembering that Sammy had seen her car driving by Lester Pintner's office, "maybe she's working with someone else who used her to get to Milton."

"And that person," Harold said, "according to what the rabbi has told me, would be the developer."

"Yes." It seemed as though they were playing a game of Clue. Colonel Mustard had murdered Miss Peacock in the ballroom with a lead pipe.

That high was erased a few seconds later when Julia realized that while they had made great progress on the arson case, there still might be a poisoner on the loose.

Harold approached the bed, and in a more subdued voice told her that the lab results had come in. The liver had, indeed, been laced with Bella Donna, a poisonous flower that could cause the symptoms suffered by the *seder* victims. Odd that the Italian words meaning beautiful lady could be responsible for murder.

He put his finger under her chin. "Now Julia," he said, "you've got to let the police solve this one."

He didn't wait for a response. "The boys are waiting. We'll all be under one roof tomorrow night."

She wondered if they'd all be safe under that roof.

Blessed home. Julia felt as though she'd been away for an eon instead of a few days.

Harold had canceled Matt's tutoring for the rest of the week. He wanted Sammy to have some time to calm down from his escapade. He even got Jordan excused from school so they could all drive their mother home together.

They entered a sparkling clean house. "I washed the kitchen floor," Jordan announced.

Sammy raised his hand. "I vacuumed."

Both boys looked as proud as peacocks.

"And, they cleaned their rooms." Harold cuffed Jordan and Sammy on their heads.

"And I cooked." Shayna, wearing a leopard-spotted apron, sashayed in from the kitchen accompanied by the aroma of her mouth-watering roast chicken. "Now, hands off the chicken until dinner," she warned everyone.

"For lunch I have prepared your mother's favorite asparagus quiche along with a goat cheese beet salad. For hardier stomachs I've got grilled cheese sandwiches."

Shayna led Julia to the living room couch where she had set up a temporary bed. The doctors had decided that the steep stairs up to the bedroom might not be the best idea for a few more days. Julia's knee was in an ace bandage. She was schlepping herself around on crutches which didn't help the sore ribs one bit. Moving was a misery. For no particular reason at all, she decided this might be a good time to go on a diet.

"Nonsense," Shayna tsked when Julia mentioned it to her. "Now is the time to baby yourself and build up your health. The whole Torah group has compared notes and you'll be receiving two different meals each day for two weeks. We'll see what happens after that."

She propped up the pillows after Julia lay down. "Guess what night it is?" Shayna asked.

"I have no idea," Julia responded.

"It's Thursday," she said gaily. "We're going to have Torah class here tonight."

Julia must have looked horrified. Shayna put her hands on her hips and gave her "the look".

There is no defense against "the look". The CIA should use her as a secret weapon.

"The snacks and drinks are already here. You don't have to do a thing. You'll have something to think about instead of pain. If you're up to sitting at the table for a while, fine. If not, that's fine, too. Everyone wants to be here, Julia. Rabbi Fine, too. He said he might come a little early to talk to you. Can you imagine, Rabbi Fine actually early?" She walked back to the kitchen laughing.

Julia slept the afternoon away, waking only to breathe into a plastic machine with a ball in it to exercise her lungs, and to limp around for a few minutes. At 6:30 p.m., Harold escorted the rabbi to the living room and she was ready for a change of scenery.

"How are you feeling, for real?" Rabbi Fine asked.

"Well, the pretend me for the Torah group feels great. She's going out for pizza after the meeting. On the other hand," Julia said, "the real me feels like a dead skunk."

"Very descriptive."

"Actually, I'm getting a little better each day. Today, it's just terribly painful to move around, as opposed to horrendously painful yesterday."

"See," he smiled. "You're improving." He sat in Harold's black naugahyde chair, the only piece of furniture left over from his bachelor days. They had pulled it closer to the couch.

"Any news?" she asked.

"Yes, though it's not good. Fire Chief Grenchler has taken pity on me because, he says, I helped save your life. Today he told me that they can't hold Shirley-Sweet Cheeks - aka Coralee - any longer. They can't prove she's committed a crime yet. She's still in custody, though. The other states are fighting over who gets her first. And they've had to let Milton go for lack of evidence."

"Darn it," Julia was exasperated.

"Um, Mom?"

"What Sammy," she snapped.

"Remember those fire pictures you were looking at?"

"Yes."

"Well, I used my Dr. Bizarro Science Kit magnifying glass and think I found something."

"Let me see," Rabbi Fine took the photo and used the magnifying glass from Sammy's magic kit.

"I don't see anything but the faint reflection of a car," he said.

"Yeah, but let Mom see it."

Julia squinted, then quickly sat up straight. The pain was hideous, but it was worth it.

"It's her car. Sweet Cheeks' car, a beetle convertible. Look, you can even see the blotch that's her decal."

Amazing. When the fire investigators took the pictures of the front of the store, Sweet Cheeks' car was parked across the street. It was caught in the reflection of the window.

"Why else would her car be parked there at 3 a.m.?" the rabbi asked. "This is proof she was at the scene. She must have set the fire."

Julia stared at Sammy. The child was brilliant!

"But why would she leave her car there?" Sammy asked.

"That's a good question," Rabbi Fine said. "Maybe someone up there," he pointed to the ceiling, "gave us a little help."

"You mean...?" Sammy looked up and gulped.

The rabbi nodded.

Harold called Chief Grenchler. "We have possibly solved who committed the arson. What we don't know is why she did it. From your photos we have positively identified Sweet Cheek's car parked across from the deli at 3 a.m."

"Thank you, Mayor," the Chief said, "we'll double check our photos and get back to you ASAP!"

At seven o'clock on the dot the entire Torah group came en masse, including Devorah's Aunt Rose and Tzippi. Even Harold sat with them. It was like a homecoming party. Instead of having a lesson as they usually did, Rabbi Fine gave in and he and Julia answered questions about the fire.

"So, Sophie didn't burn down her own store?" Bubbe asked.

"Bubbe, stop," Malka protested.

"Well, who knows?" Bubbe went on. "Once I knew a tailor who couldn't sew a straight seam for the life of him. So, one night, he maybe leaves a candle a little too close to his material and pfft, the whole shop goes up in flames. Of course, he collected insurance."

"Bubbe," Chava said doubtfully, "when did this take place?"

"Oh," Bubbe waved her hands, "in the old country. From that time, I have never sewed near a lit candle."

"*Narishkeit*," murmured Tzippi.

"Maybe it's not foolishness for her," Rose whispered.

"You never sewed, period," Malka noted.

"Ah, but I used to. In the Old Country, of course."

Rabbi Fine's phone rang. He rose from the dining room table and went into the kitchen.

A few minutes later he came back to the table.

"That was Chief Grenchler. They showed Shirley-Sweet Cheeks-Coralee the fire photo that proves she was in the area at the time, and now she's singing like a warbler. She admitted to the arson and the locked room gas crime where she tried to take you and Sammy out, but she continues to insist that she didn't poison anyone."

"What's her story?" Harold asked.

"Somehow she and Lester met. I don't know how, but bottom feeders always find each other. They had an affair, and she thought she'd become the next Mrs. Pintner. Lester wanted Sophie's Deli. Sophie didn't want to sell, so he turned to the next in line, her son Milton.

"Lester sent out Mata Hari to literally bump into Milton at the comic book shop. *Schlemiel* that Milton is, he fell head over heels in love with her. Once she had her hooks into him, Lester entered the scheme. He knew that Milton wanted to open a pool parlor, so he offered to set him up in the new building if only Milton could convince his mother to sell or give him the store."

"This is better than most TV shows I watch," Bubbe remarked.

"Wait, there's more." Rabbi Fine sounded like one of those old marketers on late night TV *spiels*.

"Sweet Cheeks convinced Milton that if he could get the store, she'd marry him and they'd run the pool parlor together. He promised that he would do anything for her. Nothing happened. She started making demands. Still nothing happened. Sweet Cheeks decided to help things along. One night when Milton was asleep, she set fire to the deli basement."

"How?" Harold asked.

"It's deceptively simple," the rabbi explained. "Sweet Cheeks had a copy made of the key to the store. She went there one night armed with chewing gum, a screwdriver, and a roll of toilet paper."

"Are you kidding me?" Julia was astonished so much harm could come

161

from so little.

"Shall I swear an oath on it?" he asked.

"No, Rabbi. I think we can trust you at this point." The Torah group tittered.

"Anyway," he continued, "Sweet Cheeks moved empty cartons near the fake wood walls and opened the cover of the junction box. That's where pieces of conduit piping come together. All she had to do was loosen the wire nut for the piping." Rabbi Fine's eyebrows were furrowed as he tried to remember everything Chief Grenchler had told him.

"Then she used her gum to stick toilet paper into the junction box and reinstalled the cover. When she flipped the switch to turn on the electricity, an arcing spark from the loosened piping ignited the toilet paper which was draped across the empty cartons. The fire spread and destroyed the basement." He took a long breath.

"This is unbelievable," Malka was aghast.

The rabbi went on. "Sweet Cheeks walked up the basement stairs without a care in the world. She tried to drive back to Milton's, but her car wouldn't start, and she heard the fire sirens coming, so she took off and ran back to Milton's house. It only took about twenty minutes, and he was never the wiser. The next day she went back for the car, tightened a loose cable, and drove away. Both Shirley and Milton believed that when the fire investigator couldn't close the case and the insurance company refused to pay Sophie for the damages, she'd give up."

"But," Julia interrupted, "they didn't plan on Sophie's indomitable spirit and the savings in her mattress."

"Right." Rabbi Fine agreed.

"So what's going on with Lester Pintner?" Devorah had just speared a piece of melon on her plastic fork. "Can they connect him to the poisoning?"

"Well," the rabbi got up and began pacing, "not at this time."

"No?" Malka was up in arms. "He's got to be guilty of something."

"Not for the arson. At least not yet. Sweet Cheeks has to testify that he told her to do it, and she hasn't gone that far yet." Rabbi Fine stopped pacing and turned toward Malka. "Sweet Cheeks is really angry at Pintner. She expected to marry him as soon as his project was underway. But he recently informed her that he's staying with the current Mrs. Pintner."

"Aha," Julia said, "finally an opportunity to use something from my college English major. I believe the proper expression for this is, 'Heaven has no rage like love to hatred turned, Nor hell a fury like a woman scorned.'"

"Shakespeare?" the rabbi asked.

"No. The poet William Congreve from 'The Mourning Bride,' 1695. I discovered it during a research paper on seventeenth century poets."

Julia was feeling better by the second. One crime solved, one to go. Now the insurance company would have to pay Sophie.

"So, has Sophie accused Pintner of the poisoning?" Devorah was like a dog on a bone. She wouldn't let up.

"She has, but he has a strong alibi for the entire week before Passover. He was in Florida with his wife," replied the rabbi.

"Couldn't he have hired someone to do it?"

162

"They haven't been able to find any other suspect."

"What about Jin?" Shayna wondered out loud.

"Who's Jin?" Faigie wanted to know. "And what kind of a name is that anyway?"

Julia took that one. "Jin is Lester Pintner's father, and I doubt that's his real name. He once owned Lester's development company. After he had a stroke, Lester plotted to take it away from him. Now Jin's life goal is to destroy his son."

"To destroy him how?" Malka asked.

"We're not quite sure," the rabbi said, "but this reminds me of a story about a son and his father that might be interesting, if not instructive, in this case. It hinges around vengeance and greed "

He coughed into his hand. "Let's at least get in a little Torah learning tonight," he said as he returned to his usual seat at the head of the table. "I assume you all know King David?"

All of them answered in the affirmative.

"He had several sons from different wives. Amnon was his eldest son. Absalom was his third son, though from a different mother. Absalom was the king's favorite. He was handsome, charming, and people in David's court loved him.

"One day, Amnon raped Absalom's sister Tamar. As a result, she was completely humiliated, commanded to keep quiet about it, and eventually went insane."

Everyone in the room tsk-tsked. Aunt Rose put her elbows on the table and rested her face on her hands to listen more carefully.

Bubbe added her two cents. "That Bible is a really dirty book. I don't think young children should know from it."

"Bubbe," Malka admonished her grandmother.

Rabbi Fine continued, "Absalom waited for his father, King David to punish Amnon. Nothing happened. Absalom was beside himself with rage."

"And why is it always the woman?" Devorah demanded. "We suffer, then the men go to war."

Rabbi Fine gave a 'what can you do?' shrug, then went on.

"Absalom waited two years. He had a great feast and invited all of David's sons. While there was drinking and carousing, he sent two servants to murder Amnon. Then Absalom fled to his maternal grandfather's kingdom.

"Although King David was furious, after three years, he was ready to accept his son, again. Absalom returned, but he still was filled with rage at his father who had not lifted a finger at the rape of Tamar."

"Let me guess," Tzippi said, "the little *pisher,* Absalom, stands up against his father."

"You're right," the rabbi agreed. "Absalom declared himself king. In the years since his return, he had been amassing the support of thousands in his father's kingdom. David fled with an army of four hundred."

Faigie finished chewing her orange slice and held up a finger. "But this isn't the first time David's been in a tough spot. Remember when he went up against Goliath? He was this young kid, brave enough to fight a giant."

"It's never a good idea to count your chickens before they're hatched,"

Bubbe announced sagely before putting an entire handful of shelled peanuts into her mouth.

"Absalom waited before sending his men after David," the rabbi continued. "He wanted to be sure he had all of his thousands organized before hunting down his father. But David was a canny warrior. He carefully placed his few soldiers in position, and when Absalom's army came, there was a terrible fight."

"And who won?" Sammy had come into the room unnoticed, as usual. He had been sitting on the floor listening to the story.

"David," Rabbi Fine answered. "Not only did his little army fight valiantly, many of his son's soldiers, seeing the way the war was going, switched sides. In the end, Absalom fled on a donkey…"

"How can you flee on a donkey?" Tzippi interrupted. "They're very slow animals."

"No, I've seen some pretty fast donkeys in my day," Rose disagreed.

"I guess they didn't have any horses around," the rabbi answered. "Absalom's hair, which once had been one of his best assets, got caught in the branches of a tree. As he was trying to untangle himself, an army commander came along. Even though David had ordered that Absalom be captured alive, the commander killed him. David lamented, 'my son Absalom, would God I had died for thee.'"

"Why wouldn't he have wanted to punish Absalom? He tried to take away David's kingdom." Rose was confused.

"I would have put him in prison so fast," Bubbe's strident voice proclaimed, "he would never see the light of day again."

"That's the relationship between fathers and sons," Rabbi Fine explained. "They love each other. At a developmental point in life, they compete with each other. In some cases, they hate each other. Today, the son usually takes over for the father, helps him in his old age as the father once did with his young son."

"So what does this have to do with this Jin guy?" Harold asked.

"I'm just saying that even though Jin's a bad person who terrorizes people, at the center is a father who has been betrayed by his son. Right now, he hates Lester, but, who knows, some day things might change. We have to hope for the best."

"I don't believe they'll ever make peace," Julia said. "You once mentioned that bottom feeders always find each other. That's what they are. I don't see them changing any time soon."

She was tired and happy at the same time. This had been the longest she had been sitting up for a few days, Sophie was officially off the hook for arson, and Julia was surrounded not only by Torah group friends, Rabbi Fine, and Sammy, but Harold, too. At least now he had an idea of what his wife had been doing on Thursday nights.

He and Shayna helped Julia back to the couch and tucked her in. The women quickly cleaned up, being sure to leave fresh fruit, nuts, coffee cake, and a few more snacks while Rabbi Fine and Harold spoke quietly. Julia was asleep before everyone left the house.

Julia awoke, stiff, but was able to sit up on the rubber donut without too much pain. Sammy was sitting on the floor by the couch. When he saw that she was awake, he spoke.

"Um, Mom?"

"What is it, Kiddo?"

"You know that the poison is a plant called belladonna?" he said in his methodical way.

"Yes."

"Well, I looked it up on the computer, and I think it's one of the plants I saw in Lester Pintner's office."

"You're kidding."

Harold had just walked into the room. "You're sure, Sammy?" he asked.

"Yes," Sammy responded.

"I'll phone the police department." Harold hurried to the kitchen phone.

"Mr. Sammy, come here," said Julia.

The boy stood in front of her, as usual, staring down at the carpet. "I'm going to give you a monster hug."

"Mom, no." He backed away. "I don't want to hurt your... your anything."

"How about a kiss on the forehead."

He grinned. "That'll be okay."

He came forward and bent at the waist so his head was a kissable distance. It was one of the sweetest moments of Julia's life.

****

Later that morning she received a phone call from Sophie.

"Julia," she *kvelled*, "you're a miracle worker. Chief Grenchler just called to say that young woman admitted starting the fire. He says the insurance company will be getting in touch soon, and they'll pay out my claim."

"I'm happy for you, Sophie. And maybe we've solved the poison chopped liver mystery, too. The police are trying to locate Lester Pintner. They've already been to his office and discovered the belladonna plant he had there. All he had to do was to grind up the berries, roots and leaves, to make a very effective poison."

"Did they get him yet?"

"No. His secretary says he left town last night, and she doesn't know where he is."

"Does that mean they'll let me open my store again?"

"I don't know. It could take some time to find him and get a confession. You might want to talk to Chief Scarpelli about that."

"Julia, I can't tell you how grateful I am for all your help. You and Rabbi Fine didn't have to do this. I'm a nobody."

"You're a somebody in this town, Sophie. I don't know how we could live without your wonderful deli."

"Just for that," Sophie said, "I'm going to make you something special. Do you like chocolate?"

"I love chocolate, but please don't do anything for me. I was happy to be there for you."

"I insist. I'll just leave it by the door if you're sleeping."

"Thanks, Sophie. By the way, how's Milton doing?"

She sighed. "Milton is Milton. I gave him a month to find a job and move out, and he won't be welcome here for a long time."

"Can he manage to do that?" Julia was doubtful Milton could do anything for himself except fill his stomach every few hours.

"He'll have to. He doesn't have any real friends. His romance was fake in every way. He's going to have to learn to be responsible for himself. I think it's called "tough loving". I've been too helpful all his life, what is that word, enabling him? No more."

She lowered her voice and whispered into the phone, "When the insurance company pays me my money, I'm going to close this deli and make a clean start in a nicer neighborhood in Crestfall. There are still lots of years in this body, yet," she said.

Julia was pleased that Sophie was so hopeful. It was about time. She wondered how she would have reacted to the clouds that had been hovering over her head. No husband, a failure of a son, closed by a fire, rebuilding, then closed again. That's a lot to take, yet there Sophie was, ready to pick herself up again. What is it, Julia wondered, that makes some people strong in the face of adversity, and others slink away like jackals?

Shayna blew in to make sure her patient was eating the prepared lunch instead of junk food. She also brought a hamburger for Sammy. After she left, Julia lay down for about an hour. The ringing doorbell woke her. Sammy opened the door. No one was there, but on the porch was a plain white cake box. He lifted it up and carried it in.

"What is this?" he asked. "It's heavy."

"Probably Sophie's surprise she said she was making for me."

"Can we open it?"

"Sure."

"Wow."

Julia agreed. Inside the box was a huge, sumptuous black forest cake topped with bright red cherries.

"Can I have some now?"

Sammy wasn't a cake person. Ice cream and sugar cookies were his default dessert menu. Julia remembered when he was younger he'd refuse to eat any more of his meal, but when dessert came, he'd want some. "How can you have room for pie when you couldn't put another green bean in your mouth?" she would ask. "I have two stomachs," he would explain, straight-faced, "one for meals, and one for dessert. My meal stomach is full, but my dessert stomach is empty."

"It's almost too beautiful to eat," Julia said, taking a tiny taste of the frosting at the bottom. She let Sammy take a tiny taste, too. "Let's put it on a cake plate on the dining room table, and we'll all have it for dessert tonight."

"Okay." His heart wasn't in it, but he did as she asked. Julia limped back to the couch impatient for the day they'd put a cast on her leg and she could burn the crutches. That cake was still on her mind. How long till she cut both of them a piece? She was just about to suggest they each take a sliver, but her knee began to ache. She was wondering where the pain pills had gone, or maybe she should send Sammy into the kitchen to make an ice pack, which for no reason what-so-ever, led her to wonder when she would try climbing up the stairs. She could probably get there on her rear end, have a proper sponge bath, and choose her own clothes, except that her coccyx was fractured. Instead, maybe she could slide upstairs on the good knee side. Those simple acts would likely take more than an hour, but she thought it would be nice to surprise Harold when he came home. He'd see an almost human looking wife. Still, it seemed daunting.

"Hey, Mom?" Sammy interrupted her reverie. "Can I have permission to look at Sophie's Deli tapes? It'll be cool to check out what policemen do when they're solving crimes. I promise I won't bother you."

Why not, Julia thought. She was interested, too. She certainly wasn't ready to start house cleaning yet. Harold had gone in to the office for the first time this week. Julia was sick and tired of watching cable news, HGTV, and soap operas. Besides, climbing the stairs without proper supervision would be too dangerous, she decided. This from the little lady who faced down the Blades.

"Kiddo, why don't you bring my laptop down here and we'll check it out together."

Sammy set up the computer on the dining room table and sat in the chair beside her. He inserted a CD of the two days before Sophie closed for Passover.

The tape wasn't too grainy. Sophie obviously had paid for a high resolution system. The first views were of the back door. They fast forwarded when no one except Sophie and her workers used it. They watched customers come into the store. Nothing looked out of the ordinary. There were some odd looking people. One old woman entered, and when Sophie saw her she ran behind the counter and brought out two brown bags. The old lady thanked her. They hugged, then the lady left. Julia thought that might have been a poor person who came to Sophie's regularly for free food. Finally they came to the camera that covered the refrigerated food area. She showed Sammy where the chopped liver was.

They watched very carefully. Minutes ticked by. Some people liked to open the refrigerator door and just stare inside. Julia could picture them doing that in their own kitchens, blindly gazing into their refrigerators as though expecting an open can of peaches to yell, "Eat me before I go bad." Others, mostly men, walked up to the doors, opened them and immediately chose what they wanted. They went through Thursday, and were just beginning Friday, the day of the first *seder*. Sophie had closed early that day, about two p.m.

"Wait a minute, Sammy." Julia was looking at a man in a trench coat, even though it was a warm enough day. She remembered not wearing a sweater when she and Sammy had gone to Sophie's. This man not only had on a trench coat, but a dark baseball cap pulled down on his eyes. Julia had seen lots of men wearing caps like that, but usually it was to keep out the sun. There was no sun glare in Sophie's shop that day. He stood in front of the door, so they couldn't see what he was doing. He was holding onto a red basket instead of a grocery cart. That meant he wasn't going to stock up on much. He had pulled the basket in front of him. Julia couldn't tell if he was putting things in it or perhaps taking things out. In addition, she sensed she had seen that same man come in the day before when she and Sammy had been there.

"Sammy, can you make that CD go backwards?"

He stared at his mother as though she was clueless. "Um, yup," he said, controlling the laughter the young folk must feel when encountering old fogies. The logic that had escaped her addled brain was, of course, if the tape goes forward, it probably goes backwards, too. That's what you call rewinding. Julia was embarrassed in front of Sammy, but they struggled forward, and darned if they didn't see the same man dressed in the same trench coat and cap on what would have been Thursday. In Thursday's shot, however, Julia saw more of his face. She sat up straight.

"I know that man." She shouted, almost startling Sammy off of his chair and onto the floor.

"You do?"

"Could you please bring me the phone?"

She called Shayna.

"Can you come over and see something?"

"Sure. What?"

"A photo of someone you might recognize."

"Be there in ten."

"What's going on?" Sammy asked.

"This guy is familiar to me. I'm not sure; maybe I'm wrong."

Shayna arrived wearing a skin tight mauve and black exercise suit. As she bounced into the living room, she saw the cake on the dining room table.

"I've never seen such a beautiful cake in my life," Shayna announced. "Did you whip that up in your spare time?"

"Right. And I've got a bridge to sell you, too," Julia responded.

"Seriously, did someone from the Torah group make that?"

"Don't worry, Shayna, your skills in the kitchen are still unmatched."

"So, what am I here for, except to take a taste of that masterpiece over there?"

"I want you to look at someone. Sammy, can you make this picture bigger?"

Her son, the genius, was able to complete the task.

"Does he look familiar?" They could see a little more than a third of his face. He was swarthy skinned, with a slight dark beard. The one eye they could see appeared to be wary. He was not large in stature. The trench coat was too big on him.

Sammy offered Shayna his seat at the table. Shayna put her finger to her mouth. "He does look familiar," she offered. "Where is this? Sophie's? Is this her secret camera thing? I want to say I've seen him before…but not as a customer, she was tapping her index fingernail on her teeth and the noise was driving Julia crazy. "He's definitely not cakes and pastries…not at the cash register…Hah," she sang out. "It's Sophie's meat man, the guy who cuts so well. Remember when we went there before Passover, and he came marching out of the kitchen? When he wagged that meat trimming knife at her face? Sophie had to let him go because of the fire. That's who he is."

She turned to Julia triumphantly. Then she looked confused. "If Sophie fired him, why did he come back to her store in a coat that clearly isn't his?"

"That's what I want to know," Julia said. "I remember him, too. He's on this tape twice, once on Thursday, and again on Friday just before *Pesach*."

"But isn't the case solved?" Shayna asked.

"I'm not so sure." Julia picked up the phone. "I'm going to call Chief Scarpelli and tell him about this."

The chief came on quickly and she explained what they had discovered. "Your guys can find it on their tape. My friend Shayna and I know this man. We were at the deli when Sophie fired him shortly before Passover. He was very angry with her. In fact he threatened her by waving a knife in her face. You can see him on the tape twice acting very suspiciously. In my opinion, he not only has a motive for poisoning the liver, we may be watching him as he puts it in her refrigerator."

Chief Scarpelli was very respectful but doubtful.

"Thanks for your time, Mrs. Donnelly, but we believe Lester Pintner is our poisoner. We have his belladonna plant. In my book, that's red-handed. We're still trying to locate him. This person must have come back to Sophie's because he likes the food."

"But Chief, he's right in the chopped liver section."

"Again, Mrs. Donnelly, I hope you're feeling better. We'll be talking soon."

Harold walked in soon after.

"You don't look very happy," he said.

"You should fire that Chief Scarpelli." Shayna was indignant.

"Whoa," Harold held out his arms like a school crossing guard.

"What's going on?"

Julia told him about the CD and the wasted phone call to Scarpelli.

"My wonderful detective," he said in a disgustingly patronizing tone, "the chief is a professional. He knows what's best."

"He's short-sighted," Shayna complained.

"He's the chief," Harold repeated, "and we're going to do what he says. That's why we hired him. Let's not talk about this anymore. It'll be Shabbat soon."

Julia was blown away that her husband remembered that Friday evening was Shabbat. The Donnellys certainly didn't observe it. Was he trying to get brownie points with his irritated wife, or was he merely trying to change the subject? Sometimes politicians can be sneaky.

"By the way," he asked, "what's for dinner?"

Enough casseroles filled the freezer for several dinners. While Harold and Julia had enjoyed the dishes prepared by the Torah group, their sons had preferred fast food instead. The parents, however, still had some of Shayna's roast chicken, Tzippi's matzah raisin kugel, and Sarah's prune and sweet potato *tzimmes*, Julia's personal favorite. She knew Sol was out of town for a work emergency, so earlier in the day she had invited Shayna to stay for dinner and the *Shabbat* weekend. Sammy could bring his sleeping bag into Jordan's room.

"You know, I don't believe Sol's ever missed a Shabbat dinner with me," Shayna had sighed. "Okay, I'll stay. Of course that means I'll be here until Saturday night."

"The more the merrier," Julia had said, happy to have her friend for a sleep-over.

Jordan came roaring down the stairs. "Mom, Dad, can I go over to Andy's for dinner? They're serving sloppy Joes."

Julia took pity on him. "Okay, but do you have any homework?"

"I'll do it there. Besides, it's the weekend. Plenty of time to do it. Be back by nine." And out he zipped.

"Mom, if Jordan gets to go out, can I have something different to eat?"

"How about another grilled cheese?" Shayna appeared with spatula in hand. Sammy's eyes lit up. He loved Shayna's cooking. She always put four or five pieces of cheese on the bread as opposed to his mother's stingy one or two. Hers came out of the frying pan perfectly grilled with mounds of delicious bubbling cheese; its presentation rivaled only by professional food magazine photos.

Shayna had put a cloth on the dining room table. It was close to 5 p.m. As she rummaged through the refrigerator and heated things up, Julia crutch-bumped up the stairs with Harold's help, took a quick sponge bath and put on fresh clothes. It felt liberating. She decided she was done camping out on the couch. Julia missed her bed. She missed sleeping beside a gently snoring Harold. Tomorrow Julia was going to wash her hair and start living again. Harold agreed that she'd go up at night, and come down in the morning, but spend the rest of the day on the main floor. For now, it was enough.

They had almost finished eating their leftovers when the doorbell rang. Rabbi Fine came in looking more rumpled than usual. His face was pale. He looked worried.

"Come, join us," Julia offered. "We've got lots of food, and it's all kosher."

"No thank you. I'm not hungry. Anyway, it's Friday night and I must get home before sundown, but I had to tell you this in person."

"What's so important?" Harold asked.

Rabbi Fine sat at the table. "I've just been with the *mashgiach*."

Harold looked at Julia, "With the who?"

"*Mashgiach*. That's the guy who oversees how Nate runs his deli. He makes sure that everything's kosher, literally," she explained.

"It's not good news," Rabbi Fine looked down at his hands. "You know, there are several infractions that will cause concern for the *mashgiach*. I'll give you an example. Say a bakery is selling *parve challah* to people who are going to eat it with meat, and dairy *challah* for people who are eating dairy. What if they sell the dairy *challah* to someone who's going to use it with meat and it gets discovered?"

"Wait a minute," Harold interrupted. "What's this *parve* thing?"

"You understand you can't mix milk with meat, right?" Shayna asked.

Harold nodded.

"So," she explained, "if you plan to eat a meat meal, you have to substitute *challah* ingredients that are acceptable with meat, like *parve* margarine and honey instead of milk and butter." She emphasized, "*parve* is something that is neither meat or dairy."

"This is a crime?" Harold was slightly sarcastic. "The dairy *challah* probably tastes better."

"It does." Shayna confessed.

"Still," the rabbi said, "when someone catches the bakery knowingly

170

selling the dairy *challah* for meat dishes rather than the *parve challah*, they're put on probation."

"By the police?" Harold was amused.

"No, by the *mashgiach*." The rabbi made himself remain patient. He was trying to beat the clock and make it home before Shabbat, but he had something important to say. "It could mean that all of their cabinets would be locked, and only the *mashgiach* would have the keys. A worse infraction would be if a butcher sold non-kosher meat. You do that once, the *mashgiach* puts you on notice and spends more time in your kitchen."

The rabbi's voice rose. "In fact, some *mashgiach*s actually have the key that opens and closes the store each day to be able to check out all deliveries. But," he said, "if you do it a second time, it's over. You can't get certified as a kosher establishment again."

The room was silent as they thought about what this could mean.

"What happens then?" Harold was interested now. This was business, his territory.

"Then the *mashgiach* stops coming. He refuses to certify that the store is kosher. That can kill business if the reason people go there is because they know the authorities attest that the store follows the rules of *kashrut*."

Rabbi Fine looked as if he had lost his best friend. "I found Levi, the *mashgiach*, who told me he went into the Nate's Nosh deli kitchen a few months ago and saw a wrapping label from a *traif* chicken company in the garbage."

"*Traif?*" Harold asked.

"Not *kosher*," Shayna translated.

"So, Nate's Nosh is about to be closed as a kosher deli?"

"One more infraction and he's gone," the rabbi said. "You know," he directed his comments to Harold, "in the Torah, a man who cheats in business is called *to'ovat Adoshem,* abhorrent to *HaShem*. There are other abominations mentioned in the Torah, but only one that I know of strictly directed to a single person."

Rabbi Fine looked at Shayna and Julia, knowing they'd want to know where to find it.

"Deuteronomy 25:13-16. It's about a person, a Jew, who uses incorrect weights and measures. *HaShem* so abhorred dishonesty that He stated that anyone who used corrupt practices would not be permitted in the Holy Land."

"But what difference does that make in our modern day world?" Harold tipped his chair back so it was balancing on two legs. It always made Julia nervous when the boys did that.

"It means that the man is no longer a trusted member of the Jewish community. In the old days he could have been flogged. These days, it means he's not respected as a businessman and has no future here anymore." Clearly, Rabbi Fine was very upset.

"I'd call that motive," Shayna placed her hands on the table. "Let's say Nate knows his days are numbered as a kosher deli. Instead of cleaning up his act, he tries to buy Sophie's good name to continue in his field. She's got a great reputation around here."

"If he wants to buy Sophie's Deli, why does he poison her chopped liver?" Harold was thinking aloud.

Rabbi Fine began to go into his *davening* phase. "How do you get what you want?" he asked himself. "You make your adversary vulnerable. She's already had the fire. Business is down. She's hurting financially. Along comes Nate. He offers to buy the deli, but keep her name on it. He even suggests she continue on as manager, maybe even be part of a chain of delis. It's a rosy deal, but she's not buying it."

Shayna interrupted by thumping her fork on the table, "So he poisons her liver. The town closes her deli. She's even more down in the dumps, and now, at her lowest point, she might accept his offer."

"Your thinking is valid," Harold noted, "but Chief Scarpelli believes Lester Pintner is his man."

"Look," the rabbi said, "Lester certainly is guilty of, what do you call it, collusion to push Sophie out of her store, but beyond that, we've got nothing beside the fact that he likes exotic plants."

"Now," Julia added, "we've got two suspects left." The two women told Rabbi Fine about the meat cutter on Sophie's store surveillance tape. "Maybe they're working together," Julia suggested. "We've come so far in solving this crime," she said, "yet it's like we're still running in place."

"Let's forget about the crime for five minutes," Shayna announced. "I've been salivating over that cake all afternoon." She began clearing the table. Sammy brought out paper plates and plastic spoons.

"Rabbi, will you have a piece with us?" Julia watched Shayna eyeing the cake. She knew her friend was deciding how to serve it. Cut a smaller circle an inch or two around the edges to make sensible pieces, or go whole hog and slice it like the spokes of a wheel. Shayna went for the wheel technique.

"That certainly is a cake," Rabbi Fine was ruminating over something and didn't give Shayna a clear answer. She cut five large pieces and passed them around. There's something almost sensual about watching a knife slowly coursing its way down through a luscious chocolate cake. This one was three layers, each separated by a thick ganache filling studded with bright red pieces of cherry. If it was a television commercial, a sultry woman would be crooning, 'You want me, don't you. Forget the calories. Take me. Take me now'.

Julia's vision was shattered by the rabbi's question.

"Where did you get this cake?" His voice was sharp. Very unrabbi-like.

"It was on the front porch," Sammy explained. "The doorbell rang. I opened the door. No one was there, but I saw this white box with the cake. Sophie told Mom she was going to make something special."

Sammy was wearing his, "I didn't do anything wrong, did I?" look.

Rabbi Fine jumped out of his chair like a bolt of lightning. "Don't eat the cake," he yelled. He ran to Shayna who had just put a forkful into her mouth. She was licking off the frosting when he hit her on the back. "Spit it out now. Don't swallow. Do it," he yelled like a mad man.

Harold rose from his seat, got his phone out of his pocket, and called 911.

"Possible poison case at 1154 Hellman Drive," he said.

"Poison?" Julia was stunned. She dropped her fork. Shayna was white as a sheet.

"I hope I'm wrong," Rabbi Fine looked anguished, "but I think it's Nate or the meat cutter. Lester Pintner wouldn't dare show his face around here. He

172

knows the police are looking for him. Nate's got a lot to gain from this. Sophie wouldn't just leave a cake like this outside. She'd have rung the bell, given the cake to Sammy, said a quick hello to you, and then leave. If Sammy opened the door soon after the bell, how could Sophie, a seventy-five-year-old woman have disappeared so quickly. No one was visible because Nate didn't want you to see him deliver it. The other guy I don't know. Maybe he left the cake here, instead. It's important to find both of them, fast."

Shayna was sitting very quietly.

"Does this mean I'm going to die?" she asked in a tiny voice.

"No," the rabbi said, kneeling by her side. "The hospital will probably give you charcoal tablets or Ipecac to make you throw up. You only had one bite. I can't imagine it did much harm."

The EMT's came in. Shayna insisted on walking to the ambulance. Harold was on the phone with Chief Scarpelli. They arranged for the cake to be taken to the lab that offered quick analyses. The rabbi went home for Shabbat with instructions that if anything dire happened to Shayna, Harold was to drive to his house and tell him.

The rest of them waited on pins and needles for some information. Julia called Sol to tell him what happened and he flew back to Crestfall. Shayna did begin showing signs of poisoning; nausea and a heightened heartbeat. They weren't sure if it was poison at work or terror on her part. The hospital kept her overnight to make sure there were no other ill effects, but she went home in the morning.

Chief Scarpelli didn't take any chances this time. He immediately sent a squad car to pick up Nate and find the meat cutter before either had a chance to leave town.

Pain in the knee. Pain in the rear. A brightly shining sun announced spring really was there. Julia guessed that she had lived to see another day. She rolled onto her side and reached for the crutches that were laid across a chair by the bed. Gingerly, she put her good leg on the floor and stood up. Nothing untoward happened. She moved stiffly to the closet to find a *shmatte* that she could put on over her head. An unattractive green and orange striped cotton number caught her eye. It was from the "fat" side of the closet and looked like a small tent. It would work for a quiet morning at home.

After daily ablutions, Julia clumped around the top floor, nosing into the boys' rooms.

Jordan was still abed at 10:30 a.m. Sammy's room was empty. He was probably downstairs watching TV while eating in the kitchen, she hoped, rather than leaving a trail of Count Chocula cereal nuggets from the kitchen to the family room. Harold and the boys had been very good about cleaning up after themselves for the first two days. Now that the initial shock of the accident was over, so was their commitment to keep the house sparkling.

With great care, Julia used the crutches to get down the stairs and made her way to the kitchen. Yes, Sammy had been there. The milk had been left out on the table, but amazingly, there was no other mess. Maybe after this patch of pain was over, perhaps the entire family would chip in for home chores. Who was she kidding?

The phone rang. Julia was able to pick it up before the answering machine kicked in. It was Sophie.

"Good morning," Sophie said.

"Is everything okay?" Julia asked.

"Are you alone?"

"The boys are here," she answered. "Sophie, tell me you're alright."

"Something's come up," she said. "I need you to come here now. Right now."

"What's wrong?"

"There is a problem. A big problem, and you must come or it will be too late. Please," she pleaded.

"Sophie, are you in danger?"

"No, I'm not, but someone else is. Come as soon as you can. No one else can help us."

"But I can't drive, Sophie. Can you come here?"

"No. Take a cab, but don't tell no one."

Julia was concerned. Was Nate or Carlos holding a gun on her? Why did she need her? And why did she have to go to her house? Sophie had said 'no one else can help us.' Who was the other person who needed help? Certainly not Milton. She couldn't call Rabbi Fine. It was Shabbat. Harold had gone to some mayor's breakfast to speak on "Salt: How to Plan for Winter Woes." Julia didn't want to call a cab, but she couldn't call Shayna who was still recovering from the poisoned cake incident. What if she had to leave quickly? She'd rather have her own car, but she couldn't use the pedal and place pressure on her knee.

She could always call Chief Scarpelli, but he hadn't been very cooperative about this whole case. Besides, if Sophie and whomever were to see cops, she could be in big trouble.

Then it came to her. Jordan. He knew how to drive. He was a big lug. Strong. He had a cell phone; she had a cell phone. They could be connected, and if he heard something scary, he could immediately call the police. He was, unfortunately, too young for even a driver's permit, but that had never stopped him before. Julia whimsically imagined the boy could drive from birth.

But how could she put another son in danger? What would Harold say? On the other hand, Sophie really needed her. What would Rabbi Fine do in this situation? He would remind her of the boat. He had once told a story about a group of people who were on a boat. One of the passengers started making a hole in the boat. The others told him to stop, of course. The moral, when one person makes a hole in a boat, everyone is at risk. Sophie's boat had a hole in it.

Julia had to do her part to help. She had been brought into this mess in the first place, and she needed to see it through. Jordan wouldn't have to leave the car. He wouldn't be in danger. Julia would, as usual. She sighed. Harold would kill her. But maybe she could be back home before he ever found out.

"Sammy," Julia called, "come here."

He came trotting in with his plastic Star Wars cereal bowl. Today he had left off his swim fins. Instead, he was wearing his cowboy boots with his red plaid swimsuit.

"Yup?"

"Wake your brother, please."

"Aw, Mom, he'll kill me. It's only 10:40. That's dawn to him."

"Tell him I need him, and it has to do with driving."

Sammy's eyes almost goggled out of his head.

"You want him to drive?"

"Only if he wants."

Sammy took off to his brother's room so fast Julia was afraid he'd fall up the stairs. There was a rumble and some yelling coming from Jordan, then a yelp. Within a minute, Jordan, barely up, came barreling down to the kitchen. He slept in his underpants and a tee shirt that could stand up by itself. Where were the lovely pajamas she bought each boy every *Hanukkah*?

"Is Sammy telling the truth? Do you want me to drive? Where? I don't have a license. You and Dad were so mad at me for taking your car before, why do you want me to drive now?"

Julia put a glass of orange juice in his hand and told him to drink it and be quiet. Sammy came streaming in.

"Here's the deal," she told them. "You know I've been working on this case."

"And I've been your partner," Sammy said emphatically.

"Right, Kiddo."

"Well, last night, as Sammy knows, someone sent us a poisoned cake. You came home way after all the excitement was over and I was asleep."

"Cool, did anyone die or anything?"

"How sensitive," she said aloud before remembering to hold her tongue.

"So, Mom, what does that have to do with a car?"

"Sophie wants me to come to her house immediately. I'm sure it's about

176

the poisoning case, but I can't drive." Julia explained that Sophie cautioned her not to tell anyone else.

"So when do we go?" Sammy asked.

Julia sighed. She couldn't take Sammy. It could put him at risk again. Harold wouldn't forgive her. She was going out on a very short limb asking Jordan to drive her in the first place.

"Kiddo, someone has to guard the house in case the police call with more information on the poisoning."

Sammy was too smart to fall for it.

"Jordan doesn't know how to investigate." He stamped his cowboy boot. "What if he sees something important and doesn't understand what it is? That's what I've been doing for you."

He had a point.

"Sammy," Julia stared him straight in the eye, "it's 10:50 now. We'll leave as soon as Jordan gets dressed. If Jordan or I don't call you by noon, you call the police and ask for Chief Scarpelli. Tell them you're the mayor's son. They know where Sophie lives."

He nodded okay, but his eyes were full of tears.

"Hey," he shouted. "I know. I can stay here and be there with you at the same time. We'll do a three-way conference call. Dad's secretary once showed me how to do it when I went to his office with him. That way, Jordan can tell me what he's seeing and I can help, even if I'm not there."

"What a genius you are." Julia kissed him on the top of his head and looked up at her older child. "Jordan, if you're not up for this, you don't have to drive me. I can call a cab."

"Mom, you might need me," he said. She was so proud of her two sons.

"Well what are you standing there for? Get dressed. We're late."

Jordan took the stairs three at a time. That's what baseball practice does for you.

Sammy got Julia's fully-charged phone and helped her put on a pair of gym shoes. She took along the donut pillow. Stylish she wasn't. But then, they weren't going to a fashion show.

Jordan appeared less than five minutes later dressed in a pair of jeans and his prized possession, a brown leather bomber jacket she had bought for him at a thrift shop.

Julia found Harold's cell phone in his dresser drawer and gave it to Sammy. Although his office had forced him to have a cell phone, Harold rarely used it. Sammy started charging it immediately. Julia felt terrible leaving him home alone, but sometimes a promise to a husband cannot be broken.

Chapter Thirty: Sophie's Choice

Jordan parked a few houses down from Sophie's. They both agreed that they didn't want Sophie and anyone else who might be with her to know that Jordan was outside in the car. Then Sammy arranged the conference call and the three phones were synchronized. Julia put hers in a pocket of the dreadful tent dress she was wearing, and slowly crutched her way up the block. There was not a cloud in the blue sky. The lawns were green. All was peaceful in Crestfall. Things could be worse, like walking into an ambush, Julia thought, but for some reason she felt no fear.

That's because you're an idiot, she could imagine Shayna yelling.

What idiot? I'm going to help a friend. Julia was miffed at her imaginary friend.

What friend says don't tell no one? What friend gets you up from a sick bed to come to her house? Didn't you learn anything from that farkakteh Blade experience?

"I trust Sophie," Julia said, and a sense of peace came over her. Was she channeling Rabbi Fine? Was *HaShem* giving her a heads up? It didn't matter. Like a pinball spinning through its maze, a force had been unleashed, and she was going to see it through to the end.

Julia clumped up Sophie's front steps and knocked at her door. A pair of eyes peeked out from behind the dining room curtains. Shortly after, Sophie opened her door.

"Are you alone?" She peered up and down her street, seeing nothing but parked cars.

"Do you see anyone else here?" Julia asked. Not a lie. Close, but not a lie.

"Come in."

It was obvious that Sophie wanted to pull her in immediately, but crutches require concentration and care. Eventually Julia was seated on a dining room table chair, the little donut pillow uncomfortably squashed beneath her.

Sophie sat on the other side of the table. The white lace cloth seemed like a neutral zone between them. She was quiet, anxious, nervous.

"So you're wondering why I wanted you to come here?" She fidgeted with the edge of the cloth.

"Yes," Julia's knee was beginning to ache. She had forgotten to take her pain pills in the rush to get there.

"Something happened," Sophie began. "It wasn't my fault, but it is my fault, and I have to make it right." Tears filled her eyes.

"Tell me." Julia had learned that a calm demeanor and an open question could achieve wonders.

"See, when the store was closed because of the fire, I had to let some of my people go. Others, I kept on, paying them part of their salary until we could open again. I understood that they all had families to support, just like me."

She took out a much crumpled piece of tissue to catch her tears.

"After we reopened, business was bad, and I had to fire more of my people. Remember, on the first day I met you with Shayna, that I had to let go of my best meat counter man because I couldn't afford him any longer? It was Carlos. He was very mad at me. I knew that he had a five-year-old and a newborn baby.

He needed money." She looked at me, "But I had no choice."

"And so?" Julia wiggled on the donut, trying to find a spot that didn't hurt so much.

"And so, he tried to find another job. He finally ended up at Nate's Nosh."

Julia's antennae rose. "Are you telling me that Carlos began working for Nate?"

Sophie nodded. Somehow, she looked smaller in her much used housecoat, a washed-out yellow cotton with muted pink and purple roses.

"What happened?"

Sophie stood up. "I made some tea and *mandelbrot*. You'll have some."

She went to the kitchen. Julia was left alone. She whispered down toward her phone pocket, "Are you with me, Jordan?"

"Got your back, Mom." He was still awake, on duty. She heard the radio playing some rapper tune.

"Can you hear me over the radio?"

"Super ears, Mom. Don't have a cow."

Sophie returned to the room with a tray, three tea cups, a plate of *mandelbrot*, which other people call biscotti, and Carlos, the meat counter man.

Julia must have looked surprised, because Carlos started backing up as if to flee.

"It's okay," Sophie said. "She's my friend. She'll help us work this out."

Carlos sat at the table like a skittish cat ready to jump at the slightest sound. All one could hear was the soft clinking of spoons on glass tea cups as they stirred sugar cubes into their tea.

"Now, Julia, Carlos isn't going to hurt anyone. He's frightened and didn't know where to go. He trusts me, and I trust him. Listen to what he has to say."

"Carlos," Julia interrupted, "you must know that the police are looking for you. Why don't you turn yourself in?"

His head hung low. His black beard had grown in, and it looked as though he hadn't slept for days. "I come to this country when I was twelve. All my life I never break the law. I work, marry my Isabel, have children. I loved working at Sophie's Deli. I would never hurt Sophie. But when she fired me, I got very angry. How am I going to pay my rent, I thought? How do I buy food for my children?" Carlos seemed to be talking to himself.

"I try getting another job, but it is very difficult. Then I go to Nate's Nosh. He asks me where did I work before. I tell him at Sophie's Deli for ten years. He is very happy to hear this. 'I'll hire you,' he says, 'and I'll pay you twice as much as you made before if you do something for me.'"

His bloodshot eyes stared at Julia across the table. "I was very pleased. Imagine, two times the salary. I couldn't believe it. I started the next morning. Then I see that this man isn't like Sophie. He says he's a kosher deli, but I handle the deliveries. His meats are *traif*. I didn't want to stay. I'm not like you, Sophie. I am a good Catholic, not Jewish, but I see how you make your business work. You do things the right way. Nate is a cheat. I don't feel right working there, but I have no choice. We have to buy diapers for Ramona, and our son, Javier. He grows like a weed."

"And then?" Julia interrupted.

"And then, one night, when the others have gone, he says to me, 'It's time

180

for your favor.' My blood chills. The hair on my neck is standing up. I know this isn't going to be good for me. Nate puts his arm around my shoulder and says, 'All you have to do is put four containers of chopped liver in Sophie's Deli refrigerator on Thursday, and the same on Friday. I'll give you those two days off. When you bring the containers into her store, they'll be in the pockets sewn in a coat I'll give you. Put them into one of her red baskets as you walk around the deli, then place them into the freezer section. Take four of her containers out and buy them. Wear a baseball cap pulled down over your eyes. That's all. Four on Thursday, four on Friday. Then your favor is over'. What's in them? I asked. I was afraid, but I had to know."

"Don't you worry about that," he said in a mean voice. "I'll take care of everything."

"Is this going to hurt anyone?" I asked.

"Just give them a little gas, a stomach ache. Just enough for them to stop going to Sophie's and come here. You want that, don't you? You want to continue making money here, right? Nate, he is not a good man," Carlos said.

Julia was unconsciously dunking her *mandelbrot* into her tea, the dry biscuit absorbing the sweetness of the hot drink. She wondered if, in his shoes, she would have gone along with the plan.

Of course you wouldn't, her imaginary Shayna hissed. *It would have been immoral.*

What's morality when your children are begging for food? Julia challenged. No response followed.

"I did it," Carlos sobbed. "I put the bad liver in Sophie's Deli. I didn't know it could kill someone." He put his head on his hands. "I don't know what to do."

"We've got to go to the police," Julia said.

"No," he shouted. "They'll blame me for everything. I'm nothing here. Nate, he is the owner of a store. Who do you think they'll believe? I'll spend the rest of my life behind bars. I know how things work. Nate, he'll open his guilty eyes wide and say, 'I had no idea Carlos was going to poison the chopped liver. He only worked for me a short time. I never knew how much he hated Sophie'. And the police will believe him. Why wouldn't they? He's a businessman. He has money. He is like the police."

CI know Chief Scarpelli." Julia said. "If you tell him what you've told me, you'll have a better chance."

She changed the subject. "Carlos, did you do any baking while you worked for Sophie?"

"I can follow some of her simple recipes," he said proudly. "She taught me to make *mandelbrot* and coffee cake."

"What about a Black Forest Cake?"

"I never make them," Sophie said. "Just simple, one or two layer cakes. Carlos can pipe icing, but I doubt he could pull off a Black Forest Cake."

"What do you want from me?" Julia asked.

He gulped, took a breath. "I came here for money to run away. When I find another job in another state, I will send for my family. But Sophie says the police, they'll find me. She says, 'My friend Julia can help'. I wait for you, but you want me to go to the police, too. I think I should leave now."

181

He stood up to go. That's when they heard the bull horn.

"Carlos, this is the police. Come out with your hands raised."

Sophie and Julia looked at each other.

"You lied to me." Sophie was furious.

"I didn't call the police," Julia said.

"Then how did they know Carlos was here?"

Jordan or Sammy must have alerted them, she knew, but didn't say anything.

"Carlos," Julia used the same tone as when one of her sons was hurt, "if you and I go out the door together, I promise no harm will come to you."

Carlos was pacing around the dining room table. He was becoming more agitated.

"I don't want to lose my family," he kept saying. "The police, they'll blame me for all of this. They won't believe me," he cried.

"I'll be with you," she insisted. "I'll say you didn't know there was poison in the liver. I'll tell them that Nate did it. They won't shoot you if I stand in front of you." She remembered a movie in which the person the police thought was guilty, was actually innocent. He was protected by a phalanx of people who surrounded him as they walked toward the police.

Julia took the phone out of her pocket. "Jordan, are you there?"

"Mom, there are lots of police outside of the house."

"Is Chief Scarpelli out there?"

"I'll check." Jordan sounded frightened.

A few minutes later Chief Scarpelli came on the line.

"Julia, are you alright?"

"We're all fine, Chief. Carlos is afraid you'll blame him for everything."

"Tell him we'll listen to his story. No one wants any trouble here."

Carlos looked like a treed cat. He was breathing hard, talking to himself, mumbling "I won't let them take me" over and over. He was becoming hysterical.

She heard a commotion outside, then a knock at the door.

"Mom, it's me, Jordan."

Sophie peeked out the dining room curtains again. "It's a young man in a leather jacket," she said.

Julia nodded. "What do you want?"

"I'm here to take you home," he said, sounding scared, but insistent.

"Let him in," she told Sophie.

Jordan squeezed through the door.

"Mom, there are about twenty guys out there. They all have guns. This is serious."

"Carlos, this is Jordan, my son. Jordan, this is Carlos."

"'S'up, Dude?" Jordan extended his hand.

Like some strange etiquette lesson, Carlos shook Jordan's hand.

"Gentlemen," Julia began to rise from the table. She grabbed her crutches. The trick to making this work was to continue talking calmly, nonstop, like toothpaste smoothly oozing out of the tube, "this is what we're going to do. We're all going to go outside together. We'll form a protective line. Jordan and Sophie go first, Carlos and I second. We'll stand on the front porch and talk to

Chief Scarpelli. Then we'll all go to the police station together. Sophie, you'll drive my car. Jordan, give her the keys. We'll all be there for Carlos while he tells his story. Okay?"

They were already forming ranks when the bullhorn rang out again.

"If you're not out in three minutes, we're coming in."

Slowly, they made their way through the front door. The air was filled with electricity. Julia was praying that no policeman would have an itchy trigger finger as they waited for the Chief to come to the bottom step.

"Chief, Carlos has a story to tell, and Sophie and I believe him. He's afraid the police will hurt him, so we'd like to accompany him to the station if you don't mind. Then you'll find out what really happened. It was Nate. All Nate. Carlos put the chopped liver on the shelves, but he didn't know they were poisoned."

The Chief's face was bright red. Julia wondered if he'd had a physical lately.

"Julia Donnelly, you're making me crazy," he said in a low voice that couldn't carry over to his men, "I could put you in jail for abetting a criminal."

"But you won't, Chief, because I'm helping you get to the bottom of this. And you'll be solving a crime."

Then she shut her mouth, afraid to push the chief any further. Jordan, Sophie, Carlos, and Julia slowly walked down the steps in unison, as much as possible with the unwieldy crutches.

"This is highly improper," Scarpelli whispered after they were seated in his car.

"What's your husband going to say about this?"

She had no answer.

Sophie took Julia's car. Jordan went with her. Carlos and Julia went in the police car and they all met at the station. Carlos told his story, which did not exonerate him, but did lessen the charges. The police eventually located Nate in a summer cabin he owned in southern Illinois. They found the mortar and pestle he used to prepare the poison for the liver and the Black Forest Cake. Sophie put up money for Carlos' bail and the Donnellys found a good lawyer to defend him. Of course, the question that remained was why would anyone have gone to the lengths that Sweet Cheeks, Lester Pintner, Nate, and Carlos had?

"Greed goes all the way back to the ten commandments," Rabbi Fine pronounced as he sat at the head of the table. "*HaShem* warned us not to covet that which was not ours."

The Torah group meeting was at Julia's house again so she wouldn't have to hobble too far with the crutches. In a few weeks the doctors said they'd give her a walking cast so she could exile the crutches to a dark corner of her closet. Unfortunately, the donut pillow would be around for a long while. This group was so large, they had to add another table that extended into the living room.

The usual members were in attendance, Faigie, Devorah, accompanied by her Aunt Rose and Tzippi, Malka, Chava, and Bubbe, Lilah, and Shayna. Also with them were Sammy, Jordan, Harold, and Sophie. On the table, in addition to pistachio nuts and melon, was an array of coffee cakes, *mandelbrot*, sugar cookies with sprinkles, and banana bread. All from Sophie's Deli.

"I'm almost embarrassed to talk about greed with this amazing spread around us," the rabbi smiled, "but I will. Greed is about wanting what someone else has; desiring more."

"Like if we just had one more little *babka* cake, this would be complete," Bubbe said wistfully.

"Bubbe!" Malka and Chava chimed in together.

"That's okay," Sophie laughed. "Next time I'll bring two *babkas*, okay?"

"Just look at how greed almost destroyed Sophie. Milton wanting her deli for himself; Sweet Cheeks lying about her relationship to Milton, actually setting the store on fire; Lester trying to cheat Milton out of the deli; Jin wanting his old business back; and Nate wanting to use Sophie's reputation," the Rabbi said. "They all acted out of greed, and what did it get them?"

"*Bupkis*, that's what," Bubbe announced loudly.

"The law isn't fair," Faigie noted. "This builder person, Lester, he gets away with everything. He's the one who worked with Sweet Cheeks to scam Milton out of the deli. Isn't that collusion? He was scheming to get the store."

"But nothing happened," Malka interrupted. Her marriage to a lawyer gave her the edge in all legal discussions. "According to the strict reading of the law," she spoke with authority, "Lester did nothing illegal. Morally wrong, yes. Legally, no. Sophie still has the deli. Milton didn't do anything illegal to take it from her. Even though Sweet Cheeks misrepresented herself, she got nothing out of the deal. She will, however, have to serve time for the deli arson."

"Also, she'll have to wait while the three other states fight over who has jurisdiction," her sister Chava added. "Sweet Cheeks won't see the light of day for a long time."

"And," Julia added, "Harold says that because of Lester's actions, he's telling all the surrounding mayors not to do business with him. It's going to hurt him big time."

"We're forgetting something," Devorah said. "Even though this whole situation was rife with greed and anger, some good things happened, too. Look at what Julia and her sons did for Sophie."

Julia was embarrassed. They did what they did, as Rabbi Fine would say, because they were all in the same boat.

"Tell us about Sophie's house with Carlos," Chava pressed.

"Not that Sophie and I were in any real danger," Julia began, "but Sammy and Jordan both were listening to what was going on in Sophie's dining room. Sammy decided that Carlos was going to lose it and called Chief Scarpelli on Harold's cell. Scarpelli brought a ton of men when just a few would have been enough."

Harold coughed.

"Okay," she continued. "He brought as many men as he could to protect the mayor's wife and the owner of a Crestfall deli. So our brave Jordan jumped over the porch railing and knocked on the door before the police noticed him. When he came in, Carlos actually calmed down and agreed to go outside with us.

"Jordan, Sammy, we wouldn't have had such a peaceful ending to this if it hadn't been for both of you." The boys were heroes in Julia's eyes. Even though Harold was furious at her for including their sons in her tilting at windmills, he was proud of them, too.

"And the bad guys will get what they deserve," shot Bubbe with a mouthful of macadamia nut cookie.

"Bubbe," the Rabbi counseled, "Proverbs 24:17 says, 'Do not rejoice at the fall of an enemy.'"

"Those proverbs have nothing on Yiddish," Sophie countered. "Here's a good one for Nate. 'May he go to hell and make bagels and cakes, but never be able to eat them,'" she said with a grim smile on her face. For a deli owner, that was the worst punishment possible.

"Rabbi," Shayna appeared to be troubled. "I'm glad that we've solved the arson and the poisonings, but there's something more that's troubling me."

"What?"

Everyone went quiet.

"When Julia and I were behind the fish market, those gang-bangers hated us. They didn't know us, but they hated Jews for no reason."

Julia's friend looked as though she was going to cry.

"I'm stumped. I don't know how to feel. How should I react to someone who hates me when I've never done anything to hurt them? What answer does Judaism offer?"

Rabbi Fine took a minute to think. "There are at least two things Judaism says about hatred and forgiveness. In the Talmud, Rabbi Joshua said, 'A grudging eye, the evil impulse and hatred of his fellow men shorten a man's life.' In addition, our masters taught, 'Thou shalt not hate thy brother in thy heart,' Leviticus 19:17. That's a big deal, not to hate your brother in your heart," the rabbi said.

"Why should we turn the other cheek when someone wants us to vanish from the earth?" Sophie argued.

"Yeah," Bubbe agreed. "We already lived through that. Someone's got to pay for all this hate," she said bitterly.

"So where does that leave us?" Rabbi Fine turned to all of us at the table. "Are we just supposed to hate all those who hate us? Where would the world be if everyone held grudges? You are partly right, Bubbe. In some Jewish teachings, the offended party is not required to forgive."

"I bet that includes the Blades situation," Chava said.

"Before you count your chickens, listen to this," the rabbi politely interrupted. "There is a kind of forgiveness, *selicha*, a forgiveness of the heart. It is an empathy for the troubled offender, a consideration that he shares our human frailties and is deserving of sympathy."

Malka exploded, punching her fist on the table so hard that her cheese and crackers almost jumped off their plate.

"Why should we forgive these vermin?" she shouted. "Like Shayna said, they hate us. One almost stuck a knife in Julia's throat. They're just vicious *prostaks*."

Shayna whispered to Julia behind her hand, "*Prostak*, that means a vulgar, coarse, ignorant person."

Malka looked toward Jordan and Sammy who were sitting quiet and goggle-eyed at what she had just said. Harold also looked very surprised. He had heard a much sanitized version of their meeting with the Blades. It was clear Julia had some additional explaining to do in private.

Malka apologized to them. "I'm sorry if that upset you, but this is a serious matter."

For her part, Julia kept thinking of Black Slash. At the time, she had felt a simpatico with him. What did they know of his upbringing, what kind of life had he led? She knew that was the old liberal view, excusing crime because the offender had a difficult background. But people have free will. People choose between the paths of good and evil. Still, she had sensed that Slash was a sad, lonely boy who joined up with those animals to belong to something, anything to justify his miserable existence. She felt that there had to be some good in him, some shred of humanity.

Could she find it in her heart to forgive him? And if she could, what about the others in his gang? On the one hand, a knife was pressing on her throat. On the other hand, she was not physically harmed. The point of the knife just grazed her neck. They had made a deal and the gang kept their side of it. That meant that they could be trusted, even if it was in their own interest. And, she continued thinking along those lines, if they could be trusted once, perhaps they could be trusted again, and from that, a relationship could develop.

Rabbi Fine went on, "Personal forgiveness can be very difficult and painful, but it plays an important role." He directed his comments particularly to Shayna and Malka. "By forgiving from the heart, one can go on in life, put the event behind them. Jewish tradition asks that we rise above anger, believe in the good in *HaShem's* world, no matter how hard that may be."

Shayna looked down at her hands. Julia knew that she was warring with herself. Could she overcome her feelings of fear and anger at those dreadful people. Julia knew her friend would work on it and that they would talk about it further.

Malka, however, was a different country altogether. Bubbe and her deceased husband had both been Holocaust survivors, for which she had never forgiven *HaShem*. Her heart was a stone when it came to the Blades. Julia doubted she could ever find it in her heart to forgive them. Julia wondered what part of life she would lose because of her stubborn soul.

Their meeting ended on a quiet note, soft murmurings amongst the women.

Julia thanked Rabbi Fine for his thoughts, and hobbled back to the couch to lie down for a moment. It seemed as though they had been sitting for hours.

When everyone was gone, the extra table and chairs put away, all Julia wanted to do was crawl upstairs and slide into bed. Of course, it was the precise moment that Sammy chose to come to the couch with the list of schools his counselor had given them. Hard to believe it was only two weeks since his refusal to go to class.

"Um, Mom," he said. He had changed from his Torah class clothes to his bed-time outfit of a swimming suit and a tee shirt. "I looked over these schools, and I've narrowed them down to two."

"Two? There had to be eight on that list."

Harold entered the room and sat in his big black chair.

"What's up?"

"Sammy's winnowed down the schools to two choices," Julia said.

"Yeah. I don't want to go to a boarding school," he said. "And I don't want to be on a bus one or two hours a day to get to school and back," he went on. "And, some of them are specialized, like I don't want to go to a creative arts school."

She looked at his list. "Akiva Middle/High School or St. Francis of Assisi? These are the only two that are close by?"

"Yup," he said.

"But they're both parochial schools. Akiva Middle/High School is for Orthodox Jewish kids, and St. Francis is for Catholics."

"You don't have to be Jewish or Catholic to go to either one," Harold noted. "I went to a Catholic school and it didn't do much harm," he joked.

Julia ignored his ham-handed humor.

"Do you have a preference, Sammy?" she asked, praying that their son would not choose the Catholic School.

"I have," he looked at them solemnly.

"What is it?" Harold asked.

Sammy announced his choice, and Julia smiled. Change is a'comin' to the Donnelly home.

Alev hashalom	May he rest in peace
Aleiha hashalom	May she rest in peace
Baruch HaShem	Thank God
Bedikat Chametz	The formal search for leavened food in the home prior to Passover.
Bubbemisah	An old wife's tale
Challah	Specially braided egg bread generally eaten on the Sabbath
Chametz	Leavened food products, which traditional Jews abstain from eating during the week of Passover (Many Orthodox Jews sell or remove their *Chametz* from their homes during this time.)
Chutzpah	Arrogance, nerviness
Davening	Praying, often accompanied by moving the body back and forth rhythmically
El nah refa nah lah	God, please heal her!
Farshtinkener	Rotten and smelly
Gefilte fish	Ground up pike and/or carp mixed with onions, carrots, parsley, and eggs, formed into balls and poached in fish broth and water.
Geshrei	A loud scream
Gonif	Thief
Hagaddah	The book that tells the story of Passover and provides instructions for *seder* service, food, and prayers.
HaShem	The Name. Another way of saying God
Hechsher	A symbol on a product certifying it is kosher.
Kashrut	Jewish religious dietary laws dealing with what foods can and cannot be eaten, and how they must be prepared.
Kosher	Food that meets the standards of kashrut.
Kvell	Expressing great pride
Lashon Harah	Evil tongue, speaking ill of another; gossip
Ma'aser	Taking a tenth of something, gleaning
Mamzer	A conniving, untrustworthy person, bastard
Mashgiach	A Jew who supervises the *kashrut* status of establishments such as kosher restaurants
Meshuge	Crazy
Meshugener	A crazy person
Maitsorim	Boundaries, limitations
Mitzrayim	Hebrew for Egypt
Mitzvah	A good deed; one of God's commandments
Matzoh	An unleavened flat bread in the form of a cracker, eaten by Jews during the Exodus, and an integral part of the Pesach holiday.
Narishkeit	Foolishness
Parve	Neither dairy nor meat. Can be cooked and eaten with either food and remain kosher.
Pilpul	A method of analyzing similarities and contradictions when

	studying texts in the Talmud
Pirkei Avot	A collections of sayings of the fathers of Judaism, compiled in the early third century
Prostak	A vulgar, coarse, ignorant person
Putz	Someone easily tricked; a fool
Shabbat	The Sabbath. A day of rest from sundown on Friday night to the first three stars on Saturday night. Orthodox Jews do not work on Shabbat. Some worship at synagogues on Saturday morning, but they do not drive.
Shaina maidel	Beautiful girl
Shalom bayit	Peace at home
Sheitl	A wig or head covering, worn by married, Orthodox Jewish women
Shiksa	A non-Jewish woman
Shlemiel	A useless, inept person, to whom bad things constantly happen
Shmendrick	A stupid jerk with an inflated ego
Spiel	A prepared presentation, like a television marketer
Sleecha	Pardon me
To'eivat Adoshem	Abhorrent to HaShem
Torah	The five books of Moses and the first books of the Old Testament
Traif	Something unkosher, usually food
Tsuris	Trouble; problems
Tuchus	A person's rear end
Vilde Chaya	A wild animal
Yente	A gossip, busybody
Yeshiva bucher	A student of Judaism at a Yeshiva (an Orthodox Jewish school)
Yom Rishon	The first day after Shabbat-Sunday
Yontif	A holiday

The Passover Story (Pesach) in Brief

Pharaoh, who believed in many gods, was the leader of Egypt. The Jews, who believed in one God, were slaves in Egypt. The Pharaoh feared that Jews were multiplying at too rapid a rate. He ordered that all first born Jewish males be drowned.

Miriam, the sister to a new-born male, made a basket of reeds and put the baby in the river close to the place where the pharaoh's daughter bathed. The woman saw the infant, claimed him as her own, and named him *Moses*. She needed someone who could feed the baby mother's milk. Moses' sister sent her mother to nourish and watch over her own baby.

Moses was reared as an Egyptian. One day, as he rode out into the desert, he saw a slave master beating a slave. He killed the cruel man and fled Pharaoh's kingdom to Midian, where he married and became a shepherd.

One day as he was watching his flock of sheep, he passed by a burning bush, but the bush was not being consumed by the flames. A voice (God) within the bush spoke to Moses telling him he was to leave Midian, go to Egypt and tell Pharaoh to let the Jewish people go. Moses said that he could not speak well.

190

The voice told him that his brother Aaron could speak for him.

Moses and Aaron went to Egypt and told Pharaoh that if he did not let the Jews go, plagues would be brought down upon him and his people. There were ten plagues, the last one was the death of the first born. Pharaoh did not take the first nine plagues seriously. The Jews were instructed by Moses and Aaron to paint their doors with the blood of a paschal lamb. During the tenth plague, while God "passed over" the homes of the Jewish slaves, the first born of the Egyptians, including Pharaoh's son, died.

Finally, the Pharaoh let the Jewish slaves leave. This was the Exodus of the Jews from Egypt. They left so quickly that they didn't have time to let their bread rise. God commanded Moses to hold his staff over the Sea of Reeds, and it split in half. The Jews escaped by crossing it. Pharaoh had a change of heart and sent his army after the Jewish people. The soldiers rushed through the Sea of Reeds, but it became whole again, swallowing up the army.

When the Jewish people reached Mt. Sinai, God gave them the Ten Commandments. They wandered in the desert for forty years, and finally reached the Promised Land.

The *Seder*

The word *Seder* means order, and the Passover *Seder* is a special celebration dinner with many traditions, prayers, and rules to be followed. These are written in the *Haggadah* which means "the telling". Every year families all over the world gather around their tables to share the experience of the Exodus of the Jews from Egypt. They perform the same service with special *seder* plates, symbolic foods, and traditional dinners. Many of the symbols of the *seder* are mentioned in this book at the *seder* that Julia and her family attend with her friends Devorah, David, Aunt Rose, and Tzippi.

Here are the objects that are to be on every *seder* plate during Pesach and have been described in this book:

Beitzah – Egg

Maror – Horseradish

Z'roah – Shank bone

Karpas – Parsley

Charoset – Mixture of apples, nuts, honey, cinnamon, and red wine.

Also present on every Passover table is Matzah, flat like a cracker, it is often referred to as the 'bread of affliction'.

The *Afikoman,* half of a piece of matzah, is considered a dessert. Traditionally it is hidden someplace during the *seder* and young children hunt for it when the meal is over.

Recipe for Tzippi's Tzimmes.

Tzimmes is a little bit of this and a little bit of that, almost any combination of sweet vegetables. It is to be slowly cooked for a long time to get the best blending of flavors. It can be made with or without meat. Here are the ingredients:

1 1/2 lb. prunes/apricots
3 cups boiling water
3 lb. boneless chuck or brisket (optional)
A chopped onion (optional)
2 tbsp chicken fat (or margarine)
1 1/2 tsps salt
1/4 tsp pepper
5 medium sweet potatoes cut in pieces
3-4 carrots cut in pieces
1/3 cup brown sugar or 1/2 cup honey
1/2 tsp cinnamon

Wash prunes and soak in boiling water. (If you use meat, melt 2 tbls chicken fat or margarine in a large pot. Brown meat with onion. Sprinkle with salt and pepper, cover the pot and cook over low heat for one hour. Add prunes and their soaking water, sweet potatoes and/or carrots and apricots, sugar or honey and cinnamon. Replace cover loosely and cook over low heat for two hours. It looks and smells good in a big pot with steam coming out.

Acknowledgements

As you know, when you put two Jews together, you get three to five opinions. So in order to try for a semblance of balance in Jewish laws and traditions, I have used the invaluable services of Rabbi Amy Memis-Foler and Rabbi Yehoshua Karsh. In addition, for poison information, my thanks go to Dr. Catherine Counard, Claudia Braden, R.N., BSN, MPH, and Dr. Jarrold Leikin, Emergency Medicine, for their knowledge and advice. I am also very grateful to my writer's group, Renee James, Tracy Koppel, and Lisa Sachs. In addition, I would like to thank my friend and editor Susan Braun of Aakenbaaken & Kent. Once you read this, you will never think of Passover in the same way!

Printed in the USA
CPSIA information can be obtained
at www.ICGtesting.com
LVHW040956140124
768963LV00007B/296